SAVE
HER
LIFE

BOOKS BY CAROLYN ARNOLD

On the Count of Three

Past Deeds

One More Kill

DETECTIVE MADISON KNIGHT SERIES

Ties That Bind

Justified

Sacrifice

Found Innocent

Just Cause

Deadly Impulse

In the Line of Duty

Power Struggle

Shades of Justice

What We Bury

Girl on the Run

Her Dark Grave

Murder at the Lake

Life Sentence

SARA AND SEAN COZY MYSTERY SERIES

Bowled Over Americano

Wedding Bells Brew Murder

MATTHEW CONNOR ADVENTURE SERIES

City of Gold

The Secret of the Lost Pharaoh

The Legend of Gasparilla and His Treasure

CAROLYN ARNOLD

SAVE HER LIFE

bookouture

Published by Bookouture in 2025

An imprint of Storyfire Ltd.
Carmelite House
50 Victoria Embankment
London EC4Y 0DZ

www.bookouture.com

The authorised representative in the EEA is Hachette Ireland
8 Castlecourt Centre
Dublin 15 D15 XTP3
Ireland
(email: info@hbgi.ie)

ISBN: 978-1-83525-918-4
eBook ISBN: 978-1-83525-917-7

PROLOGUE

Washington, DC

The man was making her skin crawl. Just the way he kept looking at her, not even trying to hide his attention. He was old enough to be her father. Just *gross*. If she ignored him, he'd hopefully take the hint and harass someone else with his disgusting leering instead of her and her best friend.

"You know what? I really need to get going." She was grateful for a prior appointment if it got her away from this guy. She stood and kissed her friend on each cheek, their way of doing things, and headed for the door. A part of her felt guilty for leaving her friend behind to deal with him, but Avery assured her she'd be fine.

As she walked a cool tingle laced down her spine. She gave a casual look over her shoulder, and her heart shuddered. That man was following her. She picked up her pace, and in a few seconds glanced back again. He was closing in on her.

The sidewalk was crowded this time of day, but she'd never felt so alone. She could call attention to him and create a scene, but if it turned out to be nothing, she'd look the fool. It was no secret her imagination was a powerful tool as her English teacher often praised her for it. According to him, she had a bright future as an author if she wanted to direct her efforts there, but she had her sights set on becoming a nurse or doctor. Someone who helped saved lives, or at least brightened them. That was why she volunteered on the weekends at a nursing home.

Suddenly, she was attuned to the sounds of her shoes slapping against the concrete and beeping horns from angry drivers making their way down M Street NW. The smell of vehicle exhaust hung heavy in the air and made her lightheaded, but her destination wasn't far now.

But as she kept her focus on that, she was rushed from behind. She never even had a chance to scream before everything went black.

ONE

TWO DAYS EARLIER

Bruceton Mills, West Virginia

This was the place people wished for death to find them. Fluorescents flickered and buzzed overhead, their harsh light casting more shadows than already existed in this black hellhole. On each side, she was hemmed in by gray-painted concrete walls, and beneath her, the linoleum floors were unforgiving of rubber soles, raising the odd squeak in protest and leaving behind a strip of black.

Sandra Vos was following a corrections officer through USP Hazelton Penitentiary, a high-security federal prison, to the parole hearing room. She was here because the man who had killed her twin brother was requesting early release. Darrell Patton was only thirty-three years and three months into his fifty-year sentence. The full term wasn't enough to compensate for Sam alone, but Patton was also charged for kidnapping his own seven-year-old daughter and holding thirty people hostage at gunpoint that fateful day. He deserved to serve every single year he'd been given. For Sam, she'd do her best to make sure that would happen.

Sam had been her entire world. More than her physical twin. Her twin flame. They had telepathy as attested to in some circles but dismissed by many skeptics and those in the scientific community. He could finish her sentences, and she his. Sometimes they could carry an entire conversation with just one look. It was like he was the other half of her, and when he was taken, she lost a piece of herself.

But they'd been through hell together and back between the loss of their parents and subsequent placements in various foster homes for two years before landing with a loving adoptive couple. The Davenports were nurturing souls brave enough to take on the responsibility of twelve-year-old twins because they didn't want them separated. But just less than two short years later, the Davenports would bury one. Sandra had perched at the side of her brother's grave tossing a flower onto his lowering casket, while the Davenports wept. She was too numb to cry.

At times that felt like yesterday.

Yet here Sandra was all these years later, still putting one foot in front of the other. Though she wasn't left with much choice. The way she saw it, the best way to honor Sam's life was to make the most of the one she had and whatever time she had left. They say that time heals, but it was more like a scab, able to be ripped off again and the wound made fresh.

It didn't help that today took her straight back to that time. Not only was she forced to recall losing Sam in vivid detail, but she was about to face the man who had put him in the ground. The unfairness of it, that Patton had the nerve to request parole to claim his freedom early while her brother rotted six feet under poured acid on her grief. It had her reacting on instinct, standing up for her brother to protect his memory. She promised herself and Sam that for as long as she drew breath, she'd do her part to keep his killer behind bars.

The corrections officer she'd been following gestured for her to go into a room. Voices from inside filtered into the hallway.

She took a deep, steadying inhale, thankful her career groomed her to remain calm in stressful situations. She'd lean on that training to get her through this.

She left the officer and entered the room. It was a simple, cool, sterile environment that held no secrets as to its purpose. Another officer stopped her and verified she was in the right place. "Parole hearing for Darrell Patton."

She nodded. "I'm Sandra Vos, here to speak in opposition to release."

He gestured toward a seating area, implying she pick a chair. There were ten total in two rows, all unoccupied.

She sat down in the front, trying to ignore the fact that Darrell Patton was mere feet away. He was sitting to the side of the room next to a man in a suit, most likely his attorney. Long lines marred his face, leaving a trace of every expression he'd ever made. His brown hair was heavily threaded with silver. When he'd gone away he was a twenty-five-year-old and was now a man of fifty-eight. Somehow in this environment, and with his vulnerable posture—slightly slumped forward and rounded shoulders—he appeared harmless, plain, tired, and haggard. But she believed nothing that her eyes could see. Not until it could be backed up by fact. For all she knew this persona was an act his lawyer told him to put on for the parole board.

A table was set out widthwise at the front of the room. Two board commissioners and the deputy commissioner were already seated there. They didn't have name cards, but she had done her homework before coming and could identify each of them. They all made brief eye contact with her but remained expressionless. After all, they were serious men here for serious business.

She was surprised that Patton's daughter or friends hadn't shown up when notice would have been sent to all of them. They could have spoken *for* him. She found herself especially wondering about the daughter. She'd be thirty-nine now, since her birthday was in June. Did she ever develop a relationship with her father? Sandra imagined that would be challenging with him behind bars.

"The clock tells us it's time to get started," the deputy commissioner said in a cool tone, and the guard near the door started to close it, just as a man entered.

Sandra overheard him tell the guard his name was Lonnie Jennings, a friend of Patton's, and he was there to speak to his favor. He was directed to take a seat and claimed the end chair in the front row, closer to Patton.

The deputy commissioner called the hearing to a start and requested that Darrell Patton's attorney speak first.

He stood and positioned himself in front of the board, tugging down on his jacket and doing up its buttons. "My client is seeking approval for early release based on his exemplary record as a peaceful inmate. Darrell Patton has served thirty-three years and has lived with the consequences of his actions every one of those days. He regrets having put himself and the lives of others in danger."

Sandra stiffened at how the lawyer had whitewashed his transgression, as if he hadn't actually been responsible for the loss of life. Her fingers and arms became cold. Goosebumps rose. Chills were a common side effect when she became angry. It normally took her a long time to get there. Just not when it involved what happened to her brother. But she talked herself down by reminding herself her time to speak was coming. Then she'd make it clear just how dangerous Patton was then *and* now.

The lawyer continued. "Since his incarceration, he has been doing what he can to make up for his actions, and it is with a humble and pleading manner that he asks this parole board to approve his request for early release. He's prepared to do all he can to secure employment and contribute to society." The attorney returned to his seat.

"Very well." The deputy commissioner leaned forward, both elbows on the table, looking over his glasses at Patton as he called on him to speak for himself.

Once Patton put himself in the same spot his lawyer had been, the deputy commissioner spoke again. "What do you have to say for yourself, Mr. Patton?"

"That I'm sorry to everyone in this room that we even need to be here today, that my actions thirty-three years ago brought us to this day. I'm sorry to those I've hurt." Patton turned to look directly at Sandra. She met his gaze, determined not to disclose any weakness even if her stomach was ice and her breathing labored.

"Beyond your apologies, Mr. Patton, tell us why we should consider early parole," one of the board members said.

"I've changed in my time here. I was only twenty-five, young, naive, immature, when I carried out my crimes. In all the time that has passed, I've worked to improve myself every day and show that I'm a model inmate. You'll see from my record that I've never initiated any fights in here, and I've always listened to the direction of the COs."

"All very well, but what's to say you are not a danger to yourself or others if you get out early?" This question came from the second board member.

"With respect, as I've said, I'm a different man now. I've even found God, and I'm regularly in attendance for Bible study."

Sandra hated it when anyone pointed at their religious beliefs as evidence of being blameless. Some of the worst atrocities in history were done in the name of God or religion.

"You may return to your seat," the deputy commissioner told Patton, and he did just that. Then he glanced at a piece of paper and looked up at her. "Sandra Vos, you are here today to oppose early parole for Darrell Patton?"

"I am, sir."

He waved for her to get up. As she stood, she brushed her fingertips over the gold St. Michael pendant that dangled from a chain around her neck. It was passed on to her brother after their father's death, then on to her. Standing tall, shoulders squared back, head high, chin slightly out to denote confidence and strength but not arrogance, she spoke. "As you just said, my name is Sandra Vos. Darrell Patton did more than put lives in danger. He killed my twin brother, Sam, at the age of fourteen. Sam, like any American teenager, loved and played football. After practice one day he decided to go out with his friends for pizza. Our mother, the sweet woman who adopted us just a couple years before, said he could, but she's been haunted by that decision ever since. You see, that day, Sam never came home. All because Darrell Patton saw fit to kidnap his seven-year-old daughter and stop for pizza. His face was broadcast on a TV they had in the restaurant. People recognized him, including my brother. Sam spoke up though, and Darrell shot him just before locking down the place. Due to Mr. Patton's refusal to release him for medical attention or surrender himself, Sam never received the help he needed. Sam died on scene. In the eyes of law enforcement, Sam was a tragedy, collateral damage, but he was far more than that to me and his family. Darrell Patton stole a light that day. He didn't seem to care that he endangered lives. The people in the restaurant that day, but also his own daughter's. His own flesh and blood," she emphasized. "He knowingly packed a gun and took her into a public place, gambling with his daughter's welfare. Even when given ample opportunities to surrender, Mr. Patton refused. As a negotiator with the FBI, I know the longer an incident stretches out, the window of opportunity for peaceful resolution starts to close. Darrell Patton was warned of this, but he continued to risk everyone's life. Even his own. And sure, Mr. Patton *might* be a different man now. But consider this. He did what he did because he was desperate and down on his luck. He took his daughter because full custody had just been awarded to the girl's mother. He felt he was wronged. That makes me fear what will happen if Mr. Patton gets out and feels wronged again. As this board is tasked with considering all the practicalities of early release, where does he plan to go if he gets out? How does he intend to support himself? From my knowledge, he'd be on his own. His daughter didn't even see fit to attend this hearing. What if Mr. Patton becomes desperate again? What's to prevent him from being triggered into committing another crime? How many people will die next time? You ask me, Darrell Patton is a danger to himself and society. I urge this board to deny request for parole." She returned to her chair, satisfied with her presentation. Since the parole board's main responsibility was to weigh whether Patton was a risk to himself or society, she wanted to end on that key point. Some aspects had been impromptu, but most of it she'd practiced to tedium in front of a mirror. Even a few times before her teenage daughter, Olivia, Liv for short. She had given her mother two thumbs up, but there was far more on the line today.

"Thank you, Ms. Vos," the deputy commissioner said. He turned to Patton and asked, "What are your plans if you are released? Where will you go? How will you make a living?"

Patton stood and cleared his throat. "I'm still working out the details."

The three men tasked with determining Patton's fate all looked at each other. Their facial expressions made it clear they were not impressed.

One of the board members asked, "Will your daughter be supportive of you? As Ms. Vos pointed out, she's not even here today."

Patton glanced over his shoulder, and his cheeks burned

bright red. "I haven't talked to my daughter since that day, though I have tried reaching out to her numerous times. I have confidence if I were freed, I could build a relationship with her."

"That sounds to me like you plan to manipulate your daughter's feelings to suit your purpose, which, I'll be honest, doesn't sit well with me. What if she doesn't agree to reconciliation?" The deputy commissioner leveled an expectant gaze at Patton, and Sandra felt a spike of victory.

"If I may step in," the lawyer said, standing next to his client. "Mr. Patton has also learned a trade during his time here. Woodworking, and it's something he can utilize on the outside to support himself. Until he gets himself on his feet, I am confident his friends will take him in."

The man from the end of the row, Lonnie Jennings, now stood. "If I may say something?"

"We will be getting to you just shortly." The deputy commissioner fired him with a glare.

Jennings sat back down.

The lawyer gestured toward Jennings. "I believe Mr. Jennings was going to offer to take in Darrell Patton. Am I right?"

"Yes," Jennings said.

The board didn't look impressed at the temporary loss of control over the direction of the hearing.

"All right, Mr. Jennings, let's hear your statement," the deputy commissioner said to regain ground.

Sandra tuned out most of what the man said, aside from the fact the two men were friends since childhood, and Jennings had witnessed the change in his friend. He put it on the record he'd take Patton in if he was released.

Eventually, the hearing was called to a close with the promise a decision should be reached by Friday.

Two days from now. Whether it took that full length of time or not, every minute was sure to feel much longer.

As everyone cleared out, Patton was looking at her, and she stared right back. She saw a man who regretted what he'd done, but she wasn't sure if the reason was pure or selfish. Would he feel that remorse if he hadn't been caught?

She waited for Patton to break eye contact before leaving. As she walked down the hall toward the exit, she felt confident that by showing up here today she had made a difference. And she was prepared to come back every twenty-four months as he became eligible to appeal again. Between her intention and a thing called justice, Darrell Patton would serve out his full fifty years.

TWO

The drive from the USP back to Washington, DC, where Sandra lived, took three hours. On the way she'd received a text from Olivia asking how things had gone, and that she was at her best friend Avery's house. Leave it to a sixteen-year-old to message over calling.

Sandra dictated a response to the voice-activated system in her Mercedes. "I think things went well, and just remember to be home by curfew at ten. I'm going to spend some time with grandma before going home. Call if you need anything."

The voice of her vehicle confirmed, "Message sent."

Technology sure had changed in the last thirty-three years. Sam would be lost if he were to return to this world.

It was six o'clock by the time Sandra was pulling into the driveway of Davenport Manor. It was an estate mansion, more than any ordinary house. It had belonged to her adoptive father's family for generations and was like another member of the family. It was this generational pride that had their adoptive father insisting that Sandra and Sam take on the Davenport name, but only adding to the one they were born with. They grew up with hyphenated names before it was even much a thing. Vos-Davenport.

The Davenports had taken in Sandra and her brother after several desperate attempts to have a child of their own had failed. They had been thirty-eight at the time but had generational money going back to the early eighteen hundreds when the family got into logging and was made wealthy. This provided them with more than enough funds to afford children, and they possessed an abundance of love.

William Davenport, Bill to his friends, Dad to her and Sam, had died ten years ago of a heart attack. But his wife, Margo, now seventy-one, still lived in the manor. Despite her declining mental health due to a battle with Alzheimer's, she refused to leave her marital home. Instead, she used the family's wealth to pay for round-the-clock in-home care.

Sandra parked and ducked inside, with a quick rap on one of the double dark mahogany front doors on her way through.

Margo's live-in nurse, Dana Ford, greeted her in the entry. She was a clear example of why no one should be judged by appearance. At only five three and of tiny build, it would be an error to assume she wasn't strong. She could probably bench press Sandra's one hundred and twenty-five pounds. Dana was also in her forties, though closer to forty than Sandra, who was creeping up on fifty at forty-seven.

Dana was a registered nurse, but she also stepped in for basic household responsibilities as called upon. This included things like getting the door and serving up meals, snacks, and drinks for Margo and any guests. In addition to Dana, Margo employed other staff. A cook came in a few times a week and prepared meals, which Dana heated up and set out. There was a cleaner who came in once a month to dust down the ornate woodwork of the home and all the fine pieces of furniture. A specialized cleaner tended to the art collection that spanned the walls. And a regular maid cleaned the home a bit every day, doing so in curated rounds, so by week's end the entire place was finished only to start again. Of course, there were also outdoor crews that tended to the yard with its extensive gardens and cherry trees.

"How is she?" Sandra unwound her scarf and took off her coat, handing both over to Dana.

"More good than bad today, though you know what the evening is often like."

Sandra nodded. Any time after six PM, Margo's mind seemed to tire out and retreat. But that didn't stop Sandra from wishing to believe her mother was aware on a certain level. Even if it only brought a fleeting moment of recognition and happiness. She wouldn't want her to suffer one moment thinking her daughter didn't care enough to visit. Though, she could tell by the absence in her eyes sometimes that she didn't always know. In the least, company alone seemed to lift Margo's spirits.

Dana secured Sandra's clothing over her arm. "You look tired. Could I get you a coffee? A light snack? Your mother's already eaten."

"Both would be much appreciated," she told Dana.

"I'll bring it to you. She's in the parlor."

"Thank you."

"Uh-huh."

Sandra would grab a meal when she got home, then collapse on the couch. The coffee just might get her there. Her day had started at five AM with a run next to the Potomac. It was a personal regimen born of necessity. The fresh air and workout got her heart pumping and cleansed her mind and soul. It had a way of purging most of her demons, even if they were just put off for thirty minutes or so. She looked forward to the morning when she could get back out there again. Though the stress from today's events might require an exorcist.

Sandra walked through the beautiful house, a place she'd

called home since the age of twelve. Not that she had taken to it right away. Or to the Davenports themselves, for that matter. Her life before had been far different. Their father was a policeman and had died in the line of duty. He'd always believed it would be Sam who would follow in his footsteps. While he never got the chance, Sandra entered law enforcement. By taking the oath to God and country, it was as if she carried both men whom she had loved so very much with her. It was for the same reason the gold St. Michael pendant never left her neck. All this also brought her closer to her mother, who had fallen into an eternal slumber after taking an entire bottle of sleeping pills in grief over the loss of her husband.

Sandra reached the doorway to the parlor, a grand room, and Margo's favorite for good reason. The furnishings were antique and, like the house, had been passed along from generation to generation of Davenports. The house overall was shadowy, encouraged by the dark wood walls and fixtures, but this room was the exception. Margo insisted on the removal of the original heavy, burgundy drapes. Their absence allowed sunlight to drench the space through the floor-to-ceiling windows and offered an unrestricted view of the backyard. During early spring, it was especially captivating when the blossoms on the cherry trees were in full bloom.

Margo was sitting in a plush chair, a blanket over her lap, a book in hand, next to the window and across from the fireplace. Its mantel, defined by modern standards would be oversized and gaudy, but from an architectural and historical standpoint, it was a thing of beauty.

"Mrs. Davenport," Sandra said as she approached. She didn't want to call her Margo or Mother out of mercy in case she didn't remember her.

Margo looked up, setting her book in her lap, and a huge smile graced her face. "Sandra, dear, why are you being so formal?"

"It's how you raised me. To be a proper young lady." She smiled at the woman who had seen her through her adolescence and who was so warm a creature that she'd harm no one. She was bred to pinch the handle of her teacup with her index finger and thumb, while leaving the burden of the weight to her middle finger. One day, many years ago, Margo had told her, "It's how the British royals drink their tea." Yet despite the formal upbringing, Margo had retained her humble and sweet nature. Nothing about her was pretentious. In her older age, she'd physically shrunk, and her light complexion turned an almost translucent white and became speckled with age spots.

"Posh." She waved a hand. "Dear, sit, sit. Tell me all about your day. Mine hasn't been terribly exciting, I'm afraid."

"It was a long one for me. Lots going on." There was no way she was bringing up Darrell Patton wanting early parole for fear her mother remembered he was the one who took Sam from them. She didn't want to upset her, or have the need to tell her yet again that Sam was gone. She'd already watched that pain wash over her face more times than Sandra cared to count. That line in her speech about their mother being haunted by the decision to allow Sam to go out was the truth when moments of lucidity rolled in.

"At work?"

"Not today. I took it off to care for some personal matters. I did go for a nice long run this morning."

"That might be why you look so tired. You should be home resting instead of here with me."

"Here you go." Dana came into the room with Sandra's coffee, black, just the way she liked it, and a small plate of cheese and crackers.

"Thank you." Sandra appreciatively took a sip. The brew was strong and smooth. *Perfection.* Next, she dug into the cheese. Somewhat surprisingly, the sharp salty edge married perfectly with the coffee.

"Is there anything I can do for you, Mrs. Davenport?" Dana asked Margo.

She held a hand up and gave her a gentle shake of her head. "Not now."

Dana left, and Margo looked at Sandra with a wink and a chuckle. "She can call me Mrs. Davenport."

Sandra smiled at her. It was a crime that her brilliant mind was deteriorating. Adding to that injustice was women of Margo's generation were very much oppressed. Their role in a marriage was birthing babies and caring for the home. It would have been devastating for Margo when she'd failed to produce an heir, but Bill had loved her more than life itself. "What book are you reading?"

"*Pride and Prejudice.*"

"Ah, it's one of your favorites."

"For good reason, but enough about me. How is my beautiful little chickadee?"

That was her pet name for Olivia. It really was a good night. "She's doing well. She's at a friend's."

"And her grades? She keeps those up?"

"She's a bright girl and studies hard." She drank more of her coffee, but her enjoyment was interrupted when her phone rang. The caller's identity told her it was Elwood Rowe, aka her boss. Elwood was the assistant director of the FBI's Critical Incident Response Group and oversaw the Crisis Negotiation Unit of which Sandra was a part. When she wasn't in the field negotiating, she was applying her skill set to manhunts behind a desk at the Washington Field Office. "Excuse me a moment," she said to Margo and stepped out of the room. She answered on the third ring, "Special Agent Vos."

"I was just starting to wonder if you were going to pick up."

"I saw your name, and I had to think about it," she teased.

"Very funny."

Thankfully, she had a great relationship with her superior unlike many people, but Elwood was a fair leader.

"I wouldn't have called you today if I could have helped it. I know you had a personal matter to attend to. Speaking of, how did it go?"

Elwood knew exactly why she'd taken the day off, but she appreciated he didn't put it in so many words. She also understood as part of the FBI's CNU that the job didn't have set hours. That was the cost of being available on-call to law enforcement seven days a week, twenty-four hours a day. "I should hear by Friday, but you said you need me. What is it?"

"There's a hostage situation in Woodbridge, and the locals have requested a negotiator. You'd relieve the primary and step up in their place. Guess he needs to leave for some personal reason. I'm asking you because I think you're best suited for this one after handling similar situations in the past."

"Sure. Just tell me where I need to go, and you can give me a recap while I'm on the way."

THREE

Elwood had finished his briefing before Sandra made it to the end of the block. At four o'clock that afternoon, a 911 call came in from a woman lasting just long enough to communicate she and several others were being held at gunpoint. The dispatcher traced the call back to Corey's Grocer but was unable to reestablish contact. It was believed that the hostage taker, or HT, had intervened. Her welfare and that of the others was still unknown as negotiators on scene had failed to make contact with the HT. With no idea who he was, or what he wanted, and almost four hours into this, it had the making of a long night ahead. For that reason, she made a quick stop for a barbecue sandwich with mumbo sauce and got back on the road. She'd like to get to Woodbridge as fast as possible, but the little bit of cheese and crackers she ate wouldn't hold her. In this line of work, you ate when you could. After eating and getting behind the wheel again, she called Olivia.

"Mom?" Olivia's voice came over the vehicle's speakers. "Everything okay? I'm still at Avery's."

"That's good. It might be best you spend the night there, if that's okay with her parents."

"Mom?"

"Nothing to worry about. I've just been called for an incident in Woodbridge, and I don't know how long I'll be." Olivia was old enough to stay on her own, and the building they lived in had twenty-four-hour security, but Sandra still didn't relish the thought of her teen daughter being alone if the incident dragged out all night.

"I'm sure they'll be fine with it."

"Please, just ask them. Or I could see if Eric could come to the penthouse and stay with you." Eric Birch was a detective with the Metropolitan Police Department, and the man Sandra had been seeing for the past few years after meeting him on a call. They had what could best be described as a relaxed, undefined, yet exclusive relationship.

"No offense, Mom, you know I like Eric, but I'd rather hang out here with Avery."

Sandra smiled. "I thought you'd say that. Let me know if Avery's parents are okay with you staying over. I'll hold, or you can put me on with them."

A dramatic sigh, followed by, "One sec."

She listened as her daughter asked Avery's mother, Tammy Porter.

"No problem at all, sweetie," Tammy said. "Tell your mom to stay safe."

"Thanks. Did you hear that, Mom?"

"I did. Remember only contact me if—"

"It's an emergency. I know the drill."

"Love you," Sandra told her daughter, slightly torn between going to her and doing her job. Being a single parent was a challenge every day. It felt like even when the right decision was made, it was still the wrong one.

"Uh-huh. Back at ya."

Before Sandra could say goodbye, Olivia was gone, and the catchy beat of a nineties dance tune came over the speakers.

She turned it up and sang along, letting the song sweep away the tension from the day. It also took her to the past when it would have been popular. Sam was already gone by then, but how he would have hated it. The thought of him took her back to the parole hearing. At least she wouldn't need to face her brother's killer for another two years.

She might have pressed her foot harder on the gas. The drive from Washington usually took about forty-five minutes, and she wanted to make up the lost time from stopping.

Her phone rang, cutting off the song mid-chorus, and Eric's name splashed on the screen. She answered with a smile.

"There she is. How did the hearing go? Sorry I couldn't call sooner."

His job made his schedule somewhat unpredictable. "It went well. I think."

"I'm sure you did a great job stating your case."

She wished she had the same level of confidence, but the uncertainty of the verdict dampened it.

"When will you hear back?"

"They said by the end of the week."

"Nothing like living in suspense. I could come over and help take your mind off it."

"I'd love that, but I'm not home."

"Oh?"

"I'm on my way to Woodbridge for an incident."

"After the day you had? Didn't you book it off?"

"I did, but Elwood didn't have a choice." Eric knew her boss, and that their relationship was professional but didn't stand on formality.

"All right, well, you know what you're doing."

"Well, I have been at it a while. I pretty much have compartmentalizing down to a fine art." It was hard to believe her FBI career had started twenty-five years ago in administration at HQ when she was twenty-two. After two years in that capacity, she enrolled in the FBI Academy, and upon gradu-ating was assigned for the next four years to the Norfolk Field Office helping locate spies, before returning to HQ to work in counterterrorism. That was when she'd met Olivia's father and had fallen pregnant eleven months later. She took eight weeks off after her birth, and six months after that, left as a single parent, and transferred to the WFO. After a year there working strictly on manhunts, she was recommended for negotiation training, which led to her joining the CNU. She'd been posted at the WFO for the last fifteen years.

Eric laughed. "Well, be safe. I'm sure it will be wrapped by tomorrow night."

"God, I sure hope so."

"What do you say to meeting up for dinner at, say, six? We can go to La Gioia Ristorante."

That was her favorite Italian restaurant, and it was just around the corner from home. Its name essentially translated to "joy restaurant," and their food lived up to the promise. She felt her spirits lift with every bite. Having that to look forward to would carry her through. "Actually, how about you pick it up and come to my place?"

"*Ooh*, I like the way you think."

"Mind out of the gutter. Besides, Liv will probably be around. Though she likely won't have any interest in hanging with us old folks for long before she retreats to her bedroom."

"Liv? No big deal. I even like her. She's not bad for a teenager," he teased. "Then I'll pick up dinner for three. The favorites. Your place tomorrow at six?"

She appreciated that Eric never took issue with Olivia. "Sounds incredible." She'd hold on to the prospect of tomorrow night to get her through the negotiations. Speaking of, Corey's Grocer came into view. "I've gotta go, Eric, but I look forward to our dinner."

"Good luck. Though I know you make your own."

She turned the radio off when they disconnected. The clock on the dash read 7:57 *PM* when she pulled into the lot. It had taken an hour even to get here, fifteen minutes longer than the usual drive time, but that wasn't bad considering she'd stopped for a bite to eat.

The grocery store was in a small plaza with a bank, a hair salon, and a doctor's office. She was flagged down by a uniformed officer and directed to stop with a raised hand. A reporter beat him to her car and rapped on the driver's window.

"Diana Wesson with *PWC News*," she said through the glass.

"Go. Scram." The uniformed officer came over and shooed her and her tailing cameraman away. Next, he gestured for Sandra to lower her window, which she did. "This vicinity is closed to the public," he said.

"FBI Special Agent Vos, here to relieve the primary negotiator." She held up her credentials and was told to park closer to the road.

Police cruisers peppered the lot, and several uniformed officers stood behind them, using the vehicles as cover. Special Weapons and Tactics officers were present and easy to spot. All of them were suited for war, earning them the nickname in negotiation circles of Neanderthals or knuckle-draggers because their default was a physical response. For the CNU, it was about resolving situations with dialogue, as was their motto. But there were times a balance of both was needed. But in this case, four hours into a standoff was far too soon to seriously consider a breach or physical response.

The MCV, or mobile command vehicle, was positioned closer to the storefront. There were also a few ambulances and medics to the right of the MCV.

Twenty to thirty civilian vehicles were in the lot too and were likely registered to the hostages inside. A van marked with *PWC News* was parked across the street, and the reporter from a moment ago was gesticulating as she faced her cameraman and spoke with her back to the unfolding scene. But they weren't the only network.

Sandra would be more surprised if the media wasn't already here, but they had to go. They could make negotiations a tougher job by raising the stress level in the HT. Considering hostage takers were already under a significant amount of pressure, it was her job to reduce it. Cutting out what was controllable was crucial.

A thin man in his fifties was standing outside the command vehicle puffing away on a cigarette. He crushed the remainder of the butt on the ground as she approached.

She'd put on her bulletproof vest from her go-bag in the back of her car, but it was the FBI embroidered windbreaker over it that would announce her before she said a word. Still, she introduced herself. "FBI Special Agent Sandra Vos."

"Lieutenant Drew Garrison, team leader. I'm the one who put the call in to the CNU."

As team leader, Garrison was responsible for overseeing everything from the location of the MCV to assigning duties on scene.

"So is that Vos with one 's' or two?"

"One. It's the Dutch spelling."

"Ah. Wooden shoes, wooden head, wooden listen." He smiled, but she wasn't amused. She'd certainly heard that one before. "My apologies. I didn't mean to insult you or really mean anything by it."

"It's fine." And it was. She wasn't someone who was easily riled. It was a trait that served her well, as a good negotiator was a calm one.

"Come on, then, before I put my foot in my mouth again. Let me introduce you to the team, and we'll get you up to speed." He held the door to the vehicle for her and the smell of coffee drifted out. "After you."

Before going up the steps, she looked across the street again. "We need the media out of here."

"They're like cockroaches, aren't they? I've already sent an officer over to get rid of them, but it's hard to banish them from a public sidewalk. You know with all their constitutional rights and the 'people have a right to know' mentality."

"Depending on how things progress, they might need to preach that all the way to jail."

Garrison smiled. "I like the way you think."

Inside, the command vehicle was outfitted with the latest technology. Computers and monitor banks were on the wall with a live video feed showing the face of the building. She could see that the front windows of the store were blocked inside with what appeared to be shelving, and it told her something about the HT. The action of barricading indicated he was prepared to settle in and protect himself from the line of fire. It demonstrated intelligence and forethought. It also told her that he existed in reality, was able to calculate risk, and didn't have a death wish.

There were three workstations, and a table with a semi-circle bench surrounding it, which was ideal for discussions and briefings. The situation board was within plain view, and Sandra took it in quickly from where she stood. It only offered the basics. *Unidentified Male HT, armed, hostage count approx. 30-40.*

Once Garrison closed the door behind him, he bellowed, "Listen up, everyone. The FBI's here. This is..." He turned to her.

"Special Agent Sandra Vos."

"Vos, right." He smiled, though Sandra didn't understand why. "She's here to relieve Leon as primary negotiator."

A man in his late forties pushed out his chair from a work surface. He had been seated next to another man, who was in his late thirties, early forties.

"Fox meet Wolfe. His role is coach," Garrison said, and she understood why he'd smiled before. He must have been planning this little play on words, knowing that one meaning of Vos was fox. Sandra's father used to always say, *Sandy, you're clever as a fox, my girl.*

"Ray's my first name," the coach said.

"Sandra." She'd be working closely with Ray as the coach's job was to support her by monitoring communication and passing her notes when he picked up on something she might have missed.

Garrison abandoned humor as he circled the room, introducing everyone and their roles. "Detective Richie Osborn, scribe, and Detective Patrick Mahoney, intelligence officer and profiler. Lieutenant Amos Bowen is the team coordinator, but he's out there doing his thing right now."

The scribe would record the calls and make a short and concise script of any discussions and reactions from each side. With Patrick playing double roles, he'd jot down essential information to the markerboard and play a part in gathering background information on the HT and hostages. Sandra was more fixated on what the team coordinator was up to. One aspect of his job was to advise the SWAT commander on any developments and determine if it was time for a physical response. But if they were discussing that with any intention, she wasn't sure why they'd called her. "Excuse me, but what *thing* exactly?"

"Whether it's time to take stronger measures."

"From my understanding, we haven't made contact with the HT. Is force being considered?"

Garrison smiled tightly. "It is. Four hours have already passed, and as you just pointed out, there hasn't been any communication."

Sandra stiffened. "Radio silence is no reason to move in. If anything, it's the opposite. You'd be going in blind, and innocent people will die." *Sam.* Not that he was killed by police, but the memory of his loss rolled over her, nonetheless. It was down to people making poor choices.

"Not everyone sees it that way, but you'll be alerted if action is going to be taken."

She understood preparing for the worst-case scenario, but she had to keep her mind set on peaceful resolution. She'd also just arrived and wasn't about to insert herself as some ego-driven fed. No doubt there was a lot of skill and experience in this room. "Please run me through everything that's happened so far."

"Want a coffee while we talk?" Garrison pointed to a coffee machine in an alcove. A few mugs were beside it with a small container of sugar packets and some whitener.

"I'm good for now, but thank you."

"All right, then." Garrison gestured for her to sit at the table, and he joined her, as did the rest of the team except for Leon, who stood next to them.

"You probably know the basics. No contact, no ID, the situation came to our attention through a 911 call?" Garrison asked.

"I do know all that. Do we have a recording of the call? I'd like to listen to it."

Garrison gestured to Patrick, who responded. "We have it, and that won't be a problem. The call was disconnected before she was able to provide her name, but we traced the number to a Heidi Norris, thirty-seven. We reached out to her husband, and he confirmed she'd popped out for groceries. An officer is at his home with him now and will remain there for the duration of the incident."

"As you can see, the HT has barricaded the front of the store. That happened not long after we arrived on scene," Garrison said, moving the briefing along at a swift pace. "He used hostages to do this, but with the sun reflecting off the glass, it was hard to make out much more than silhouettes."

The early planning was an even stronger indication that the HT was thinking clearly. Rationally, however, was debatable.

"There are three ingress and egress points. One door in the front, two in the rear, counting the rollup at the delivery dock. All are locked. SWAT officers are set up to watch the rear in case he decides to slip out," Garrison said.

"We believe he's holding the hostages in an employee lunchroom," Patrick said, as he slipped her a blueprint of the store. "It's an interior room on the second floor."

It would be an intelligent choice as no windows cut back risk to himself and hostages escaping. "The board notes approximately thirty to forty hostages. How was that estimate determined?"

"There are thirty vehicles in the lot, with five belonging to employees on shift. There are five more staff in addition. We've run all the plates and have a list of names." Patrick handed her more paperwork.

"The number could be higher if people walked here, or more than one person arrived per vehicle. Have we tried reaching out to these people?" She used *we* as an intentional effort to build camaraderie. Not everyone loved it when the FBI walked in, and this was one subtle way that might ingratiate herself with them.

"No answers on numbers linked to the owners of the vehicles. We believe the HT has confiscated everyone's cellphones," Patrick said with a frustrated sigh.

Another smart move. "One of those vehicles could also belong to the HT," she put in.

"Which I'm keeping in mind, but without more to go on aside from male, that's not getting us anywhere yet. I've also pulled backgrounds on the employees. All clean." He handed her another stack of paper.

Until they knew more, they had to come at this situation from every angle they could think of, and an inside job was just one possibility. She was impressed Patrick thought of this. She looked at the top sheet. It had *Manager* handwritten in black marker. Brad Stevens was only thirty-one. She shuffled through the pages, noting everyone's names and job titles. "This is terrific. Where did you get the employee names?"

"The store's assistant manager. A Marsha Jackson. She's at home today and available to us if we need anything else."

"That's great." She was building up quite a pile of paper on the table in front of her and lifted the store's blueprint. "Jackson get this for you too?"

Patrick shook his head. "That came from the plaza owner, a cooperative man as well."

Bowen and SWAT would use this to strategize entry points. She spotted the three that Garrison had mentioned.

The blueprint had been marked up to indicate the different sections of the store. The place was one story aside from an upstairs office space and a room labeled *lunchroom*. The main level included a pharmacy, a delicatessen, a seafood counter, and a warehouse with shipping and receiving in the back. She set aside the blueprint and looked at Leon. "Tell me everything you tried to establish contact."

"No ID, so no cell phone to try. No answer on the store's landline, or through any suspected hostages' phone, as Patrick told you. We got a throw phone to the door, but he refused to accept it. He sent a hostage to check it out but had her leave it there. We could see that he was holding a gun to her from the side. No clear sightline to take a shot," Leon laid out.

Thank God for that! When she looked closer at the video monitor, she saw the phone was still in front of the door. It allowed a single-line connection from the device to a programmed number. In this case, it would feed back to a phone in the MCV. Her first goal was to get that into the HT's hands. "When was the last time you tried to make contact?"

"An hour ago," Leon said, "using the bullhorn again and trying to get him to retrieve the throw phone."

"And where would I find that bullhorn?" Sandra cocked her eyebrows.

Leon pulled it out of a cabinet and handed it over. "Good luck, Vos. You'll need it. But if that is all you'll be needing from me, I'm gonna go." Leon looked at Garrison, who nodded his approval for the negotiator to leave.

She followed Leon out with the bullhorn in her hand. She stood at the front of the MCV to shelter herself from the ever-present media, but it also put her in a vulnerable position. Regardless of her bulletproof vest. But with the amount of fire power around, if the HT showed himself to take a shot at her, he'd likely be taken out before he had the chance. She turned the bullhorn on and held it to her mouth. She knew just how far away to position it to avoid feedback.

"I can only imagine how afraid you must be. It looks like you don't want to talk. Maybe you fear if you come out to collect the phone, someone out here will shoot you. I won't let that happen. I'm Special Agent Sandra Vos with the FBI, and I'm sure you don't want to spend your entire evening in there. Tell me what you'd like to end this, and let me help you." She spoke slowly and used a calm tone to project authority and trustworthiness. It was unlikely to trigger a defensive reaction. "I'd like to help get you home safe and sound. If that sounds good to you, just collect the phone, and I'll call you." She intentionally didn't set a clock to it. In hostage situations, if actions or decisions were rushed, that was when people got hurt, or worse, dead. She also addressed a basic human need by assuring his safety. She clicked the bullhorn off and turned to go back inside the command vehicle.

"Excuse me!" a man yelled out, his voice ringing with panic.

She pivoted and saw he was being held back by a uniformed

officer. But she was curious what made him risk jail by breaking through the cordon.

"Please, wait," she shouted to the officers. "Let me hear what he has to say." She guided the man behind the MCV for cover just in case things took a drastic turn.

"Thank God. No one else is listening to me." The man was breathing heavily, his chest heaving. "My pregnant wife is in there!"

FOUR

When hostages were involved, the stakes were always high, but a pregnant woman ratcheted up the urgency. Sandra stuck her head inside the command vehicle to have the information officer come out and talk with the man, while she returned to her post in case there was a development with the HT.

A few minutes later, Patrick Mahoney was back and passing on what he'd learned. "His name's Joshua Cobb. His wife, Megan, is eight months pregnant with their first child."

Their first... Somehow, that made it even more crucial Sandra find a way to get her out of there. Once she established communication with the hostage taker, she'd do her best to have her sent out first.

Patrick continued. "She had a craving for ice cream, he was watching hockey and wouldn't go get it. So she did. He caught the incident on the news and hurried over."

"The guy must be full of regret," Richie, the scribe, put in.

"Oh, he is."

"Look!" Ray pointed at the monitor.

The door of the grocery store opened, and one of the

hostages came out and grabbed the phone. It all happened quickly.

"Oh, that's a good sign," Ray said. "Our guy's ready to talk."

"We'll let some time pass. If he doesn't call, then I will." Sandra set the timer on her phone for ten minutes. If the HT hadn't called by then, she would initiate contact.

"Why wait?" Garrison asked.

"I want to give him the opportunity to feel like he's in control."

"He should be feeling nothing but. Let's face it. We've just been hanging around waiting for him to do or say something," Garrison lamented.

She let his opinion go without response, and instead put her headset on, turned to Ray on her right, then to Richie on her left. "When this timer goes off, I want to call," she told them. They'd both be listening to every conversation she had with the HT.

Ray quickly ran her through their system and how to make the call. "We'll be ready when you are," Ray said, giving her a pressed smile.

She set her cellphone on the worksurface in front of her, watched the timer tick off a few seconds, then glanced away to look at the video screen. No further movement to be seen inside. Back to her phone, the timer was on the last ten seconds. It beeped, and she put the call through.

It rang once. No answer.

A second time. No answer.

A third, the same. But on the fourth, the call was picked up. There was silence on the other end.

She anticipated this possible response, but at least the HT took her call. "This is Sandra." She was keeping it light. "Just in case we get disconnected, you can always call me back by hitting the *Call* button. It will patch you right through to me. Do you understand what I'm telling you?"

Silence.

"I'd like to help you," she said a few seconds later. "Are you all right in there?"

"Yeah."

She glanced at Ray and Richie. Both men were smiling. After four hours, the HT had just said his first word. More an utterance that came out mumbled. But it counted.

Ray passed her a note. *It sounds like he's tired.*

She gathered the same. Without hearing more, it wasn't possible to tell if he was affected by drug use or if he'd helped himself to alcohol from the store's shelves. She also couldn't distinguish any accent to his voice. "Well, that's good to hear. You sound tired though." By saying this she was showing more empathy. The goal was to get him to trust her, and as a result, she'd gain influence. "Since we're going to become friends, what should I call you?" With his name, they could access his background and dig into his life situation to see if either could explain how things had spiraled to this point. This knowledge could also help determine his motivation and thereby aid where she steered the negotiation.

"No names."

Two words and still not enough to determine if he was local. "You're doing all right, but what about everyone who's with you in there? Are they doing okay?" Megan Cobb wasn't far from mind but she couldn't rush the dialogue along.

"Yes."

"Wonderful." She let a small smile lighten her tone. "This means you're in a great place for all of us to walk away from this. Obviously, no one out here wants to see you or anyone hurt. We're all in this together. What can I do so that we can all go home safe?" She'd intentionally painted a happy picture, then waited. She let the silence stretch some, hoping he was calculating his demands.

The line went dead.

"At least you got him to pick up," Ray said to her.

"Better than Leon," Richie put in, while Patrick noted the time on the markerboard.

"It's not a reflection on Leon. The HT is just ready to talk now." She wasn't about to disparage anyone's reputation. Let alone someone she didn't even know.

A hulk of a man entered the command vehicle. Buzzcut, tight pants that encased thighs the size of her torso... *well, not quite as thick.* He wasn't in SWAT getup, so he must have been Lieutenant Amos Bowen, the team coordinator, and she could feel his testosterone from the door to where she was seated near the other end of the vehicle.

"She got through," Garrison informed the man. "This is FBI Special Agent Sandra Vos." Then to her he said, "This is Lieutenant Bowen."

The team coordinator looked down at her, not just due to his towering height but in a clear move to intimidate. His hard gaze leveled judgment as if to say, *So you're who they sent.*

He was about to be disappointed if he expected a reaction. She wasn't one to cower, especially to the likes of him. She'd been dealing with inflated male egos since she became FBI. Law enforcement was still very much a man's world.

"'She got through...' Based on that enthusiastic recap, I'm to guess he wasn't too talkative."

She peacocked her body posture at his sarcastic assumption. "We established contact. That's a good start."

"I know you just arrived," Bowen said, "but the rest of us have been here for nearly five hours. Tell me you at least got his name."

Technically, four hours and forty minutes... "Oh, I got more than that."

Bowen smiled. "That's a no on the name, then?"

She shrugged, letting it be clear he wasn't getting to her.

"All right, I'll bite. What did ya get?" Bowen crossed his

arms, and his biceps popped like melons. It looked painful. There was muscular, but then there was this. His life outside of work had to be spent in a gym lifting weights.

She almost wished he didn't ask. The fact the HT wasn't willing to discuss going home safely may suggest he didn't have intentions of walking away. But that was far from being conclusive this early on. She'd give Bowen one offering, and then ricochet an inquiry back to him. "He said no one's hurt, but I suspect you have experience with hostage situations. I'm sure you've made your own observations thus far." The compliment and invitation for him to share his wisdom was tactical empathy at work. The hope was it would spark reciprocity while helping him see he could benefit from the team around him.

Bowen didn't bite this time. "If that's all you got from your ten-second interaction with the HT, you didn't get much. When Garrison wanted to call in the FBI, I didn't understand the need. Now even more so. You haven't gotten any further than us."

Ray and Richie shifted in their chairs. She saw them look at each other. Both were curious how she was going to handle this man. Patrick was avoiding eye contact.

She nudged out her chin. "I sense you're a man who likes to hear it how it is. Well, contact was just made, so as far as getting started, that clock just began ticking. If it's okay with you, I'd like to discuss the call further with the team and listen to the nine-one-one call. That is, unless there is something else you need, Lieutenant?"

Bowen clenched his jaw and left.

"I think that's the first time he's ever been speechless. Impressive," Ray put in.

She was just standing her ground so Bowen would know he couldn't tromp on her. With people like that it was best to make your position clear up front. "Could you play that nine-one-one call?" She directed this at Patrick.

"Sure." Patrick brought up the recording and hit play.

"Nine-one-one, what's your emerg—"

"He's got a gun... He's— Oh my—"

Crying and people shouting in the background.

"What are you doing?" *a man said, and the caller cried out.*

Then the call ended.

Everyone was looking at her. She gathered her thoughts and shared her observations. "It's brief, and the HT is clearly distressed. I don't think he planned for this to happen, or he would have thought ahead to confiscate everyone's phones. But at the same time, he did decide to hold people before law enforcement arrived."

"So he was backed into it, but wasn't?" Ray asked, his brow wrinkling up.

"Something like that. There's just so little to go on yet," she said.

"I just keep asking what turns an outing for groceries into this?" Garrison weighed in.

Without even having so much as the HT's identity, the question was purely rhetorical. It wasn't even certain what brought him here. Any response would be best guess. "I'm going to try calling him back, see if he answers." She got situated again, as did Ray and Richie.

Her call was answered on the second ring. "Leave me alone."

Aggressive words, but he hadn't hung up. "I would if I could, my friend, but that's a bit hard for me to do until I hear that everyone is safe in there." She was after more than his earlier *yeah.*

"Everyone's safe," he said firmly.

"Can I talk to them?"

"There's no need for that."

A lilt to his voice was now distinguishable and disclosed a

Virginia accent. He was from the area. "All right. Will you tell me how many people are in there with you?"

"Dunno. Thirty or forty."

Sandra noted that he hadn't taken the time to count them, which potentially wasn't a good thing. To him, they weren't people and that would make them dispensable. "You're sure, thirty or forty?" Repeating his words showed she was listening to him.

"Yeah."

That was close enough to *that's right*. Such a response would unconsciously embed in his subconscious that she was on the same page as him. "We have a husband out here, Joshua, who is really concerned about his wife, Megan. She just had a craving for ice cream." By using names, relationship, and something so basic as why Megan was at the store, it would encourage the HT to see his hostages as real people like himself. If he viewed them that way, he'd be less likely to hurt anyone. "Could I talk to her, at least?"

He didn't respond, and there was no background noise whatsoever. Not even the sound of anyone crying. He must be in another room from the hostages. But then how was he keeping them there? She continued. "Megan's thirty-three, and she and her husband are expecting their first baby."

He sniffled. Allergies, a cold, or emotion? It was hard to tell, but it was a break she needed.

"But she is okay, so I can tell Joshua, her husband, that?" she prompted.

"She's just fine. I swear I didn't hurt her." He thrust the last sentence out with a note of disgust, as if injuring her would have been detestable.

Ray wrote, *Detect empathy*.

She did too, and that was a breakthrough. Sharing Megan's story had worked. "You didn't hurt her?" She intentionally parroted his words, serving them back in a curious tone. By repeating him, it confirmed she was listening when he spoke, and it was a tactic that would encourage him to elaborate. In this case, she wanted to ensure there wasn't anything between the lines of what he'd said.

"No. She's just fine."

"That's great news..." She left room for him to volunteer his name, which he didn't. She wasn't going to push it when he was still talking. "I'll let her husband, Joshua, know that she's okay, that she isn't hurt."

"Whatever. Everyone's good," he reiterated.

"You sound like you're tired and could use some rest."

He laughed, dry and full of irony. "The feds are here for me. I'm not going anywhere!"

"Sandra. I'm the only fed here, and I'm on your side, like everyone else here. All this can end peacefully now, no one gets hurt, including you, and you can go home and get some sleep. You haven't done anything you can't walk away from."

"Nah, I saw them out there... The men dressed in Kevlar, carrying big guns. No way they are going to let that happen." He sniffled again, and Sandra sensed desperation. And that bred impulsive action.

"Nah, we've been talking. I'll let them know you just want to end this peacefully."

There were several seconds of silence.

She spoke again. "Please, just let me do this for you. It's the least I can do, but I'd really like to know what I should call you."

"Gavin."

Richie wrote this down with a fast hand.

"Gavin, we can do this now. As I said, you can still walk away from this. Do you want me to arrange for you to come out, all safe and sound? Then you can put all this behind you and get some rest."

"No, I'm not doing that."

While she'd wished for a more positive answer, she hadn't

expected one. "All right. I'm still here for you, and as long as you continue to keep the hostages safe, we can keep talking. Is there something I can do for you? Anything that might make you feel more comfortable?"

"I just wanted the drugs," he burst out. "That's all, but they wouldn't give them to me. I had no choice but to…"

Richie, ever the dutiful scribe, was furiously writing.

Ray gave her a note that read, *Felt backed into a corner… Prescription?*

"No choice but to what, Gavin?" She had to know what he was referring to. Taking hostages? Hurting someone and lying about it?

"Locking things down."

"Okay. Tell me what drug you need, Gavin, and I'll get it for you. Was it a prescription?"

Gavin hung up.

"At least the guy's predictable. You ask a question he finds uncomfortable, he ends the call," Patrick said.

"Seems so," Richie put in.

"I say at least he's talking. Even if it's piecemeal," Ray added.

She took some comfort in that. "At least we have his name now."

"Well, there's no Gavin attached to the vehicle registrations," Patrick said.

"I still don't think we're without resources," she began. "I'd put money on this drug being prescribed. Could you ask the assistant manager if she has any way of getting into the pharmacy system from the outside?"

"I'll get on that right now," Patrick said.

"And if she can't get in, call Lakisha Hester. She's with the Science and Technology Branch at FBI headquarters."

"Her number?"

Sandra brought up Lakisha's contact card in her phone. "I'll shoot you over her info. Your number?"

Patrick rattled it off, and Sandra forwarded it along. She then texted Lakisha a quick heads-up that she might be getting a call from Patrick Mahoney with the PWCPD and added, *connected to ID'ing HT in live incident.*

Within a few seconds, she had a response.

I'll do my best.

All I can ask.

"Okay, she knows you might be calling," Sandra told Patrick.

The intelligence officer nodded with his phone to his ear.

FIVE

"'They wouldn't give them to me.'" Sandra repeated Gavin's words, after listening to the playback of the call. "He's desperate. For whatever reason, he needs those drugs."

"Only thing is he's screwed the pooch on this," Garrison said. "No way he can expect to just walk away free and clear. I know that's what you're promising, but even a village idiot would know he needs to account for what he's done."

"I'm not promising that at all. The point is to minimize the punishment, diminish his fears about the outcome of surrendering," she said.

"Fair enough," Garrison said. "But I suppose my point is he had to know he couldn't just walk out of the store with his pills, even if he limited his force to the pharmacist and the clerk there. The store security guard would have stopped him."

"The store has one?"

"Yep. Norman Brady," Patrick said, weighing in on the conversation. He'd already filled them in that the assistant manager couldn't log in to the pharmacy system, so he'd reached out to Lakisha. No ETA there. Patrick flipped through his paperwork. "Brady's a direct employee of the store, not an outside firm."

"It could be where Gavin got his gun. That's if Brady was armed," Sandra said.

"He was. A Smith & Wesson M&P. I got that information from the assistant manager."

It might have been nice to have had this information earlier, though it was impossible to know if Gavin had managed to get the gun off the security guard or if he turned up with one of his own. But the main point was Gavin was armed, which she'd been informed about when she arrived.

"The HT could have lied to Agent Vos," Ray began. "It's only logical a physical altercation must have taken place between him and the guard. Whether that be during a play to take the guard's weapon or to have him relinquish it. Someone might be hurt in there."

"Could be." The admission was bitter. Just the possibility of it chipped at the early camaraderie she had going with Gavin. He'd most likely lied to her already.

"On another note, was anyone else freaked out by how quiet it was in the background?" Richie asked.

She nodded and turned to Patrick. "What do we know about the lunchroom? Does it lock from the outside?" It was only a theory that's where the hostages were being held, but she'd treat it as a fact for now.

Patrick shook his head. "No, but the assistant manager said there are two doors and they both have long pull handles. The HT could have slipped something through them to prevent people getting out."

"Which would allow him to wander the store as he wished," she said.

"I suppose so. Heck, he could be watching us. There's video surveillance in the upstairs office."

That wasn't a heartwarming thought, and she wouldn't have minded *that* piece of intel before.

The door swung open, and Bowen stepped inside with another man who was dressed impeccably in suit and tie. The flaps of his long dress coat were open, and he carried himself with an air of authority and had a pleasant resting face. Considering the circumstances, that demonstrated impressive emotional restraint and earned Sandra's immediate respect.

"Special Agent Vos," Bowen said, "this is Police Chief Buchanan with the PWCPD."

"Either Jeff or Buchanan is fine," he told her as he shook her hand.

"Sandra."

"I've been told this situation has been ongoing for hours. Lieutenant Bowen thinks it might be a good time to end this by force." Jeff pried her with intelligent eyes and clearly wanted her take on this.

"Gavin, that's the hostage taker, is talking, and I believe I can bring this situation to a peaceful resolution." She provided his name to humanize the HT to the police chief. There was hope he'd take that reminder and be less eager to have SWAT rush in there and do what they would.

"A pipe dream," Bowen scoffed, pulling his phone from his pocket when it chimed. "You've been in contact a couple of times and the last was over an hour ago. An hour of silence."

"Which is nothing in the grand scheme of things." Lulls in communication were common during crisis negotiation, and one hour was nothing. Gavin would be questioning what was going on outside and becoming more worn down by the minute. To an exhausted hostage taker, the thought of surrender started to look appealing.

"Chief, Agent Vos gave him the opportunity to surrender peacefully. He ended the call. He's not even willing to discuss it," Bowen said, vying for favoritism from the chief.

Sandra had noticed Garrison on his phone earlier. He must have updated Bowen.

Jeff looked at her. "Is that true?"

"I'm sure you have experience with hostage situations," she began. "Rarely does the HT give up right away. Based on what he keeps saying, he felt backed into this situation." She passed a glance at Ray since she'd used the wording from his note. The theory didn't explain why or how he escalated to this point though. But even if he arrived armed, it didn't mean he'd meant for all this to happen.

"Hmm." Jeff narrowed his eyes, clasped his hands in front of himself, and angled his head. "What do you think the chances are this will end peacefully?"

"Honestly? There's no way to know for sure, but I've been trained by the finest at the Bureau and will use that education and my experience to do all I can with that end goal in mind." Negotiation training lasted for two intense weeks covering the process, abnormal psychology, and case study review. The coursework was put into practice with role-playing exercises.

"Speaking of end goals, what does the hostage taker want?" Jeff asked. "Do we know yet?"

She shook her head. "Just what set him off. He was refused medication." As she recapped this, it sank in that it was more likely Gavin hadn't arrived armed with the plan to hold hostages. She could hear his voice in her head, and he'd sounded genuinely shocked when he couldn't get the drugs.

"The HT is clearly unstable and unpredictable," Bowen said. "What impulsive decision is he going to make next? Personally, I don't think we should be standing around waiting to find out."

"As you've made your stance very clear several times," Jeff said coolly.

"If I may," Sandra intercepted, looking at Jeff as she spoke. "Working as a negotiator for fourteen years, I have learned to read certain signs. Gavin gives me no indication that he planned this today, and I don't read off him that he has a death wish either. I can work with both those things. We're on the path to getting his full identity too. Once we have that, we'll be able to form a broader picture of the man who is holding hostages. It's necessary to think like him if we're to bring this to a good ending."

"We know where Bowen stands, but what do you think, Garrison? You're team leader, from what I understand," Jeff said.

Garrison passed a timid look at Bowen. "Agent Vos has the HT talking. We've been at this for hours already. What's a bit longer if everyone walks away?"

"Those are my thoughts on the matter." Jeff's brow knitted with deep thought, as Sandra imagined him weighing real life cost against budget constraints. Eventually, he added, "All right, I say you keep on it, but if things change... By that I mean if hostages get hurt, or it's confirmed someone has been, I want to be informed." The police chief started off talking to her but clearly directed that latter bit to Bowen. He then left the vehicle with Bowen tailing him. If he intended to change the chief's mind, she wished him luck. Jeff Buchanan seemed like a man who knew his mind, and once he'd made it up it would be tough to change.

Garrison turned to the intelligence officer. "Tell me, Patrick, any advancement on getting into the pharmacy system?"

Patrick's phone had been pinging throughout the conversation. "Lakisha said she has a colleague helping her with it. She gave me his number too. It's a Simon... Somebody. Sound familiar?" He looked at Sandra.

"Simon Pratt. He's good. I'm sure we'll be somewhere soon with that. In the meantime..." She got up and returned to her post, and that alone signaled Ray and Richie to theirs. "I'm going to try to reach Gavin again."

Gavin answered before the second ring.

"I'm sorry I keep hanging up on you. It's just that..."

The silence had worked to make Gavin think on his actions. He also sounded more tired than before. All of this was good. "You must be processing a lot in there, Gavin. How are you doing?"

"I'm tired. I... I didn't want to do this, but I didn't have a choice."

From the sound of it, the passing time poked his conscience too. Another positive takeaway. She still wasn't going to let her guard down and assume he was weakening though. In fact, his repeated claim was striking her as disingenuous and had her wondering if he had hurt someone. "You didn't have a choice about what, Gavin?"

"I just wanted the meds." He sniffled.

His avoidance was reassuring. There was most definitely more that he wasn't telling her, but calling him out would be counterproductive. "You sound like you never meant for things to get to this point."

"I told you that. They refused to give me my meds."

"Help me understand. Why did they turn you away?"

"It was my insurance. It should have covered them still, but they said it was canceled. They must be lying, but I don't have the money to pay out of pock—"

Ray passed her a note that read, *Lost his job?*

There was scuffling in the background, and the sounds of a tussle.

Sandra looked at Ray. "Gavin, can you tell me what's going on?"

The line cut out.

She slapped her headset down.

The door to the command vehicle opened, and Bowen walked in. His gaze traveled from her workspace to her eyes. "I take it things aren't going well on the negotiation front?"

He had an uncanny ability of showing up at the most inopportune time. "It's the long game," she said.

"Uh-huh. Just how long do we have to sit around?"

Bowen was clearly bitter about the chief siding with her, and the team coordinator was really reminding her of her ex, Olivia's father. Nolan Copeland worked with the FBI's Hostage Rescue Team, or HRT, and that unit was mission-based, full-time, and focused on counterterrorism. They were the brawn to the CNU's diplomatic approach. While the CNU's motto boiled down to resolution through dialogue, the HRT's was simply to save lives. It sounded noble and could be, but in saving lives, there were often casualties. Nolan didn't like being overruled either. "As long as it takes."

"Hmph."

Bowen snapped his mouth shut, and turned to leave. He opened the door with such force the vehicle rocked.

She had to shake the negative energy from that man, and the best way to accomplish that was focusing on the job. She turned to the board where Patrick had written *Canceled insurance*. "As Ray pointed out to me, Gavin may have lost his job recently. But he could have paid cash for the drugs..."

"Not if he didn't have enough money. The medication might be more expensive than he can afford," Richie pointed out.

"Or that. Could I see the transcript of the conversation?" she asked Richie, and he handed it to her. She scanned down to the part she was looking for. "'They must be lying.' He was surprised that he didn't have coverage."

"That doesn't reconcile with him losing a job," Patrick said. "He'd know his insurance would be canceled."

"Which he did," she said. "But Gavin's words were the meds should be covered *still*. So he wasn't surprised the coverage was coming to an end, but that it already had."

"That's rough," Richie put in, "losing your job a couple

months after Christmas. Who knows if he got himself into debt for the holiday and now has no way of paying it off?"

"Which would only compound his feelings of failure." From a psychological standpoint it was simply known as an inadequate personality. "We need to paint this guy a rosy future, or this thing could blow up in our faces. Unfortunately, I have a feeling if he doesn't start cooperating soon, my hands may be tied. Let's give this another go." She turned to Ray, and she put the call through.

Gavin answered quickly, screaming into the phone, "I didn't want to do that!"

Adrenaline flooded her system, and she rode it to a place of flow and acceptance. "It's all right, Gavin. We can work through this, whatever it is. Just tell me what happened, and I'll do what I can to help." She intentionally phrased it so her words couldn't be twisted and seen as her shifting blame to him. Even if he was responsible.

"I hurt someone!" His voice raised. "There's... there's a lot of blood."

SIX

He snapped off the top on two more beer bottles. He'd drunk six already, but he wasn't in the mood for much else. He'd had a bad day, a bad week, month, year, *years* before that, and he didn't see it getting any better. There was no job, no prospects, no sunny outlook for the future. The definition of a loser by anyone's standards but he refused to accept the label.

He dropped onto the couch next to his companion, handing him one of the bottles.

The television was on, and they were mindlessly staring at whatever played out on the screen.

"Son of a bitch!" he let loose.

His companion turned to him, slowly, which was his way of going through life. He gave the expression *slow as a slug* meaning. "I'm not sure what we can do about it."

"No, no, I can't—" He swigged back some beer. "I just can't accept that. We've suffered for long enough."

His companion was staring at the TV as if he never heard him. It was just the news, and one would think it was the most fascinating entertainment the way the guy was practically drooling.

"What the hell, man? Can we at least watch something worth watching? Hand me that remote." He flung out his hand, palm open for his dumbass friend. All he had to do was drop the clicker in there. But it was hard to tell if he was even breathing. Drugs would do that to a person. He did some hard stuff too. "Clicker!" he screeched when his companion still hadn't handed it over.

"Oh, sorry."

But just as he was getting ready to turn the channel, a news-cast came on about a hostage situation in Woodbridge. The chyron at the bottom read, *FBI Crisis Negotiation Unit called in.*

He drank more beer as he watched things play out on screen.

"I thought you were going to put something else on," his companion whined.

"Shut up, will ya?" He cranked the volume, following an inner instinct that was telling him to watch this.

An armed man is holding several hostages at Corey's Grocer.
It's been ongoing for hours, but there is no progress for police...

A video playback, tagged hours earlier, showed the store's parking lot full of emergency vehicles. Then there was a closeup of a Mercedes trying to gain access. The woman behind the wheel looked familiar, but it had to be his mind playing tricks on him.

The reporter chimed in with words that supported the chyron and not long later, there was a shot of the woman in an FBI windbreaker.

"No shit." It *was* her. That bitch who threatened their futures. Seeing her splashed on his screen after just thinking about her was like a divine blessing. Maybe they should shake her up, make her see actions have consequences. Yeah, that's exactly what he'd do. But how to go about it? Go directly for her or from another angle? But what other angle?

He swigged back more beer, polishing off that bottle, and wiped his hand across his mouth. *The internet!* The epiphany hit like a tsunami. Who said booze wasn't good for anything?

He took out his phone and googled her name. Old articles came up, talking about the loss of her brother in a hostage stand-off. Well, boo-hoo. She wasn't the only person to lose someone. He certainly wasn't offering any condolences. She'd screwed everything up for him and his buddy here, and she should feel their pain. Killing would be over and done, which made hurting her and bringing her to her knees more appealing. Besides, who couldn't use a fed in their pocket? But how to get her attention and make her cooperate?

He continued digging online while his companion snored next to him. Shortly later, he found out that Special Agent Vos had a teenage daughter. She was a pretty little thing too. Yes, Mommy Dearest would probably do anything to save her.

He flicked off the TV and slapped his companion on the leg. "Time to sober up and get some sleep. We have work to do when the sun comes up." One thing that Vos would soon discover was he wasn't open to negotiation. If she didn't do what he wanted, he'd put a bullet in her beautiful girl.

SEVEN

At Gavin's admission, time came to a stop. "Gavin, we'll figure this out," Sandra told him, still the projection of calm. "I need for you to relax some, if you can. Please just tell me exactly what happened. Are they badly hurt?" There hadn't been a gunshot, but that didn't mean a fatal injury hadn't occurred.

"He tried to take my gun. But I... There's... there's a lot of blood..." The repetition and fragmented and choppy speech indicated Gavin was panicking.

He. The victim was a man. "Just take a few deep breaths, Gavin. Can you do that for me? Everything will be all right." She needed to bring the tension down, to a place that was easier to manage. De-escalating was crucial for a peaceful resolution.

"Okay, okay." Deep breaths traveled the line.

"Good, good, are you feeling any better?"

"A bit, yeah."

"Good. Is the man still breathing?"

"Yeah, and he... he won't stop looking at me!"

"Can you tell me his name, Gavin?" She knew better than to suggest deep breaths again. A second time would be seen as patronizing and insincere. "Gavin, please, let's just talk, and we'll figure out our next steps together. But I'd like to know the man's name. The man who is hurt." Again, she intentionally left out finger pointing, almost making it sound like the hostage had injured himself.

"I don't know."

"Well, can you ask him?" She waited anxiously for the answer. Was Gavin downplaying what he'd done? Then she heard a man's voice in the background, but it was slurred and garbled. A lot of blood and affected speech could suggest a head injury.

"I can't understand what he's saying," Gavin said.

"Can you put him on the phone? Could I talk to him?"

"No. I don't think that's a good idea."

Asking why would put Gavin on the defensive, and he might shut down. Instead, she asked, "Is he the only one hurt, Gavin?" She put that out there gently, almost nonchalantly, as if she'd still be on his side even if he had injured someone else.

He was silent at first, which Sandra didn't find reassuring, but then he spoke. "His name is Vern Wilcox. I got his license off him."

"Vern Wilcox?"

"Yeah."

The scribe was writing down the name, and Patrick was flipping through his paperwork, likely remembering that he'd pulled a background on the man.

"Okay, Gavin, that's a good start."

"I didn't mean to hurt him," Gavin pleaded.

"You and I know that, but not everyone out here will see it that way. But I'll stand up for you if you are willing to work as a team. Are you willing to do that?"

"Yeah... ah, sure. What do I do now?"

She felt tension release. Trust had been established, and his question suggested she held influence. That meant progress. "To start, I want to make sure you realize that I'm only honest with you all the time, Gavin. Do you believe me?"

"Yes."

Ray passed her a note that said, *Ready to surrender?*

She nodded but would continue to focus on the next steps, one by one. "I'm so happy to hear that, and since you know you can trust me, I think it's fair to stress how some people out here really aren't happy. They will make everyone's life miserable, and we both know what that means. They will do what they can to force you out, even if it's in a body bag. And I don't want to see that, Gavin. I want you to leave safe and sound. Would you be willing to surrender peacefully?"

"No, no, I can't."

"Okay, that's fine if you're not ready yet. I wanted to ask you though." She was bound to repeat that question to ensure the FBI's ass was covered. That way if the night spiraled to hell, it wouldn't bite them. "But there is something you could do that would be a good sign of faith, Gavin. Send Vern out so we can treat him." She'd love to request the release of Megan Cobb, but as far as she knew the woman was uninjured, making Vern more of a priority at this moment.

"No, you'll find a way to shoot me."

"I'd never do that, Gavin."

"You know what I mean. *Them*, the guys with the guns."

"I talk with them, and they listen to me." Somewhat of a lie which she hoped she'd carried off. "But a sign of good faith goes a long way. It's time for words to be put into action."

"What about me? Where's my sign of good faith?"

"That's us talking for hours, Gavin. I'm here for you as long as you need. All I ask is that you continue to work with me."

"What do you want?" he eventually asked.

"Let Vern Wilcox go so he can get the medical attention he needs." Flashes about her brother's fate moved in. How the situation hadn't been resolved in time, how the negotiator had failed to get Darrell Patton to release him for medical attention. If only he had, Sam might be alive today. But she'd learned a long time ago that entertaining *what ifs* was futile and destructive.

Silence hung across the line. She could have said something, but her mind was busy dredging through the past. How she had driven herself to the brink of obsession trying to unravel the timeline of events that ended with her brother in a body bag. Even at fourteen, she had been hungry for a reason, unable to fathom how her beautiful brother, with his infectious laugh, could just be gone.

Ray tapped his finger on the notepad in front of her. She'd spaced out for a second, and he must have sensed it. He'd written, *Offer him something in exchange, chance to find out if he has an endgame.*

She nodded her thanks to him. "Gavin, you didn't want any of this to happen, and that tells me that you're a good person in a bad situation. Let me help you. How about you release Vern Wilcox, and I do something for you? What do you want?"

"I just want to take the meds and leave."

"I can only imagine that would be appealing. It's been a long day, but it's all up to you, Gavin. You can go home if you want to. Right now. Just say the word."

Gavin hung up on her again.

"What are we supposed to make of that?" Ray asked her.

"We wait and see." In her experience she found trying to read minds pointless, if not potentially dangerous. Profiling had its place, but in the real world no person fit perfectly into any one box.

EIGHT

"Meet Vern Wilcox, customer," Patrick said, passing Sandra his background. "His car's the Audi."

She read down the report. Sixty-one, resident of Woodbridge, single. The picture attached to the background showed a man with silver-streaked black hair and of serious expression. He looked the image of a powerful businessman.

"Just in the wrong place at the wrong time," Patrick lamented.

No one added to that, and they proceeded to listen to a playback of the last conversation. What struck Sandra was one of the last things Gavin had said. "'I just want to take the meds and leave,'" she reiterated and added, "This could be interpreted as he has the meds in hand now. In the least, he wants this over with. Is that desire selfishly motivated or does he need to get the meds to someone?"

"Patrick," Garrison, the team leader said, "follow up with the FBI on the pharmacy system. Find out what's taking so long."

"Will do." Patrick put his phone to an ear.

Sandra only half-listened as he spoke to Simon. She was sipping coffee and watching the video monitor and debating whether to try calling Gavin again when the front door of the store opened.

An injured man stumbled out. From what she could tell, it was Vern Wilcox.

"Hallelujah!" Richie said.

"Now, that is terrific progress," Garrison said.

She kept her thoughts to herself. It was a step in the right direction, but she wasn't letting her guard down yet. Really the *party* was just getting started. Gavin had relinquished a hostage without securing something in return. Was this a sign he planned to take her up on her offer and surrender?

Armed SWAT officers moved in to secure the man and get him to an ambulance out of the line of fire.

Patrick wrapped up his call and shot out the door of the command vehicle. As the intelligence officer, his job included gathering information. And Vern Wilcox would be a golden resource as the first person to come out of the store.

She watched on the screen as Patrick walked to the man, who was now seated on a gurney at the back of an ambulance. As she observed the interaction between Patrick and Vern, and an irritated paramedic, thoughts of her brother rolled in again. At least Vern was getting the help he needed. Hopefully, his injuries weren't serious.

When Patrick returned several minutes later, she was fast to question him. "Is he going to be okay?"

"He has a concussion," Patrick told everyone. "Guess he rushed the HT and got pistol-whipped for his troubles."

"Did he know what kind of gun?" she asked, curious if their earlier theory held weight.

"He just described it as black and compact, so it could be the security guard's Smith & Wesson M&P."

"If so, it's unlikely he'd have that without the guard putting up a fight," Garrison said.

"There are other ways of manipulating people that aren't physical," Sandra countered.

"Except we can't ignore that Gavin responded physically to Wilcox. Being turned away at the pharmacy counter probably evoked a similar immediate reaction. And we can't overlook where we are now," Garrison pointed out.

Sandra looked at Patrick. "Did Wilcox know if anyone else is hurt in there?"

"He didn't."

Sandra had been wishing for a more definitive answer. "Did you ask specifically about Megan Cobb?"

"I did and, apparently, she won't stop sobbing, but Gavin brought out some cushions from the manager's office to make her more comfortable. And before anyone asks, Wilcox told me everyone's being held in the lunchroom."

"Just as we thought," Garrison said.

"Uh-huh. He secures the doors by putting a mop through the pull handles. He pops in and out of the room. He did collect their phones and took them with him."

"Was he able to tell you anything about Gavin's description that might help us ID him?" Ray asked, beating Sandra to the question.

"He says he looks to be in his twenties. He also added that he's losing it in there. When he's around, he's pacing, waving his gun in the air, and making threats."

"He's stressed, trying to think of a way out of this," she elaborated. "That could be a good thing. Anything else?"

Patrick shook his head. "Well, just that your colleague Simon doesn't have a name for us yet. I just got off from him before talking to Wilcox. But apparently, he's close to getting all the warrants in place to access the system, so it shouldn't be long now."

"More progress. I love to hear it," Garrison chimed in.

"Let's try our luck for more." She got into position and patched through to Gavin.

He answered on the second ring and held the line in silence.

"That was a really smart decision, Gavin, letting Vern Wilcox go."

"Is he going to be all right?"

The fact that Gavin was asking told her his conscience was working. Also that he had developed empathy for his hostages. There would be no advantage in mentioning Vern's concussion. It would put Gavin into a tailspin and cause him to lose hope. "Yes, he'll be fine. You did a good thing, letting Vern go for medical attention. You're still in a terrific position to walk away from this."

"I'd love to believe you."

"Well, you said before that you trust me. There's no reason for that to have changed. I haven't lied to you, and I never will. I'm telling you the truth, Gavin," she stressed. "I'll see what we can do for you. Are the meds for someone else, Gavin?"

Seconds ticked off. No response.

She took that as confirmation the meds were for another person and decided to run with that assumption. It was a potential risk but one that she was comfortable taking. "I understand you're nervous. But how about we get those meds to the person who needs them? Just tell me who they are for."

"No. You'll— No, that's not happening. I tell you that, you'll know everything about me."

No one could say Gavin wasn't intelligent. "But if this person needs their meds, let me help them. It's obvious you care deeply about them."

"She's my whole world."

She... It could be a significant other, but there's only one person Sandra would describe as her whole world. Her daughter, Olivia. Was that why he empathized with Megan? He related with her and had a soft spot for children? "Are you a father, Gavin?"

More silence, but she wasn't letting it derail her.

"Let me help you, help *her*."

"Okay."

Sandra's shoulders relaxed. He might as well have said outright the medication was for his daughter. The position of power shifted more to her. "Does that mean you're willing to come out? I will get the meds to her."

"I let that man go. What else do you need?"

She didn't take well to the fact he'd removed Vern Wilcox's name from his statement, referencing him by a label instead. That could be a deliberate choice to distance himself. "What is your daughter's name, Gavin?"

"I'm not telling you that, and I'm not ready to come out."

One step forward, one back. If he wasn't willing to surrender yet, the hostages became her top priority. "I can tell you're a good guy who has just found himself in a tough spot, but you're not in this alone, Gavin. And those people in there with you all have families who will be worried about them too. And Megan—"

"She stays."

His quick rebuttal confirmed his attachment to the pregnant woman. He'd instantly recognized her name and thankfully hadn't reduced her to a label. But he'd also seen where she was headed with a request and nipped it. "Okay, but all those other people in there... if we could find out who they are, we could let their families know they are all right. This would go a long way with my superiors, and they'd be very willing to help you and your daughter." She had to be careful how she put this and how she said it. The phrasing needed to be genuine and not manipulative. She intentionally didn't say *family* because she didn't know his home situation. A fractured relationship could have him feeling more like a failure and trigger him into taking further destructive action.

There was a stretch of silence.

Sandra moved ahead. "Is there someone we can contact for you? To let them know you're okay."

"No. It's fine."

So he either had an unstable home life or still feared disclosing his full identity for some reason. "All right, that's fine. I just thought I'd offer. If you won't let me talk to the hostages, will you please just get their names and a number for their closest family member?" This exercise would go a long way to humanizing the hostages.

Gavin didn't say anything for a few beats. His breathing became deeper and traveled the line. "Okay. Fine, but I will need some time." He ended the call.

Sandra sat back. She was making headway, but it wasn't time to celebrate just yet. There was a lot she still had to find out. In the meantime, the knowledge she lacked could be detrimental.

NINE

Another hour scooted by, taking them to eleven PM, and Sandra and the team were still in a holding pattern. Bowen remained eager for SWAT to move in and bring the situation to an end. But she had enough experience to know that *end* wouldn't be a pretty one if they rushed things. Thankfully it didn't sound like the police chief had changed his mind despite Vern Wilcox being hurt. She had no doubt Bowen had passed that news along.

The line for the throw phone rang, and Sandra answered.

"I have all their names," Gavin told her.

"Great. Let me get a pen and paper." She looked at Richie, who was ready to note everything down.

"Not so fast. I thought of something I want."

"It's not good faith to change what's at stake partway through, Gavin, but I'm listening." She wanted to denote a cooperative spirit while maintaining control.

"I want my daughter to get her meds, but I want to take them to her."

"I'll see what I can do." She knew there was no way that would fly.

"And I want a hundred thousand dollars and the freedom to walk away from this free and clear."

"I'm sorry, Gavin, but I'm not sure how I'm supposed to make that happen." It was a passive-aggressive approach, but the apology paired with the use of his name added warmth. This response also flipped things back to Gavin for him to solve the problem.

"Fine. I don't need the money. It's for my girl. Get it for her. Isn't there someone you could talk to about this?"

He'd just elaborated and revealed his primary emotional driver was his daughter's welfare. "Sure, Gavin, I can talk to my boss about this and explain your side. I can tell you're a good dad, just trying to do right by your daughter."

"That's right. This is all for her."

"Your daughter also needs to learn there are consequences for her actions. It's a valuable life lesson that could save her a lot of grief. If you surrender peacefully right now, the charges against you will be light, Gavin. I'll speak on your behalf."

"Just get the money and the meds for her. You have an hour to decide." He hung up, and Sandra set a timer on her phone for sixty minutes.

"Well, he seems to have *that* move down," Bowen griped.

Of course Bowen had to be in the command vehicle for that interaction... "At least he's given thought to what he wants."

"Whatever delusions he has, there's no way this guy is getting away scot-free," Bowen seethed. "And a hundred K? Not a chance."

She wasn't going to discuss the money with Bowen. "You and I know he will pay for what he's done, but he needs to be convinced that the charges against him will be light. If we succeed in reassuring him in this regard, we get everyone else out safe and sound too. I believe zero casualties is the ultimate goal we all share."

Bowen mumbled incoherently and said, "I can't believe we'd offer this guy a deal."

"It and the money are worth entertaining if it gets him and the hostages out safely."

"Tick tock," Bowen said and tapped a finger on his watch face and sat down at the table with a coffee. "The HT gave you an hour. I'd say we'll know everyone's fate at that time."

Patrick wrapped up a phone call and spoke to everyone. "So I heard back from Simon. He got into the pharmacy system and found a few Gavins listed. I narrowed it down to one that fit Wilcox's description. Gavin McConnell. Twenty-five years old, no criminal record, has an address in town. No phone number on record or noted in the pharmacy system."

"No record is great news." This suggested Gavin would be less likely to take things to the absolute extreme. It was probable he wasn't prejudiced against law enforcement. Not that he'd given her any indication of that during their talks, aside from some fear the FBI was on scene.

"I'm not sure how much comfort I take in his clean record," Patrick said. "Most law-abiding citizens don't hold people at gunpoint for hours."

"The sad part is, Patrick, we're all capable if we're pushed to our breaking point," Sandra said. "What about any spouse or significant others?"

Patrick typed more. "He shares an address with Karen Bing..." More clicking away. "She's the mother of a two-year-old, Cassandra. Both are also attached to Gavin's account with the pharmacy. Simon can't get into the prescription records side of things without another type of warrant though."

"Likely no need to worry about it. Get an officer over there to talk to her," Garrison told the intelligence officer. "Tell her what's going on and have the officer find out what they can from her about Gavin. We've speculated he was recently fired from his workplace. See if the officer can find out the circumstances and specifics, if that's even the case. If not, then why the medical insurance was canceled. Also if the meds are needed urgently."

"You bet." Patrick got on the phone.

Sandra needed to have a frank and honest conversation about granting Gavin McConnell's requests. That wasn't going to happen with Bowen. He might not like what she had to do next, but she had a job to do and lives to save.

She stepped outside to call Assistant Director Rowe.

TEN

Sandra's phone continued to count down the minutes in the background while she was on the phone with Elwood stating her case.

"So you think we should be prepared to hand this guy a hundred *thousand* dollars?" Elwood put emphasis on the amount. It was a lot from one perspective, but very little if it saved lives.

"I do. Besides, it's not like we'd let him leave with it. It's more a bait-and-lure type of situation."

"Clearly."

"And I'll buy us more time by saying we need to gather the money together. If this all works out, we won't even need to show him the cash."

"Though we should have it in case he wants to see it."

"Yes."

"But the deal... You want that to hold up?"

"I do." She wanted to keep her word to Gavin in this regard. She mentioned a lighter charge and wanted reassurance that would be the case.

"For any of the above to happen, McConnell needs to

surrender peacefully and the rest of the hostages must walk away unharmed."

"I'll make sure he knows that." Though she'd have to watch how she played this. She certainly couldn't present the criteria to Gavin in case there were injuries she didn't know about. Then he'd feel boxed in.

"There is the chance he's not prepared to surrender just yet either, which if that is the case..."

"I know what to do." She'd request another sign of good faith.

"Good. Keep me posted."

"And you me. I need to know when the money will get here."

Elwood was gone, and she got off to look at the timer. She had five minutes left and returned inside the command vehicle.

"And there she is," Bowen said caustically. "No question of where you've been or what you've been up to."

"Guess as long as you know, I don't need to bring you up to speed." She walked past him, ignoring his sneer, and some of the team whose mouths gaped open. She sat at her post and turned to Ray beside her. She had forty seconds left on the clock but called.

Gavin answered but didn't say a word.

"I've spoken to my boss, Mr. McConnell." She could feel Bowen listening to her every word.

"Huh. So you found out who I am."

"Well, a colleague of mine did. You don't have a record, Gavin. What do you say we end this peacefully now?"

"Right after a hundred grand goes to my girl and my freedom is assured. Those are my terms."

"And as I said, I have spoken to my boss. We're going to need a little more time to get the money together."

"Bullshit. You're the FBI. You have money."

"That's why we're able to get it together, but these things

take time. And..." She paused for dramatic effect. "My boss is being a stickler, truth be told. He wants your word that you're prepared to surrender first."

Silence.

Ray wrote, *It feels like he's not ready.*

Sandra nodded, concluding the same. "I know that you want to leave so you can get to your daughter, Gavin, and I want to help you do that. How is your daughter? If she needs the meds urgently, let me get them to her."

"No."

"That's fine. If you're not ready to surrender just yet, give us a sign of good faith."

"What do you want?"

"My boss would love the rest of those names, Gavin." She waited out an ensuing silence.

Eventually, Gavin started to rattle off names and numbers. Richie was writing them down furiously. They had about five names when a phone rang in the background on Gavin's end.

"Oh, shit! What the— No, I don't want to talk to her."

She had to guess it was someone calling his personal cell-phone given how he'd responded. But Patrick told them Gavin didn't have a number on his file. Though it was possible he had a prepaid phone, which weren't catalogued the same. "Gavin, talk to me. Who is calling you?"

"It's Karen. What the— Did you put her up to this? Did you tell her what I'm doing?"

The girlfriend calling held no advantage. Rather the opposite. He'd feel exposed as a failure to someone he'd likely rather impress. "You don't need to talk to her, Gavin. Just don't answer the—"

"I'm doing this for our daughter!" Gavin roared.

There was gunfire. Then the line cut off.

"Shit, I knew it." Bowen's cheeks were a bright red as he shot to his feet. "We should have moved in hours ago. I've tried playing by your rules, Vos, letting you talk everything out, but that ends now. I'm going to get SWAT to move in."

She was stunned. "Don't do that."

Bowen, who had taken steps toward the door, turned back around. "Why shouldn't I? Are you going to contact your boss at the FBI again? Tattle on me?"

"This isn't about us, LT. It's about Gavin and his hostages," Garrison put in.

"To hell, it isn't."

Sandra stood and walked over to the team coordinator. "I'm here because I was called in to help, but I report to the assistant director—"

"La de da. And here to help?" Bowen spat. "We're hours further along in this mess, and there's a backslide. His fucking girlfriend calls on a phone that we didn't even know existed."

Garrison stood. "I think we should all take two steps back." He turned to Patrick. "I need to know everything that took place during that conversation between the officer and the girlfriend."

Patrick glanced at Bowen but responded to the team leader, "I'll find out the exact details of their conversation, sir," and picked up his phone.

"Make sure someone goes and sits with her too," Bowen wedged in. "I don't want this screwup happening again."

"Yes, LT," Patrick told him.

Sandra was watching all this unfold, feeling the situation fall through her fingers. She typically would have cautioned about this exact thing when telling Patrick to get an officer over to talk to the girlfriend, but as far as they knew Gavin didn't have a phone. Leaving the hostage situation to the negotiator was what worked.

She turned to Bowen. "We don't know exactly where Gavin is currently holed up. It's likely near the hostages, but there were times I spoke to him there was silence in the background.

You want to secure Gavin, without hurting anyone, we can't afford to go in blind."

"Likely near? He's probably not wasting a bullet on the ceiling," Bowen protested.

"There's no way to know. Let me try contacting Gavin again and see if I can find out what's going on in there."

Garrison looked at Bowen, who waved his hand. "Give it a go, Vos," Garrison said.

Sandra put the call through, and the line rang repeatedly. She sat back.

"Let me guess. No answer?" Bowen said. "Surprise, surprise, he's not talking now. He knows he just screwed up his chances of getting out of there."

After the long day and night Sandra had, this guy was testing her last nerve. "You can't know exactly what he's thinking."

"I can't, but you apparently can," Bowen kicked back. "And we can't just ignore the fact that a gun was fired." He drilled Sandra with a glare.

"No one is," she said.

Patrick cleared his throat and cut in. "I spoke to the officer who talked with the girlfriend. He never saw her call but said she excused herself to use the washroom in the back of the house."

"Did he get McConnell's number?" Garrison asked.

"Yeah, and I'll make sure the service is cut."

"What else?" Sandra asked Patrick. "He must have learned something from her we can use."

"McConnell doesn't have any savings. In fact, the opposite, he's in debt for twenty grand. He was let go from his factory job Monday of last week," Patrick said, referring to his notepad. "Replaced by AI."

"It's going to replace all of us one day," Richie put in. "The rise of the machines is more real than you might think."

She wasn't touching that comment and no one else seemed to want to either. "And the health insurance? Did the officer ask the girlfriend about that?" she asked Patrick.

"Oh, yeah. The girl became blue swearing. She said Gavin told her they'd have medical insurance until the end of the month. Guess she kicked him out last week, but he asked for a chance to make things right. The girl's got a chest infection that's in danger of turning into pneumonia. He told his girlfriend to stay with the girl while he got the meds."

None of this was good. No job, canceled insurance, a broken relationship, one chance to prove himself a good father and it blows up in his face... Receiving a call from Karen would have been the cherry on top. It would have emphasized his feelings of hopelessness, reducing the chances of ending this peacefully. "Patrick, could you reach out to Gavin's former employer?"

"It's the middle of the night," Bowen chimed in.

"Does that matter right now, because I don't think it does," she countered. She picked up speaking to Patrick. "I'd like to know what happened with the insurance."

Patrick glanced at Garrison, who nodded, then he got on the phone.

"Please, just a bit longer," she said, appealing to Bowen. "Let me see if I can establish contact with Gavin again." She didn't wait for a response but put the call through. *Answer, answer,* she mentally coached. If she didn't get through to Gavin, she wasn't sure she could stop the powers that be from tromping in there.

Gavin answered. He said nothing, but he was breathing heavily.

"Gavin, I need you to talk to me. Tell me, is anyone hurt?" She balanced diplomacy with the goal of her job, toeing that fine line of being the shot caller and Gavin respecting her enough to relent to her position.

"No one is—"

A woman cried out, and from the sound of it, she was in extreme agony. Sandra shut down her imagination and focused. Cool, calm, collected. "Who is that, Gavin? Tell me what's going on so I can help you."

"It's nothing. It's just that..."

Sandra let the silence ride out for several beats, then said, "I need to know that everyone is okay, including you."

"I... I'm fine."

The woman cried out again. Whatever was the cause, it sounded like the pain was excruciating. "Was someone shot, Gavin? If so, just let me know and we'll work on this together to move forward. No one else needs to get hurt."

"No one was shot. I just got mad. My girlfriend... she thinks I'm a loser. But she's right. They would be better off without me."

The girlfriend and the daughter... "Gavin, I can appreciate how you might feel that way. You haven't had a good couple of weeks. I can see why opting for a way out might be appealing, but just hang in with me for a bit longer, please." This aspect of negotiation ran contrary to what those uneducated in the craft might deem the right move. But in cases where an HT brought up suicide, talking about it wasn't planting the thought in their heads. That was already there. Speaking about it demonstrated that the negotiator understood them, further ingratiating them with the HT.

"My life sucks!"

The woman continued crying out in the background. Another person yelled, "She needs a doctor!"

"Gavin, you have the opportunity to be the hero right now and turn things around. I have faith in you." She tapped into her inner calm. She couldn't let the chaos in the background affect this interchange.

"*Pfft*. I don't. How could you? You don't even know me!" he spat.

"I'm good at reading people, Gavin, and I can tell that you're an amazing dad who would do anything for his daughter." She would dredge up every redeemable quality, no matter how minuscule, to wield in her arsenal if it could resolve this situation without any more injuries or casualties.

"I love Cassie. She's my everything, my world."

"I don't blame you. She's a beautiful little girl with a bright future. And, Gavin, you can be a part of it."

"No, I'm not coming out there. I'll be shot."

"You have my word. You will be safe."

"No. I just can't. Not yet."

Sandra breathed easier with that concession. Gavin had clearly entertained the idea of surrendering. He was likely getting tired and worn down. "But Cassie needs her medication. I know you want to get that to her."

"I do, but I..." He started crying. "I had no choice, and now..."

"Is everyone okay?" she asked again and then added a twist, "Would you let me speak with the hostages?" They still didn't have all their names. He'd been interrupted when he'd tried to hand them all over. When he didn't respond, she said, "I'm sure there's something you'd like right now. Coffee, maybe? Do they have coffee in there?" The unrelated diversion would shake up his thoughts, throw him off.

A few beats, then, "Just crap stuff."

"Great, let me get you coffee. How do you like it?"

More crying came through in the background.

"Two sugars and cream."

"You got it. We'll round one up, some good stuff, and get it to you. But I do need to speak to the hostages first."

"What about my getting out of here and my hundred K?"

Just when she thought those demands were put aside... "Let

me speak with the hostages, and once I know everyone is okay in there, I'll speak with my boss again, follow up on the money. Will you do that, Gavin?" She hadn't even disclosed a deal was possible yet, and she wouldn't unless it became necessary.

"Okay," he mumbled.

"I want to talk with that woman who is crying first. Who is she?"

He didn't respond, and she heard shuffling on the other end. The crying became louder and dampened to a hiccupped sob. Then a woman's voice cut across the line. "Get me out of here!"

"I'm working on that. I'm FBI Special Agent Sandra Vos. Who am I speaking to?" All of this was spoken calmly to soothe the hostage.

"Megan"—she howled and hissed in pain—"Cobb. Please, help me. I'm in labor."

A month early... "Megan, I will do what I can to get you out of there. How far apart are the contractions?"

"I don't—" She winced loudly.

More rustling on the other end, then, "This is Gina Andrews. I'm a nurse, and her baby is coming. Her contractions are strong and every five minutes. She needs urgent medical attention."

Patrick kicked into motion, once again riffling through reports he'd pulled.

"Okay, Gina. Thank you. I'm Special Agent Sandra Vos. You're by her side, and he's letting you help her?"

"Best I can."

Patrick gave her the printout on Gina Andrews. Thirty-five, resident of Woodbridge. Her photo showed a redhead with a freckly face. "Is everyone in the upstairs lunchroom, including the man holding you?"

"Yes."

Sandra made eye contact with Garrison, and he nodded.

They had a second confirmation on where the hostages were being held. "Was anyone shot when the gun was fired?"

"I don't know."

"That's enough." Gavin was back on the line. "You spoke with Megan and her friend. Both are fine."

"Megan's not fine, Gavin. She is going into labor a month before she's due. She needs urgent medical attention."

"Her water just broke!" Gina yelled in the background.

"Come on, Gavin," Sandra said. "You must be terrified, but you let her go and that will go a long way to helping me help you."

"She'll be fine. I just heard this woman say she's a nurse."

"Gina, yes. But just because she's a nurse, it doesn't mean she's able to deliver the baby safely there. As I said, Megan is in premature labor. You're a good father, Gavin, and you must see the dangers. Infection... complications?"

Silence for a few seconds. "My freedom and a hundred and fifty K for Cassie and everyone walks."

His price went up... "I'm going to tell you right up front, Gavin, because we have this friendship now, this trust between us, but I don't see my boss going for that."

"Get him to go for it, or she'll be having her baby right here!" He ended the call.

Ray swiveled his chair to face her. "Never saw that coming."

"Makes two of us." In fact, it was the last thing she expected, and it made her uneasy. Gavin's emotional state was all over the place. One minute, he was caring about Megan Cobb, and the next sounded prepared to kill her. Sandra needed to find some way of making Gavin see that he needed to start cooperating with her, for everyone's sakes. Including his own.

ELEVEN

Sandra tried calling Gavin right back, but he wasn't answering.

"Tell me if I have this right, Vos? A woman is in labor, and he's refusing to talk or let her go?" Bowen asked.

She didn't say anything. He'd summed it up.

"All right, then. It's time to move in." Bowen shot to his feet, no doubt to wrangle SWAT into action.

"If you go in there now, there will be lives lost. Possibly Cobb's and the baby's," she rushed out.

"She does have a point," Garrison said.

Bowen stopped for a moment, shook his head at his colleague, and left the command vehicle.

Sandra sat at the table to make a call to Assistant Director Rowe. It rang a few times before he answered.

"Have any good news for me?"

"Wish I did. It's the opposite. Things are escalating. He wants more money, and the pregnant woman I told you about is in labor. *Premature* labor."

"You need to find a way to get McConnell to let her go."

"You don't think I've been trying?" She massaged her temple and had an idea. It was a tiny offering but could warm

Gavin into a more cooperative mood. "A while ago, he said he'd love a good coffee."

"He's shutting down and you want to reward that behavior?"

"I know this is going to come across contradictory to the rule of negotiating, but I feel if we show a small kindness to him, it will go a long way. He did release Vern Wilcox without anything in return. This would show that I remember, and that the small act mattered."

"You better hope it's a miracle brew, and he suddenly feels super cooperative. But if you feel good about this, then I trust you. But, if this doesn't work out, it might be time to cut our losses and let SWAT move in."

"Not you too." Her shoulders sagged, and at her words the others in the command vehicle looked at her but quickly turned away again.

"Even you can't win them all."

"I still feel I can talk him out."

"And you would because you can be... How to put this delicately?"

"Why start now?"

"Stubborn. Hard-headed."

"I like to think of myself as determined and focused."

"Well, whatever it is, use it."

"And the ETA on the money?"

Elwood grumbled incoherently and hung up.

She returned to her chair and steeled herself to call Gavin when Patrick spoke.

"I got a hold of Gavin's former employer. Guy's name is Michael Underwood. He said that Human Resources was supposed to cancel the health insurance at the end of the month. He apologized if they made an error and said he'd reinstate it for another month if it would help."

"Might be a matter of too little, too late," she said but called Gavin.

He answered with, "I'm not letting her go."

A woman screamed in the background, "You bastard!" It sounded like Megan Cobb.

Sandra's proposition would wait. "This is Megan's first child, Gavin. She's scared, and I don't blame her. The baby will be a month premature. There can be a lot of complications with that for the mother and child. As a father yourself, I can't imagine you'd want that baby to be hurt."

Silence, which she took as him waging war with his conscience.

"Gavin, you said you would never hurt her," she said, piercing the quiet and reminding him of the words he'd spoken hours ago.

"I wouldn't."

"Good. Think of your daughter, and your future together. You have the chance to save a mother and her child. Cassie would respect that. You could even decide to walk away right now and have tomorrow."

There was a lot of crying and panicked talking in the background. Sandra could make out that it was Gina reassuring Megan. This played out for some time and were the only sounds coming across the phone line.

"Fine," he said.

"You will walk away?" Sandra tried to keep her voice level, but it wasn't easy. Those in the vehicle were all watching her with expectant gazes. Negotiation was like walking across thin ice. You could be going along fine one moment but break through the next.

"Not me, but Megan. On one condition."

And there it was... The crack in the ice. "What's that, Gavin?"

"That you'll remember this act for what it is. Good faith. Use it to get me a good deal."

"You bet, Gavin." At least he'd returned to reality and knew he'd face consequences for today's actions.

"I'll send her out the front door by herself, but if I sense any shady business, I will put a bullet in her head."

Any relief that came with the prospect of Megan Cobb's freedom was instantly doused by Gavin's threat. Before now, Gavin talked about himself as if his actions were forced and reactive. "I hear you, Gavin. But when you let her go, I'll get you that coffee with two sugars and cream right away, and we'll talk more about getting you out of there." She locked eyes with Patrick, who sighed but got on the phone. He'd have an officer source one from a coffee shop. They couldn't exactly offer up some in a mug from the command vehicle.

"What about my money?"

"I'm still working on that."

"Okay."

"I'm going to stay on the line with you while you send Megan out, all right? You have any concerns then you talk to me."

Things in the command vehicle became livelier. Bowen left to notify SWAT of the impending hostage release.

"Okay," Gavin said.

She listened while it sounded like Gina was coaxing Megan to her feet. She was crying, and then the soles of shoes hit the store's flooring. A few minutes later, the front door opened, and Megan stumbled out.

SWAT officers moved in to get her.

"They're getting too close!" Gavin yelled.

Sandra recoiled, her eardrums throbbing. "They're just helping Megan. You're safe, Gavin. I promise you." God, she hoped that's all they had planned! But surely, they wouldn't try anything with a pregnant woman in the crossfire.

"That better be all it is. I don't want to hurt anyone." His voice was quivering.

Sandra held her breath as she continued to watch everything play out on the monitor. It wasn't long, and Megan Cobb was safely with paramedics. Her husband was guided over to his wife by a police officer.

"That was a great thing you did, Gavin. Your coffee is almost here." She turned to Ray, who turned to Patrick, and picked up the phone again.

A second later, he was nodding.

"Gavin, I was just informed it's here now. We can leave it at the front door, but we need your assurance no one will get hurt."

"I promise, but I don't want to see anyone with a gun. If I step out, someone's going to shoot me."

Sandra knew there would be no convincing any of the SWAT officers to disarm themselves to deliver the coffee. "I don't think they will go for that, Gavin. You have my word that when you duck out for the coffee, no one will fire at you." She was lying through her teeth here. This wasn't a promise she could make. There were powers higher than her, and some of them wanted this standoff over and done, no matter how it shook out for the HT. His life wasn't their priority, but that's why it had to be hers.

"I'll send a hostage to get the coffee."

"You can do that, Gavin. Up to you. Enjoy your coffee." She looked at Garrison, and he got on the phone. She overheard him filling in Bowen.

A few minutes later, the coffee was put in place, and the officers retreated.

When they cleared, the door opened, and a woman stepped out, moving slowly and looking around.

Sandra recognized her from the photo she looked at moments ago. *It's Gina Andrews*, she wrote on a piece of paper.

She had a white bag in her hand.

"What does she have, Gavin?" Sandra asked.

No response.

"Hurry up!" Gavin yelled, clearly directing this at Gina, but it rang through the phone piercing Sandra's ears.

Gina continued to pivot her head like an anxious rabbit trying to avoid becoming prey. Then she tore off, upsetting the coffee, and running down the plaza out of his sightline, with the bag still in hand.

Patrick left the command center.

"Fuck!" Gavin cussed.

Richie had received a call and scribbled, *SWAT was just cleared for the shot if one opens up* on the markerboard.

"Gavin, listen to me. Please. Surrender peacefully. Think about your daughter's future. Yours."

"It's too late for me now. Just get the meds, they're in that bag, to Cassie."

"We can still resolve this peacefully." But she had a sour feeling in her gut. He'd originally said the pharmacist wouldn't hand them over. Had he since helped himself or had he lied? Was the pharmacist long dead or a casualty of the gunfire? If the latter, he would have been confronting the man again when Gavin's girlfriend called. Talk about bad timing. "It's great that you have the meds, but Cassie needs her father too, Gavin." As she spoke, she saw shadows dance behind the glass of the door, and that meant SWAT would see them. Even better than her, as they'd be equipped with high-powered scopes.

She picked up the employee list and scanned down to the pharmacist. Stanley Moody. His background showed a balding, middle-aged man, married, mid-forties. "Gavin, how did you get the meds?"

"The pharmacist."

He was keeping his responses short, and she needed more information. "The pharmacist gave you the meds?"

"That's right."

"When was this?"

"A while ago."

Still not definitive enough. "Is Stanley okay, Gavin?" She used his first name only for added familiarity. It would have been the name on his tag.

"I'm not going to talk about Stanley." He might have used his name, but his voice and tone were cold and detached.

Not good at all. "We have a rapport going, Gavin. You help me help *you*, remember?"

"I didn't mean to. He was just being so stubborn and wasn't giving me what I needed. Then Karen called." He wailed out.

"Did you shoot him, Gavin?" she repeated.

"He's fine," Gavin said.

Sandra could feel herself losing hold on the negotiation, and she didn't like the hesitation any more than his word choice. "Let me talk to Stanley."

"I can't let you do that." Gavin hung up.

Sandra closed her eyes and pinched the bridge of her nose. She wanted to go for a very long run, purge the last six hours and fifteen minutes from her system, and come back recharged. She was considering grabbing some fresh air when Gina Andrews was led inside the command vehicle by Patrick and Bowen.

TWELVE

Sandra took her headset off to talk with Gina. Patrick and Garrison had already offered her a seat at the table. She sat down next to her. "How are you doing?" She needed to drill down to what was going on inside the store, but there was always time for human compassion. In her line of work, it was imperative.

"Holding up." Gina wiped her cheeks. They were damp from the wet snow that was coming down. "But it's not good in there." She faced Sandra, and her eyes filled with tears.

"Is everyone in the lunchroom still?"

"Yeah, but he's losing it. He, uh, left with the pharmacist, and he was different when he came back. He's walking in circles and talking to himself. I think he might have taken something from the pharmacy that's messing with his head."

Sandra could feel Bowen's gaze cutting through her, but she wasn't going to give him the satisfaction of meeting his eye. "And the pharmacist? Did he come back?"

Gina licked her lips. "I think he's dead."

"Because he never came back?" This question got Sandra

judgmental looks from Garrison and Bowen. The latter shook his head, as if to say, *Do you need to see the body?*

"I heard a gun go off when they were gone, and no he didn't."

Piecing together Gavin's account and Gina's it didn't look good for Stanley Moody. "Okay, thank you, Gina. You did really well. You need to go with the paramedics and get looked at."

Garrison saw Gina out, and Sandra steeled herself to face off with the team coordinator.

Bowen was armed and ready with, "SWAT is prepared to take the next available shot."

"I know that."

"The only reason they haven't is because they couldn't get a clear line of sight."

"Can't say I'm sorry to hear that."

"This guy lied to you, Vos. And he's a killer. Doesn't that mean anything to you?"

Defending Gavin was becoming increasingly difficult. She was fighting for a hostage taker who she no longer had faith in, but that was the job. She was to act in the hostages' best interest *and* the hostage taker's regardless of her personal feelings. The entire premise was if the HT was working with the negotiator, peaceful resolution was possible. But that wasn't the case here anymore. Their foundation had a fault. "I'm going to try him again."

"Whatever floats your boat." Bowen flailed his arm in the air.

She returned to her chair, coaching herself to release her frustration from being lied to. She took a few deep breaths and called Gavin. The line rang a few times before he picked up. He didn't speak, and she rushed ahead. "Is Stanley dead? Just tell me the truth so I can help you."

"I didn't mean to hurt him. He just wasn't doing what I asked him to do."

She was tired of his lame fallback excuse, like everything was happening to and against him. He failed to take any responsibility for his actions. Stepping into his shoes, his life didn't have a lot going for it recently. A man with nothing much to lose was dangerous. "I need to ask again, is he dead, Gavin?"

"Yes, yes, I think so. I... I shot him."

Pointing out that he lied in so many words wouldn't be advantageous. She couldn't ignore it either. "Well, I won't lie to you, Gavin, so I admit this puts me in a tough spot. I went to bat for you. My boss was prepared to give you everything you wanted." A lie, but it was par for the course and an effective tool if she could pull it off convincingly. Thankfully, she had that skill down to a fine art. "But now, he's pissed off. Me? I'm trying to talk him down and tell him you didn't mean for any of this to happen. Just a bad month is all." Thinking about the pharmacist, possibly on the inside fighting for life, while she continued to talk, pierced her heart. Her brother, Sam, had been a casualty of the same.

"Yeah."

"We spoke to your former boss, Michael Underwood, and he's sorry. Your medical insurance will be reactivated for another month. There was an error made at their end, and he apologizes."

"There was a— Oh my God!"

"It's all right. Everything can still work out." All of that was a complete fabrication.

"How is that even possible?"

"I told you I'd go to bat for you, Gavin. And I have. More than once. You've surrendered a couple of hostages, but someone is dead now. A deal is still possible, but only if you surrender right now."

"I can't."

"Gavin, I need you to start being honest with me. Is anyone else in there hurt or dead?"

"No, I swear. Stanley's the only one, and..." Gavin started crying. "I didn't mean to."

The admission landed heavy on her shoulders. Someone had died on her watch. The night was a long one, and even she was wearing out. "Let me get those pills to Cassie. My boss says if you walk out of there now, she'll get her medication right away."

In truth, an officer had immediately taken the pills to Cassandra.

Gavin sobbed heavier.

"Let me help you," she said gently. "Just walk away from all this. You'll still get a future with your daughter, and she'll get the meds she needs."

The seconds seemed to tick off in painful agony as she waited for Gavin to respond.

"Okay."

One word, and she was breathing easier. It was another step closer to victory. But they weren't quite there yet. "Okay, great. I will let everyone know that you are coming out peacefully. To make that clear to everyone though, you need to kick the gun out the door and come out with your hands up. Then lie face down on the ground. Can you do that, Gavin?"

"Yeah."

He ended the call, and she tried calling him back, but he didn't answer. Before she could make too much of it, the front door opened, and the gun was kicked out. Gavin followed, hands in the air, as he lowered himself to the ground.

Officers moved in and apprehended him.

A while later, the small flood of hostages streamed out escorted by SWAT officers. Each of them was directed to waiting paramedics to be looked over.

Everyone in the command vehicle hooted and hollered, high fives all around.

Ray held out his hand to her. "Great job."

"You too." She blew out a breath and took his hand, shook it. Everyone else did the same.

Sandra left the vehicle, braving the cold early morning air, and watched Gavin being led to a police car. What she saw was a desperate father with a warped sense of how to provide for his child. And it was those actions that would send him to prison, likely for the rest of his life since no deal had been extended. But at least he was alive to draw breath.

He looked at her as if he sensed her watching, and she swore when their eyes met, he knew who she was. Had he seen her when she'd first used the bullhorn or looked her up online before they cut service to his phone? She supposed it didn't really matter.

The incident had taken ten hours and forty-five minutes from start to finish, but this night was finally over. And she couldn't wait to crawl into bed.

THIRTEEN

Sandra's strides ate up the sidewalk as she jogged along the Potomac River through Georgetown Waterfront Park. She inhaled the morning air, though she'd gotten a later start than she normally did due to last night. It was eleven AM and most people in the city were at work, set up behind their desks in their corporate offices. She was lucky to be outside and moving.

Her doctor recommended she do something else for exercise "at her age," but she refused to accept that advice. She was in great physical shape, and there wasn't a history of joint trouble in her family tree. It wouldn't matter if there was though. Running was her meditation. Fresh air, moving, and breath expanding her lungs. Not only did the exercise revive her body and mind, it fed her soul. Out here, on the path, she was in her own world, left to her own thoughts. And with her line of work, with her past, she had to do something to keep the demons at bay.

He's gone, Sandy. Sam's gone... The thought fired through her mind, and she ticked up her speed. Her darkest memories often rose up and regurgitated old feelings for her to observe and heal. She expected the flashbacks would be worse after yesterday. Not just because of what she had done but the ensuing uncertainty while waiting for the verdict on Darrell Patton's parole request to come through.

Images and recollections had hit after she tucked herself into bed last night, chasing off sleep. The standard endorphin rush that lingered after a negotiation had left her system, but her mind remained awake, molested, and churning. She'd had to stare into the face of the man who had sentenced her brother to death. His bullet, fired from his gun. The intent, the carelessness... Her loss. The entire world's really. Her brother was a bright light who would have changed things for the better, if only he'd been given a chance.

They said there was nothing they could do...

She clenched her teeth and pushed herself even harder, feeling the burning in her thighs and calves and sinking into it. Her heart was holding a fast, steady rhythm, and a quick peek at her smartwatch confirmed she was in the sweet spot of her cardio zone. But even here in this euphoric state, the recollections wedged in.

She had felt his life leave his body. It was seven o'clock in the evening, and she had been out at the mall with her friends. Sirens had penetrated the corridors an hour earlier. Even then, she somehow knew something was wrong.

"Sandra?" My friend Lisa turns to me. "You look like crap. Are you okay?"

I can't find my voice. My chest is so heavy, and my stomach is clenching. "I need to... to call home."

"Okay..."

Sandra ran past a mother pushing a baby in a stroller and dipped her head, before buckling down and pushing harder yet.

I call home on the nearest payphone. Reynold, the Davenports' major-domo, answers. "Is Sam there?"

"No, miss, he's out for dinner tonight with his friends. Do you wish that I leave a message for him?"

I shake my head but quickly realize Reynold wouldn't have seen me. "No. Do you know where he went?"

"Romano's Pizzeria."

That is only a few blocks away. The sirens that had rung through the corridors and hallways of the mall... Were they for Sam? I'm going to be sick...

"Miss?"

I hang up and run from the mall. Police have the pizza joint surrounded and cordoned off.

Hours later, my horrible premonition is proven true.

Sam, my twin brother, is dead.

He was the only casualty that day.

Her exhales became heavier, creating clouds of white in the cool air. If only she had heeded that earlier feeling, could she have done something to change his fate? It was a question she revisited repeatedly and always landed in the same spot. There was nothing that she could have done. No warning signs, rendering her powerless to prevent his death. It was too late the second that bullet had entered his chest. If only Patton had surrendered sooner, maybe her brother would be running next to her now. Though that thought made her smile. There was no way. As much as he loved sports, he'd hated running.

Her smartwatch beeped, alerting her to the fact her heart rate was too high. She slowed her pace. Her brother was long gone but always with her. Not only was he in her mind, heart, and soul, and the pendant she wore, but he was by her side every day she did her job. Every time she helped hostages walk away. And while she should take consolation from the fact the majority survived yesterday's ordeal, the fallen weighed heavily on her.

Stanley Moody, the pharmacist, had left behind a wife and two children. That poor family would be burying their beloved husband and father. Was there something more she could have done or said that would have altered the course of events or make it so he was still alive?

The security guard had walked away unscathed, and when the final word reached her, she had the full story. When denied the medication, Gavin had instantly become agitated and started to threaten the pharmacist. He escalated to physical threats when the verbal ones were ineffective and pretended to have a gun in his pocket. At that point, the security guard showed up. Gavin grabbed a woman near him and said he'd shoot her if the guard didn't relinquish his gun. He complied, and Gavin seized the weapon and had everyone gather in the middle of the store. He'd locked the door, and surprisingly no one got away before he shut the place down.

She'd replayed the incident in her dreams when she eventually fell into a restless sleep. She didn't always get the complete background, but it felt like closure when she did. But none of this made her immune to feeling the loved ones' grief. And maybe that was because she let herself get too close by *seeing* people for who they really were. But this empathy was also a strength, letting her view things from perspectives other than her own. This ability might have been sharpened by her own loss. They say there is a blessing in everything, and while it's hard to see in the face of grief, it's easier to discern when the clouds start to clear.

She also learned that life could change in an instant and not to take a single moment for granted. Something she was reminded of every time she was called in for crisis negotiation.

Her phone rang, and she stopped running and slowly jogged in place. It was her boss.

"Hello." She'd save the professional greeting. He knew who he was calling.

"Good afternoon."

"Not quite but getting closer." She smiled. Being precise was hardwired. Another aspect of her personality that was well suited to the job.

"I meant it as sarcasm. You know what? Never mind. Are we going to see you at the office today?"

"You bet."

"And when would that be?"

She looked at her smartwatch. *Eleven thirty now, so...* "In an hour." She'd head home, shower, grab a bite to eat, and get to the field office.

"All right, well, I'm starting the stopwatch now."

Either he was making a poor attempt at playing a micro manager, or it was a testament to her punctuality. She said an hour, it would be an hour. Not a minute more. Not one less.

"I got a call routed to me from the front desk. They were looking for you but..."

Sandra stopped jogging in place and held her breath, waiting for him to finish that sentence. The assistant director had a bad habit of starting to say something and letting it dangle out there. "Who was it? Is there a message?"

"A man named Joshua Cobb."

"The husband of the pregnant woman."

"That's right."

"What did he have to say? Is she okay? The baby?" *Don't tell me they didn't make it...*

"Both are fine." His smile traveled over the line. "It was a girl, five pounds, three ounces. They named her Gina. The way the father announced it, I got the impression that name might mean something to you. Does it?"

Sandra grinned, her gaze going over the Potomac. "It was

the nurse who was by Megan Cobb's side and saw her through things on the inside."

"All mushy stuff. Well, this Joshua wanted me to thank you for what you did."

"I just did my job."

"It's far more than that, Vos. You saved people last night."

This morning... technically... She'd let him have this one. "Just doing what I was trained to do."

"And the world thanks you. Now, get your butt in here."

"Yes, sir." She ended the call. Her boss was many things, but conventional wasn't one of them. At least he let his guard down with her on occasion.

She turned around to head home and had a near miss with a tall man and his oversized fluffy dog. She hoped to never be grilled on canine breeds. She was more of a cat person. "Sorry," she called out, but kept moving.

When she got to her building, the concierge saw her through the glass and opened the door for her. "Thanks, Earl."

"Don't mention it, Ms. Vos." The older man dipped his head. "Good day."

"And to you." She headed to the elevator bank to take it to the penthouse. There were days she could hardly believe this was her life and she planned to never take her blessings for granted.

FOURTEEN

Sandra arrived at the Washington Field Office at the hour mark, as promised.

"'Bout time you showed up, slacker." Brice Sutton was her colleague and essentially her wingman. He was three years younger than her, but that age gap made no perceptible difference. Though she liked to think she was more mature. He'd been at the WFO for two years, and his desk was across an aisle from hers.

"Oh, yeah. Where were you at two in the morning when I was in the heat of a crisis negotiation?" She watched his face transform into comical expressions while he tried to come up with a witty response. "Like I thought. Wetting your bed and sucking your thumb?" *Maybe not more mature...*

"Very funny, Vos."

She smirked and shrugged. "I thought so." After that, the conversation died, and they busied themselves with their work. Like her, Brice worked on manhunts when their negotiation training wasn't called upon. Today, her priority was typing up an incident report and getting it to Elwood's inbox before the end of the day. That alone would take her hours to put together, as she always included as much detail as possible.

She had recounted up to midnight when her cell phone rang. She caught a glimpse at the clock on the wall, and it told her she'd been at it for three hours. She should scale back on some specifics if she didn't want this taking all night. But her attention to detail was a curse of her infallible memory. When she saw USP on the screen, her heart ticked up speed. "Sandra Vos," she answered.

Brice looked over at her rather informal greeting. She batted a hand at him. He didn't know why she wasn't in yesterday, or even about her brother. At least, she hadn't told him, but they were in the information game. It wouldn't surprise her if he'd dug into her background. She had his. He grew up in Green Bay, Wisconsin, had two older brothers and a younger sister, and as far as she could tell, he'd never been in a serious relationship. That latter bit wasn't in any docket but was something she'd picked up being around the guy. Same too for the fact she was safe from any sexual advances because he liked men and feared the next epidemic was inevitable.

Her caller said, "Ms. Vos, I'm calling from the deputy commissioner's office in regard to the verdict on Darrell Patton's request for parole."

Her caller paused for several seconds, which stretched into days for her before he gave her the result. At the end of the hearing, they said it could take until Friday for the ruling to be decided. Was the fast turnaround a good thing?

"The committee members were moved by your testimony and, in considering all aspects of the appeal, Mr. Patton was denied parole."

She squealed in her head and slapped a hand over her mouth. Brice glanced over again, one eyebrow cocked, forehead furrowed. She shook her head and took a few seconds to compose herself. She cleared her throat and thanked her caller.

"You're welcome. Have a good day, Ms. Vos."

"You too." *I will!* She'd do a happy dance if Brice wasn't still watching her like she was some animal in a zoo doing something out of character. She ended the call and positioned her hands over her keyboard, looking studiously at her monitor. Her gaze was on the screen, but instead of focusing on the report, she saw her reflection and smiled at herself.

"What are you smiling about? And you're really not going to say a word? Who was that? Clearly it was good news." Brice swiveled his chair to face her. "And good news needs to be shared."

"Not when it's none of your business. Don't you have work to do?" Her words were harsher than her tone. Brice's obsessive curiosity served him well in the job, but it was a touch invasive when he aimed it at her personal life.

"Go ahead, and keep me at a distance, Vos, but one day we're going to be great friends."

"Anything's possible. Pigs might fly too." She smiled at him. She didn't truthfully dislike the guy, but the playful banter and rapport they had going was fun.

She returned to work, but her mind was on that call. It had given her a real reason to celebrate tonight.

FIFTEEN

Sandra became a Georgetown girl after the Davenports welcomed her and Sam into their lives. Well, after some adjustment. Her early childhood never offered up luxury living. Summer vacations were trips to a park, or running under the sprinkler in the backyard. One year, their parents enrolled her and Sam in a camp program that had them away for a week, *roughing it*. That was an adventure she never cared to repeat. She found out at a young age she wasn't really the outdoorsy type. Running in nature was the closest she came. But she decided to take advantage of what life had given her, and took a portion of her trust from the Davenports and bought a glorious two-story penthouse overlooking the Potomac River. It even offered unobstructed views of the National Mall and Key Bridge.

The place was over six thousand square feet with an additional three thousand square feet in outdoor terraces. But what really sold her on the place was the floor-to-ceiling windows. During the day, sunlight drenched the home, and at night, like now, she appreciated the moonlight's reflection on the river.

She was in the kitchen, pulling a bottle of champagne out of her Sub-Zero fridge when she heard her daughter's voice coming from the entry.

"Marco?"

Sandra smiled. She and Olivia would play up the size of the home. "Polo!"

Olivia and Sandra chorused back and forth a few more times before her daughter stepped into the kitchen. She had her phone in her hand, the device's cradle. "Ooh, champagne? Fancy date with Eric tonight?"

"Well, he is coming over, but that's not why I took this out." She gestured to the bubbly that was a few thousand dollars a bottle. "Patton's parole was denied," she cheered.

"Great news, Mom!" Olivia walked over and gave Sandra a hug.

The whole time Sandra was thinking how special this girl was, even if she took after her father in her looks. She had his brown hair and eyes, whereas Sandra was a natural blond despite the war she was starting to wage against the gray. And her eyes were gray. But Olivia was a good kid, and Sandra loved spoiling her. She'd given Olivia her own suite in the house, and while Sandra realized she had more than most girls her age, maybe more than some adults, none of it had gone to her head. She couldn't have asked for a more down-to-earth girl.

"So, champagne, a reason to celebrate... does that mean that I get a glass?" Olivia put on a cheesy smile.

"A small one."

"Ooh, this night got even better. But Eric is coming over, isn't he? You look amazing, Mom."

She wouldn't take offense at the implication she didn't put effort in otherwise, but she had changed when she got home. It was just a white linen getaway set though, nothing too fancy. She'd tied the shirt into a handkerchief knot to expose a bit of her flat abdomen, which she credited to running. "Thanks, and he is." She looked at her gold watch, one she'd put on in place of her smartwatch. "He should be here any minute with dinner. He's picking up from La Gioia Ristorante." She added flourish to the name, letting it roll off her tongue.

"Sounds delicious, but I was kind of hoping Avery could come over, and you'd let us order in pizza and watch movies in my room." Olivia winced.

"You were with her last night."

"So? She's my best friend."

Sandra couldn't see a reason to say no, but it might be her fantastic mood making her more agreeable. "That's fine by me."

Olivia beamed and clapped her hands together. "I'll text her and let her know. Thanks, Mom."

"You're welcome, but remember, it is a school night." She imagined her daughter had stayed up late last night at Avery's.

"Yeah, yeah." Olivia tapped a quick kiss on Sandra's cheek and swept out of the room.

"Eric or I can drive Avery home later or arrange a ride for her," Sandra called out to her.

"Okay!"

With her exuberant energy gone, Sandra felt the aftermath of the hurricane. Still. Quiet. She pulled out some dishes and cutlery just as the doorbell rang. Eric had a key but insisted on giving her a heads-up of his arrival. For visitors not on her list, the concierge at the front desk would call up and notify her.

"Sandra?" Eric called out a moment later.

"Kitchen." She pulled down four champagne flutes. She knew Avery's mother well enough to know she wouldn't mind if her daughter got a splash.

"Oh, look at you. I'm feeling a little underdressed." He set two bags of food on the counter and came over to her, placing his hands on her hips, his thumb near her exposed navel.

"It's just casual wear, Eric. Like yours."

"Somehow my stonewashed dark jeans don't seem to stack up."

She shook her head with a smile. "You're being ridiculous." She tugged on the lapel of his dinner jacket, and he was wearing a collared shirt underneath it. Knowing him, the former wouldn't last long as he tended to run on the hot side.

His gaze traveled past her to the counter. "Champagne. Does that mean that—?" When she nodded, he grinned. "That's great news."

"I think it's worth celebrating."

He grinned. "I second that."

She prepared to pop the cork. Eric moved in behind her, nuzzling into her neck. "You might want to stand back while I do this," she told him, but he stayed put. *Can't say I didn't warn him...* She pulled the cork, and some bubbly ran down the bottle. Thankfully not much. She looked forward to drinking her fair share tonight. Upon further thought, Avery would probably be delivered home by cab or spend the night. She poured out glasses for them and raised hers to his in a toast. "To keeping the bastard behind bars."

He clicked his glass to hers. "Amen."

"Now, let's eat," she said. "I'm starving, and the smells coming from those bags are heavenly. Oh, and since Olivia's going to be fending for herself, there's more for us."

As they dished up the food, she was filled with gratitude. Life wasn't always easy. She'd faced loss, suffered setbacks, rode waves to great heights and crashed when they broke, but the journey itself was very beautiful. And in this moment, she felt extremely blessed.

SIXTEEN

The next day was a slow one and just what Sandra needed. Most of the morning her head was fuzzy from the champagne. She was considering packing things up at the office when her cell phone rang. The name of Olivia's violin teacher flashed on the screen, and Sandra answered.

"Sandra, it's Penelope Randall, do you know where Olivia is? I've tried reaching her but keep landing in her voicemail."

It took a second for her mind to process Penelope's words. Olivia's lesson was from five to six and when she'd just looked at the clock it was ten after five. She'd drilled punctuality into Olivia from a young age. There was no way she'd be late unless she didn't have a choice. The mother in her panicked. The FBI agent thought about it rationally. "She could have been held up getting there. You know what traffic can be like." She had an hour's journey from her school back to their neighborhood on a good day. It was possible that had delayed her.

"But she's never late."

To have that stressed hushed her inner agent's voice of calm. And Penelope said she'd tried Olivia without success. So why wasn't she answering? "Let me see if I can reach her."

"I'll wait for a bit longer, but every minute that passes is cutting into her lesson. I have another student scheduled after her."

"I understand." The location of the lesson alternated between the penthouse and Penelope's rowhouse, which was only two streets east of theirs. "Just give me a minute. Do you want to hold the line and wait, or have me call you back?"

"Either is fine." Penelope let out a rush of breath, clearly frustrated.

"I'll call you back." Sandra ended the call and hit Olivia's name. The line rang. *Come on, come on, pick up...*

"Hey, you've reached Olivia's voicemail. Leave your message, and I'll call when I can."

Something *was* wrong. It was a feeling that started in the pit of her gut and worked its way up to her chest. She gripped her St. Michael pendant. "Liv, it's Mom. Call me. Penn's wondering where you are, and so am I."

Sandra hung up but didn't release her phone. There had to be a logical explanation for this. Maybe Olivia had left her phone in her locker at school. But the likelihood of that was zilch when the device was attached to her daughter like an appendage.

"Vos, everything all right over there?" Brice was looking at her.

"I don't know." The cold, honest truth.

"Anything I can do to help?"

"I don't know yet. It's probably nothing." Sandra looked at the phone in her hand. Olivia had made her promise she wouldn't install a tracking app on her device. Sandra had kept her word despite it working in conflict with her instinct. Now she wished she hadn't. Being with the FBI she wasn't without resources but if she acted without navigating the proper channels, she'd violate her daughter's rights and break the law. Legally, she needed a court-ordered warrant. If she brought this to her boss, he'd be sympathetic, but it was hardly time yet to raise the alarm. He'd argue she was a teenager and had lost track of time. Not that it would explain her failure to answer her phone. And her daughter loved the violin and wouldn't miss a lesson unless she couldn't help it. That right there was enough reason to be concerned.

Breathe, Vos...

She pinched the pendant tighter, shut her eyes and took some steady, even breaths. Nothing good ever resulted from losing focus or clear thinking.

"You're panting like a fat man on a hot day over there. Clearly, it's not nothing."

She opened her eyes at Brice's offensive comment. "Speaking of panting"—she pulled back—"I feel your breath on my arm."

"What is up?" he persisted.

"I can't reach my daughter, Olivia. She should be at her violin lesson right now." She snapped her mouth shut. Just saying *violin lesson* sounded uppity. Her family money wasn't something she ever flaunted. It was one reason she dropped Davenport from her professional name. The nice home and car were things she got for herself because she loved them. Simple as that.

"And I'm guessing that was her teacher who called?"

"Uh-huh. Actually..." She held up her index finger to Brice and called Penelope back. When the woman answered after the second ring, Sandra said, "I can't reach her either, but I'm sure she's fine. If she shows up, please have her call me. Obviously, bill me for today's full lesson."

"Thank you, Sandra. I hope you get a hold of her. I just have this... Well, I probably shouldn't say this to her mother, but there's a burning in my stomach, like a premonition that something is wrong."

Sandra shielded herself from the woman's psychic hunch. "I'll call you once I get her."

"Take care, Sandra. Bye for now." Penelope ended the call, and Sandra racked her brain for an explanation.

What if her daughter had been injured in an accident and was unable to answer her phone? What if she was lying in the street somewhere? Or in a hospital?

Calm down, Vos. Breathe.

She was grateful for the rational little voice in her head. It was her reliable companion and guide when she needed it most.

"Have you tried her close friends?" Brice perched himself on the edge of her desk.

"Would you kindly get your ass off my—"

"Well, you haven't lost your sense of spunk." Brice remained planted for a few seconds longer, likely just to defy her. "Her friends? Have you called them?"

"You've heard all I've done so far." She selected Avery from her contacts. The line rang once and hit voicemail.

"Avery, it's Ms. Vos, *Sandra*, Olivia's mom..." She was rambling, not at all like herself. After all, Avery would know very well who she was. "I'm looking to talk with Liv. Please have her call me."

Another dead end. And was Avery involved in an accident with Olivia? Were both girls unable to get to their phones? But even as the thought cycled through, she knew that wouldn't explain why Avery's phone had gone straight to voicemail. That indicated her phone was either off or she was on the phone and her call waiting line was tied up, which was completely possible.

"Given the smoke coming from your ears and the look of constipation on your face, you're thinking far too much."

"What would you know of it, Sutton?" She dredged up his surname. They really had the stereotypical brother/sister relationship at times. Not like the one she had with Sam though. She and her twin were simpatico.

He waved his hands. "Sticks and stones."

"My daughter is missing, and you're bugging me at a time like this?"

"You don't know that she is missing. Not yet. You're leaping to the worst conclusions."

"Thanks for putting those in my head."

"They were already there. Just talk me through a normal Friday for her. She has her violin lesson, school before that, I presume?"

"Yes. Until three thirty." She didn't know if she cared for how he'd articulated *violin lesson* but maybe that was a judgment on her part. Sometimes people viewed those with money in a harsh light, or as being above regular-people problems. Which was all utter crap. Everyone was the same. She'd hold back that her daughter attended one of the most esteemed private elementary schools in the country.

"And then...?"

"She and Avery, that's her best friend who I just called, either pop into Georgetown Cupcake or go to DiversaBlend down the street from where we live."

"DiversaBlend?"

"It's some new coffee shop that pledges to donate a portion of their proceeds to diversity causes and claims to be environmentally conscious. They've opened a few test locations in DC."

"Targeting Gen Z."

"Yeah, I guess. Anyway, every other Friday, she heads out to Penelope's rowhouse, which is where she was due tonight." Olivia could have popped home for some reason, to grab her violin, though she often carted it to school with her, and left her phone behind. Sandra was grasping for some innocent explanation.

"All right, we can work with that."

She gave Brice a blank look. Whether they could or not, it was what they had. But at what point was it okay to worry? If this was an investigation related to her job, she'd have a calm, level head right now. But this was her baby, Olivia Grace. She had to be all right. She just had to be.

SEVENTEEN

"I've got this, Brice, if you have plans." Sandra would rather be left alone to muddle through her thoughts. She had some ideas of how to track down Olivia before getting her phone traced.

"I'm not going anywhere until I know your daughter's safe and sound."

"Of course you're not," she deadpanned.

"You act like I bug the living hell out of you, but I know it's all an act."

"Is it, though?" The flicker of a smile, despite her resistance. She couldn't let her barrier down. It seemed to work well for their camaráderie.

He pointed at her mouth. "I caught that. Just the tiniest of smirks."

"You need your eyes tested, but could we pick this up another time?"

"Nope. What can I do to help?" His voice held a serious tone, and his eyes were marked with concern.

There was one thing she dreaded doing, and she feared verbalizing it. "I'll get back to you."

"Sure. I'll be right here." He lowered himself onto her desk again.

"Don't even think about it."

He popped back up and went to his desk. She called the concierge desk at her building, and when Earl answered, she said, "It's Sandra Vos." She'd typically add *from the penthouse* but not with Brice listening to every word. Earl would recognize her by name anyhow.

"Yes, ma'am. What can I do for you?"

"Did you see Olivia this afternoon, early evening?"

"I did not."

So where the hell... "Thank you." She hung up before Earl could say anything further and rubbed her forehead. An epic headache was rolling in. *Where are you, baby?*

"Sandra."

She jumped as Brice bent over and said her name into her ear. "What the—"

"I'm not even going to ask about that phone call."

"Good."

"What is it I can help with?"

There would be no more putting it off... "We need to call the hospitals in the city and see if she's been admitted."

"Sure. Olivia, right?"

"Uh-huh." She mentioned her name to him a moment ago and at least a hundred times since Penelope's call.

"I'll handle it."

She shook her head. "We'll split them up. I think there are a lot."

As it turned out, there were seven general hospitals in DC. Brice took four, leaving her three. For every call Sandra made, she cringed as she waited for the nursing staff to come back on the line. Every passing second was like receiving a fresh sting from a bee. When they returned to the line to say they had no patient by that name and hadn't received any unidentified females of Olivia's description, Sandra wasn't sure whether to be relieved or not. It didn't exactly mean that Olivia was safe.

When she finished her calls, she sat back in her chair and looked over at Brice at his desk. He shook his head, a subtle smile on his lips, and thanked the person he was on the line with. "That was the last one for me. I'm guessing you learned nothing either?"

She shook her head, not able to bring herself to admit it out loud. Where did this leave her? She couldn't just sit here going mad. "I'm trying Avery again." *And now I'm announcing my next move to Brice... Dear God, if you're up there...* She selected the girl's name from her contacts and listened to the line ring. *Once, twice, three—*

"Hello. Ms. Vos?" Avery's high-pitched teenage voice came over the line.

"Is Olivia with you?" She didn't care about an unreturned phone call, or whether the girl heard her message. It also didn't matter that she told Avery to call her Sandra, not Ms. Vos, at least a hundred times.

"No. Should she be? Doesn't she have her violin lesson now?"

So Olivia had remembered... Sandra shook her head at Brice, who was looking at her. "Did you hang out with her at all after school?"

"Yeah. We went to DiversaBlend for an iced decaf..." Avery's voice trailed off. "Why are you asking about Liv? I'm sure if you just called her, she'd answer."

Sandra didn't want to scare the girl, but it was past that point. "I've tried reaching her, and she's not answering her phone."

"Huh. That's strange."

The girl obviously wasn't jaded yet, unlike Sandra, who imagined the worst-case scenario. Good for her. Sandra hoped she'd keep her protective bubble intact her whole life without it ever having a need to pop. Though that wish was unrealistic. The odds were life would beat her down at some point, and possibly sooner than later. "What time did you leave DiversaBlend?"

"About fifteen minutes ago, but Liv left at four forty-five."

"Which DiversaBlend?"

"Our regular one. Ms. Vos, why are you asking me all these questions?"

From the coffee shop to Penelope's rowhouse was about a ten-minute walk. She would have headed straight there. "I haven't been able to reach her, and her violin teacher hasn't seen her."

"Oh. Is she... okay?"

And just like that the girl's bubble popped as the real world penetrated it. "I don't know, Avery. Tell me what you can remember from when you were with her. Anything stand out?"

"I don't think... Oh. Well, it's probably nothing. We get pervs checking us out all the time."

The back of Sandra's neck tightened. "Was one watching you guys today?"

"Ah, yeah. He seemed mostly interested in Liv, but he gave us both the creeps."

"Can you tell me what he looked like? What he was wearing?"

"He could have been Liv's dad. Actually, he was older than that. Brown hair, lean. He was wearing a jean jacket, ah, lined with plaid flannel." She didn't do well hiding her disgust for his wardrobe choice.

"And what was he doing? Just watching you? Did he ever talk to you or approach you?" Her stomach was turning.

"No."

"Did he follow Olivia when she left the café?"

"I..."

"There's no wrong answer here, Avery. Just tell me what you remember."

"I don't know. I'm sorry, but when she was leaving, my phone rang and..."

Sandra held the silence, realizing the value of it. Avery's mind was working.

"Actually, I was looking out the window," Avery tagged on. "Olivia waved at me, and I waved back. Then I looked back to where the guy had been sitting, and he was gone. Oh my God, did he do something to her? Did he— I should have left with her. I could have protected her."

"You don't know that, and we don't know if he did anything to her." That's what Sandra said, but her mind wasn't buying a word of it. She was past thinking positively. Something had happened to her daughter, and the reason she wasn't answering her phone could very well be due to that man. If so, he was in for a world of hurt. With what Avery told her, and the fact Olivia was the daughter of an FBI agent, that was enough to support a court-ordered warrant to trace her cellphone.

"Okay, but it's so odd for her not to answer her phone."

"I know." She ended the call a moment later, aware that she had scared the girl, but there was no helping that.

"Did some creep take her?" Brice asked. "Just going by what I gathered from listening to your end."

"You could have put that a little more delicately."

"Sorry."

"I can't think that way yet." Even though her mind was screaming that exact thing. Some freaking pervert had her beautiful girl. She had a strong grip on her pendant and rubbed her thumb on the backside of it. "Avery said a man was watching her, and he left DiversaBlend not long after Olivia did."

"That's enough to support a trace on your daughter's phone. I'll get on the line with a judge."

"Thank you." She felt numb as her mind processed everything. It was like she was in an alternate reality. Olivia was unreachable. She could be— No, she couldn't think that way. Not yet. The emotion would strip her of power. She'd best pull on her training as a negotiator. The basis of which would have her calm under pressure.

Brice was on the phone talking to the judge now. She hopped on the tracing system, so she'd be ready the second they had the go-ahead. He gave her a thumbs-up just before hanging up.

Sandra keyed Olivia's number into the system, and it wasn't long until she had the results. But as she narrowed in on the map to bring up the location of her phone, her breath froze.

Brice leaned over her shoulder, and she didn't even protest how close he was to her. "Okay, that's pointing to Key Bridge. A trail from Georgetown Waterfront Park runs under it. She could be hanging out there."

Sandra knew the park and that trail well as that's where she ran in the mornings. She appreciated that he was trying to alleviate her concern, though it was ineffective. Without saying more, she grabbed her coat and headed out into the brisk evening.

"Hold up. I'm coming with you."

EIGHTEEN

Sandra let Brice drive because he had insisted, and she couldn't present a solid argument against the arrangement. Her mind was too preoccupied to safely get behind the wheel. The second the bridge came into view she leaned forward as if she could magically see her daughter or something that would end this mental torture.

Brice parked on the street near Georgetown Waterfront Park, and they walked from there along the path to reach Key Bridge. The wind coming off the river was biting and sent shivers down her spine. She burrowed deeper into her coat.

She scanned the area, looking around for her daughter, hoping she'd find her, and that she'd be ready with some clear explanation for being there and not at her lesson. Also for not answering her phone. But her heart knew Olivia wasn't here.

Still she yelled out, "Olivia!" while shrugging further into her coat and stepping off the boardwalk to the brush. The ground was mostly dirt, and some areas were wet. With it being winter, it was a beige and brown landscape aside from green vines of ivy wrapped around some tree trunks.

"Olivia!" Brice echoed her.

No response. Even the path was barren right now. Not a single jogger.

Sandra pulled out her phone and called Olivia's number. She listened carefully for her daughter's ringtone.

Nothing.

Panic surged through her. She must be too far away to hear it. Then again, between a breeze whipping through the trees, the sound of the moving river, and vehicles passing overhead they created a white noise that could have drowned out the ringtone.

"Shit." Sandra stopped walking, a hand to her forehead, scanning the area. There was nothing to see. Despite sunset getting later, the sun was already weak and sinking in the sky today. Curse the winter months. She turned on her phone's flashlight and cast the beam ahead of her. It brought something to life from the shadows. A pile of blankets and cardboard? The lumpy shape of a human body underneath?

Sandra started to run toward it. "Olivia?"

A bearded man with a dirty face peeked out. She saw now that she'd disturbed a homeless man.

"Sir, have you seen this young woman?" She fumbled to bring up a photo of Olivia.

He shook his head but said nothing and retreated beneath his makeshift tent.

"We keep looking. We find her phone, and it might give us a clue as to where she is." Brice came up beside her, and she wanted to catch his optimism. "There's no giving up, Vos."

They were talking about her daughter. "Never."

"Is her phone in a special case that might stand out?"

"It's just solid pink."

"All right. Got it. You start working a grid from here, and I'll go over there. We'll work our way toward each other."

"Yep. And I'll keep trying to call it too." She froze on Olivia's contact card, her heart cinching at the attached picture taken last July. Olivia was standing at the back of her grandmother's speedboat and smiling broadly. She loved the water and the summer sun on her face, the wind through her hair. Sandra hit the call button.

There was faint ringing. She pivoted around and saw a jogger had manifested and was pulling his phone from a pocket.

"Hello," he said.

Sandra let out a deep breath. *No giving up!* She ended the call and resumed walking again, doing so slowly and letting the beam from her phone's flashlight illuminate the steps ahead of her. She followed the imaginary outline of a rectangle, working in a grid formation. Brice would do the same from his end, and by the time they finished, they would have covered a large area. After that they'd chop off another section and repeat the process for as long as it took.

She continued calling Olivia's phone. Never meeting with success.

Sandra's phone rang and had her flinching. "Special Agent Vos." She answered without consulting the caller's identity.

"Sandra, it's Eric. I'm at your place, but you're not...?" He left it dangling as if that were a question.

It took a few seconds for it to dawn on her. He was going to meet her there, and the two of them were going to go out for dinner tonight. "Something has..." Her throat swelled shut with fear. Just for a moment. How so much had changed since that happy state she was in last night. "I can't reach Liv. Her phone pinged back to the east end of Key Bridge." She told him the precise location.

"I'll be right there."

"We can use all the help we can get. Could you bring a shirt or sweater from her room, something from the hamper that she would have worn? Just in case we need to involve the K-9 unit." She heard herself speaking and felt like she was living someone else's life at this moment. Her mind kept haunting her with

Avery's words. The ones about the man in the flannel-lined jean jacket. The one who had shown so much interest in her daughter.

"Will do. Just hang in there, okay? See you soon." He hung up before she could say another word, but she certainly wouldn't have discouraged him from coming. It was also probably past time they had the area cordoned off and called in for additional assistance anyhow.

Brice waved her over. He'd covered a fair bit of ground.

"Did you find it?" she called out as she galloped toward him.

"I think so." He was standing with his legs hip-width apart and pointing at the ground.

She followed the direction of his finger, and sticking out from the base of a shrub was the corner of a pink phone case.

She bent to pick it up, and Brice nudged her arm. "What?"

"You'll want these." He was holding out a pair of gloves, and she took them with a "thanks" and a lump in her throat.

It was official. Olivia's phone was evidence in a crime. Her daughter had been abducted.

NINETEEN

Sandra cracked Olivia's phone case open and woke the screen. Staring back at her was a picture of Olivia and Avery smiling in red T-shirts with their school's name and logo on the front in white. She traced her fingers over the screen. If only her desire to have her daughter back possessed the power to make it happen.

"Basis Independent?" Brice let out a whistle. "Nice school."

She quickly flipped the cover closed, though it was too late to prevent his observation. "It is."

Brice was looking back at her, his eyes dancing over her face. His mouth opened like he was going to say something, then closed again.

She gave him a few seconds, but he didn't add more to his comment. That fact was a relief. It wasn't a cheap school by any means, and she didn't want him to treat her any differently. "We should call the K-9 unit." She couldn't think about them finding her daughter's body, but they might turn up more of her things that may, in turn, give them a clue as to her whereabouts.

"I'll handle that. You should probably call AD Rowe."

"I will." She stepped away, sliding Olivia's phone into a plastic evidence bag Brice had given her and took hers out. She selected Elwood Rowe from her contacts. He answered on the second ring, and she got right to the point. "Olivia's missing, possibly taken."

"What? When?" A swift response like he'd been slapped.

"After school, sometime between four forty-five and five ten."

"We'll get out an alert for her."

She was momentarily stunned. *This is really happening...* First, it was her brother, and now her daughter was going to leave her. No, she couldn't think that way. *Never give up!* "Thanks. Brice is working with me, and we traced her phone to Key Bridge. We're in Georgetown Waterfront Park now and have found her device. He's calling in the K-9 unit, just in case..." Her mind betrayed her, skipping into the darkness. There was no way she could finish that sentence with what it had conjured.

"Dear God."

"Yeah."

"Sandra!" Eric was running toward her, and she worked to bridge the distance. One of Olivia's favorite shirts was draped over his arm.

"Who's that?" Elwood asked.

"Detective Birch, MPD." There was no need to disclose she was seeing him.

"So they've been pulled into this before you even bothered to come to me?"

"Not like that, boss."

"I'd ask what it's like, but considering you're going through a tough time right now, I'll let it go."

"Thank you."

"Did you get the area locked down then?" Elwood asked.

"It's in the works." She planned to ask Eric to make this happen.

"I'm going to bring in more agents on this, Vos. We can't ignore the possibility of larger things at play here. The daughter of a federal agent has been taken."

Indistinct, separate... as if she isn't mine. She'd store that away to pull up to help her step back, detach, and gain some objectivity. "Do whatever you can. I need to find her."

"Will do, and keep me in the loop, as I will you."

"Okay. Thanks." She ended the call, and took the shirt from Eric. She buried her fingers into the fabric and sniffed the collar. Olivia's Viva La Juicy perfume filled her nose with its sweet and fruity scent. "Thank you for bringing this. K-9's being called as we speak." She glanced over at Brice, who was on the phone.

"How are you holding up?"

"As well as can be expected." She turned at the sound of footsteps behind her. "Eric Birch, this is Brice Sutton, a colleague from the WFO. Brice, Eric is a detective with the MPD."

The men regarded each other, arms starting to extend for a handshake, but both settled for a head bob. It was odd circumstances to be meeting under.

"K-9's on their way," he told Sandra, but then turned to Eric. "I don't mean to sound like a prick, but why are you here?"

Eric flicked his gaze at Sandra, who subtly shook her head. She didn't really want him to know about their relationship. "I caught wind that a young woman is missing. As Sandra just told you, I'm a police detective."

She breathed easier knowing Eric picked up on her unspoken message.

"Uh-huh, who just happens to arrive with her daughter's shirt?" Brice's gaze fell to the one now in Sandra's hands.

"Nothing gets past you. We're... I'm not sure exactly what we are." Eric smirked, passed a mischievous look at Sandra. It was a devilish one that revealed his rebellious streak.

"Bed buddies?" Brice said.

Eric laughed. "I guess you could say that."

Sandra had wished to be somewhere else before. This strange interaction intensified the feeling. "Okay, if you two are finished. Olivia."

"We'll find her." Eric put an arm around her. He took the shirt and the phone from her and handed them over to Brice. "I trust you can handle all of this and get the shirt to the K-9 handlers once they arrive?"

"Sure." Brice took them and walked a few feet away to give them space.

"You can't say the guy doesn't read the room or pick up on subtle cues," Eric said to her.

"That's if you call handing everything over to him a subtle dismissal and not a neon sign."

"Whatever works. That's what matters."

What *mattered* was getting to Olivia before it was too late. She took a deep breath, coaching herself to approach this from a detached viewpoint. If only she could convince herself the missing girl wasn't her beautiful Olivia but someone else's daughter. Just like Elwood had said. *The daughter of a federal agent...* After all, that was a situation she was trained to manage and navigate. She just had to approach this as she would any manhunt or crisis negotiation.

"What do you know so far, Sandra?" Eric's question cut through her thoughts.

"Avery was with her at DiversaBlend, about five minutes from home. That was about four thirty or so. Olivia left at four forty-five, but apparently there was this man who was watching her. He gave the girls the creeps. Avery said she thought he left not long after Olivia. It just seems too coincidental to me. My gut tells me he took her or..." She couldn't finish the rest of it. While there was hope of finding Olivia alive, she could hold herself together. For now, she couldn't even entertain an alternative. Her energy would be better spent focusing on what could help. She could even apply the basic principles she used for hostage negotiation and manhunts. "We need to figure out what this man wants." The base starting point. "And don't say he's just some sick pervert taking advantage of an opportunity. I can't even think that way."

Eric was silent for a few beats, then, "Well, it might have appeared random, but Olivia could have been targeted. This could be a ransom thing. You do have money."

"It could be, I suppose. Elwood raised another point. I'm FBI. This could be some act against the Bureau." Not that she had a clue how that progressed things.

Eric smiled tightly.

"What?" she asked him.

"Don't take offense at this but the FBI, as a whole, tends to overreact."

"For good reason. We make a lot of enemies." Now the subject was raised, the sheer volume of people who could harbor ill will toward her was nauseating.

"Okay, now that right there might be helpful. Has anyone threatened *you* recently?"

"I piss people off on a daily basis with my job."

"Well, so much is online these days if people know where to look. This person could have found out your personal information and how to get to you."

That thought was terrifying. She did what she could to stay offline, even warned Olivia to watch what she did. After this, she was going to pay someone to make all digital traces of them disappear, though she wasn't sure that would go over with Olivia.

"They'd go for your most vulnerable point. Olivia," he added when she didn't respond. "The only good news is if this man's beef is with you, you'll likely be hearing from him."

"If that's the case," she reiterated in a mumble. "It's just hard to wrap my head around who this guy could be. I've put my fair share of bad guys away in my twenty-five-year career as an agent."

"Making revenge a possible motive. You said he was at DiversaBlend. Well, they'd have security cameras. Let's go down there and take a look. You can see if you recognize this guy."

"If we're going down this road, I should get someone looking into who was recently released that I had a hand in putting away."

"Sounds like a good idea to me."

"It's just sickening to think whoever took Olivia planned this. They likely know where we live, her schedule..." She shivered at the thought of strangers paying such close attention to her precious girl. It also made her angry. "I'm just going to make a call." She picked Elwood from her contacts, and he answered right away. "It's Vos. I need your help."

"Just name it."

"I need someone to look at my past cases, and see if anyone I had a part in putting away may have recently gotten out."

"Good thinking. How far back do you think I should go?"

She was going to suggest her entire career but reconsidered. "Just during my time with the WFO."

"That narrows it down some, but not a lot. I'll get some agents on this right away."

"Thanks." With that, Sandra hung up and turned to Eric. "It's time to piece together Olivia's last movements and follow them through. Obviously, we'll start with DiversaBlend and go from there."

"Let's do it. I'll drive."

Eric's voice was drowned out by a lumbering transport truck rumbling overhead. The sound was almost deafening. But it drew her gaze upward and filled her with a new fear. Key Bridge carried US Route 29 out of the city and the state. Olivia's phone was found at the side of the bridge. Had it been tossed from a moving vehicle? If so, Olivia could be long gone.

TWENTY

Keeping busy was the only thing helping Sandra retain a fine grasp on her composure. The K-9 unit was arriving as she and Eric were leaving. Brice was sticking around for a bit. He promised to call if anything turned up.

Eric held the door at DiversaBlend for Sandra. It was after eight o'clock by this point, and she couldn't believe how fast time was going. The sun had fully set, and her heart was breaking as she thought about her daughter not being at home.

Thankfully the coffee shop wasn't too busy at this hour. Sandra walked straight up to the counter and the smiling young woman standing there. Her brown eyes were bright with intelligence and vitality like Olivia's. Like her father's... Speaking of, Nolan deserved to know what was going on. But one thing at a time.

Sandra held up her badge, announced herself, and asked for the manager. The girl's smile disappeared, and she signaled a passing barista.

"Could you get Charlene? The FBI is here for her." Sandra wasn't going to correct things and point out that technically Eric wasn't with the Bureau.

The barista, who was in her thirties, stopped walking. She took Sandra in, then her gaze traveled to Eric. "Why?" the barista said to the clerk as if they weren't there.

"I don't know." The clerk looked at them.

"There's a matter we'd like to discuss with Charlene," Sandra said. It was possible these women could have something to offer if they were here earlier, but it probably wouldn't go beyond what Avery had already told her. Then again, the creep could have been a regular. Though if so, wouldn't Avery have mentioned that? Still, there was no such thing as a stupid question. "Actually, before you get Charlene, maybe you ladies could help us."

"Ah, sure." The barista came toward the counter, clearly eager to assist.

"Were you two working earlier today from four thirty to five?" she asked.

They both nodded.

"Do you recognize this girl?" Sandra showed them a picture of Olivia. Eric tapped her shoulder, but she dismissed him with a shake of her head.

The young women leaned in, looked at the photo, and quickly pulled back.

"That's Liv. What about her?" This was from the clerk.

Liv... It was clear she was rather close to her daughter. "You know her?"

"She's in here a lot around four thirty with a friend."

"And were they here today?" she asked, though knowing Avery's answer.

"They were," the clerk said.

"Did you happen to notice if a man was watching them? Someone paying Olivia a lot of unwanted attention? A guy in a plaid flannel-lined jean jacket?"

The clerk passed a side glance at the barista, then looked at Sandra. "Hey, did something happen to Liv?"

Sandra resisted spinning out at that question. *Calm at all times.* That was her way through this. How she did things for years with the Bureau. With her professional hat on she was good at isolating her stress and fears, putting them into a tight, dark box, and getting on with things. *The daughter of a federal agent...* It was outside of herself. In that context, it wasn't her world being destroyed.

"We're trying to reach her," Eric said, stepping in when she didn't respond.

"Ah, okay." The clerk ran her bottom lip through her teeth. "But, yeah, I remember a guy wearing that coat."

The barista nodded. "I remember him too. He had a creepy vibe."

Sandra would push aside that latter tidbit and focus on moving forward. Nothing good would come from dwelling on *creepy vibe.* "He a regular by chance?" Her heart fluttered as she waited for the response.

"Nah, I've never seen him before," the clerk said.

"Me neither," the barista echoed.

This supported the theory he had targeted Olivia, possibly followed her here. "Can you describe him to us? Beyond the coat?"

"In his fifties," the barista said, "with brown hair, brown eyes."

The vanilla description wasn't going to get them anywhere. They needed the video. "What about an accent?" Her posts with the FBI had been in a rather close geographical vicinity but the question was still valid.

"Nothing noticeable," the barista said.

Then he was likely from around here, but that certainly didn't narrow things down.

"Ladies." A woman in her late thirties walked to the front, clearly the one in charge here.

Sandra was ready with her badge. "FBI, ma'am. I just had some questions for them. Are you the manager, Charlene?"

"I am, and I'd be fine with them talking to you if it wasn't for the line forming behind you." She raised her eyebrows and pointed.

Sandra turned, and as she did, she made the briefest eye contact with Eric. He gave her a pressed-lip smile. He'd poked her shoulder earlier to alert her to waiting customers. The woman directly behind them rolled her eyes. Facing the manager again, Sandra said, "Could we talk with you in your office?"

"Certainly. Follow me."

Sandra and Eric were led to an office in the back of the store. The space was compact but organized and tidy. Charlene took a seat behind the desk and leaned forward. "I'd offer you a seat, but as you can see..." She opened her arms to indicate the lack of any other chairs in the room.

"Not a problem," Sandra said, "but thank you for thinking of us. We need to see some video footage from earlier today."

"Yeah, well, I'm going to need more than that. Our entire corporate mission statement is about protecting people's rights."

Sandra had a feeling they might run into this issue. "I'll get you a warrant."

"You'll need to, otherwise this will never fly with corporate."

Sandra could relate. She had to watch her steps with her job to make sure the FBI didn't face backlash. "We'll get you one and come back."

"I'm sorry I couldn't just handle this for you, but if we don't stand up for others, who will?"

What about standing up for victims? But Sandra didn't respond. Instead, she led the way from the room and headed to the barista. She was frothing milk, and the woman who had rolled her eyes at Sandra was standing there waiting along with a few other people. "Excuse me," Sandra said to get the barista's attention.

She stopped what she was doing and looked up at Sandra.

"Just one more question. Did you happen to notice if that man left after Olivia?" If she could confirm that it would go toward supporting a warrant request. Right now, they had a suspicion and a probability.

"I saw Liv leave and, come to think of it, I don't think he was far behind her. She was just out the door when he popped up."

"Good memory," Eric put in.

"It helps with the job." The barista smiled.

"I bet. Did you notice if he followed her down the sidewalk?" she asked.

"I'm going to be here all night," the customer mumbled.

Sandra turned to her. "FBI, ma'am, but we're almost done here."

The woman didn't say anything, but her cheeks flushed.

The barista was shaking her head at Sandra. "Sorry."

"Okay, thank you, and here"—Sandra pulled out a ten-dollar bill from her pocket and handed it to the woman—"your next coffee's on me."

The woman glanced down at the bill in her palm and smiled. "Thanks."

"Don't mention it." Sandra left the store with Eric.

"Not sure if that statement is going to help with getting a warrant approved," he told her.

"I have to try." She pulled her phone and called a judge who she knew and had worked with for years. Nigel Morse had started out as a friend of a friend back when she was attending George Washington University. They'd stayed in touch over the years, and he often extended her leeway. The number she was calling was his personal cell phone. When he answered, she got to the point. Their friendship didn't trump the man's desire for succinctness. "It's Sandra. I need warrant approval for video footage."

"It's going on nine o'clock at night. This must be important."

"Olivia's missing, and the video I'm after may be our first solid lead."

There was silence at Nigel's end. "Olivia's missing? When did this happen?"

His shock manifested much the same as Elwood's had. She appreciated that he knew better than to ask if she was sure and how she knew. They had a solid foundation though, and Nigel was also a realist. "This afternoon between four forty-five and five-ten. The early end was the last time she was seen by her best friend at the DiversaBlend on M Street NW. Her phone was found under Key Bridge. Someone's taken her, Nigel. I know it as a mother and a fed."

"Run me through exactly what you need."

"A warrant for the surveillance video from DiversaBlend." She provided him the street number and added, "Eyewitnesses describe a man about fifty leering at Olivia and leaving just after she did."

"Did these eyewitnesses see him *follow* her?"

"Not exactly."

More silence spread across the line, then, "Sandra, I'm not sure what I should do here."

"Just say 'granted.'"

He didn't even take five seconds to deliberate. "Very well. You have my approval. I'll get the paperwork over to you as soon as possible."

"Thank you."

"And, Sandra, I sure hope Olivia's okay. She's an amazing girl."

Emotion kept Sandra from responding immediately, but eventually she was able to push out, "That she is, and thank you."

Nigel was gone, and the silence of the empty line thundered in Sandra's head.

"He's getting you the warrant?" Eric asked.

"He is, but it might take a minute or two. We can't just stand still waiting on it."

Eric nodded. "You got it. We know when she left Diversa-Blend, and she would have likely been heading home or...?"

Sandra shook her head. "Based on when she left, she was likely going straight to her violin teacher's rowhouse. Besides, I had already spoken to Earl, and he said he hadn't seen her."

"All right, but I say we still pop by in person. We can have him looking out for her if she does turn up."

"Okay."

"Does the violin teacher live far from you?"

"No. Just over on 30th Street NW."

"That narrows things down some."

She nodded, but her legs were temporarily unable to move. Fear had her grounded to the sidewalk.

Eric slipped his arm around her waist. "We'll find her, Sandra."

"I wish that was a promise you could make, but there is a chance that..."

"Nope. Don't even go down that road. It's far too soon."

She heard his words, his advice, and they held merit. "You're right. Olivia needs me to stay strong so she can come home safe." She started walking toward her building. Normally, Georgetown's old-town charm filled her with a sense of security and blanketed her with warmth. Not tonight. The cold night air bit her nose and assaulted her cheeks. She tucked her head down and trudged along the red-brick sidewalk.

Olivia, your mom's coming.

TWENTY-ONE

Sandra stepped into her building, and Earl was behind the concierge desk. He dipped his head when he saw her.

"Still no sign of Olivia?" she asked.

"No, ma'am. Dare I ask, is everything all right? You look shaken." Earl wasn't one to miss a thing. He could have been law enforcement for his canny ability to see and recall detail.

"I'm afraid that something might have happened to her." She downplayed it to prevent her emotions from flaring up and seizing control.

"Ma'am, I'm so sorry. If there's anything I can do to help...?" Earl let his gaze pass over to Eric and gave him a sorrowful look.

"You're doing it. Just call me if she does turn up," Sandra told him.

"You got it."

She turned and walked away with Eric, feeling hopeless.

"She went missing somewhere between DiversaBlend and Penelope's," Eric recapped. "Want to walk the area again?"

"We can." That's what she said, though it wasn't necessary. Olivia likely would have taken the direct route down M Street NW to 30th Street NW. Was she entertaining wasting time because she was afraid and hurt? And for priding herself on being self-possessed, she took some offense at what Eric had said. "She's not missing, Eric. We need to say it how it is. She was *taken*. That man *took* her."

Eric met her gaze. "I'm sorry. You're right. I shouldn't have made it sound like she ran off on her own."

"Thank you."

"I can't even imagine what you're going through." He took her hand in his.

"I'm struggling. I think going into mission mode is the only thing that can help me."

"We'll get her back."

"Or die trying. But you can't know that we will. What we need is access to the CCTV footage along this stretch." Her phone rang, and it was Nigel.

"You should have that warrant in your inbox."

"One sec." Sandra checked and was relieved to see it was there. "Yep, it's here. Thanks for making this happen so quickly."

"Don't even mention it. This is Olivia we're talking about. If you need anything, I'm just a phone call away."

"Thank you." She hung up and filled Eric in on who she was calling. Lakisha Hester answered on the second ring. When Sandra heard the tech's voice, she hated that she'd have to run through everything again. Just as she was about to, Lakisha spoke.

"Sandra. My God, are you okay? I heard about your daughter."

That was fast... "Assistant Director Rowe?" she asked, taking a stab at who had told the tech.

"That's right. He told me that she was last seen at Diversa-Blend on M Street Northwest and asked me to bring up the CCTV for that area."

She let out a breath of relief at the news that it was already underway. "Have you?"

"I'm getting to it and will let you know the second everything comes through."

"I'm not sure all that Rowe told you but extend the camera footage to cover this area as well." She told Lakisha the route Olivia would have likely taken to Penelope's address.

"Will do. I'm sorry, Sandra. I don't know what else to say."

"There isn't much that can be said, but thank you. Just do whatever you can."

"You know I will. I'll call the second I have something to share."

She ended the call and let out a long, deep breath. "So, Lakisha from the Science and Technology Branch is working on the CCTV for the area. My caller was Judge Morse, telling me a warrant for the surveillance footage should be in my inbox. Let's go present it."

Sandra and Eric stepped toward the counter, and the DiversaBlend manager came to them and waved them back to the office.

"That was fast," Charlene told them as they set up in her office. "I'm assuming you have a warrant?"

Sandra held her phone's screen up to her, and Charlene scrolled down, reading the entire document at a quick pass.

"That should appease corporate. Can you email it to me?" She gave Sandra her email address, and she fired it along.

"You should have it now."

"And I'll get that footage brought up. What time do you need it for?"

"Between four thirty and five this afternoon," Sandra told her, providing a buffer on the time slot.

"All right." Charlene moved the mouse around, clicking here and there. "Here we go. Actually, if you two wanted to just... well, one of you could take my chair." Charlene got up, and Sandra sat after Eric insisted. "You just need to hit the play button there." Charlene pointed it out on the screen.

Sandra did so, and the video came to life. The camera was mounted behind the counter and afforded a view of the entire coffee shop, including the front door and windows. Customers poured in and out in a constant stream. Sandra increased the speed of the playback and watched Avery and Olivia enter the frame.

Her heart pinched at the sight of her beautiful daughter. If only Sandra could reach inside the screen and pluck her to safety.

All hope seeped from her with the appearance of a man walking behind her daughter. He was tall and wearing a flannel-lined jean jacket. He had a mop of brown hair.

"That must be him," she said and stopped the video.

"Charlene, could you please excuse us for a moment?" Eric said kindly.

"Ah, sure." The manager left, closing her office door behind her.

"He's looking down. We can't see his face." Panic was threatening to suffocate her.

"Just resume playback at less than regular speed," Eric told her.

Sandra did so, and even when he placed his order at the counter, creepy guy kept his head down. "He's avoiding the camera on purpose. He followed Olivia here. He targeted her."

Eric laid a reassuring hand on her shoulder. "Let's just keep watching the video."

Olivia and Avery got their drinks and claimed a table. The man followed not long after and chose a spot within plain view of the girls, but he continued to keep his face from the camera. All they saw from this viewpoint was the back of his head.

They continued to watch as Olivia and Avery chatted, and

then Olivia got up to leave. She grabbed her backpack and violin case and waved goodbye to Avery. As Avery had told her, she got a phone call and was lifting the device to her ear as Olivia made it to the doorway.

But then, sure enough, the man got up, stuffing his hands into his pockets, as he followed in Olivia's steps.

The video afforded them the view that Olivia had turned left on the sidewalk, the right direction for Penelope's. Sandra was holding her breath as she watched the man go out the door and turn left after her.

"He took my baby girl." Anything else she might have said dried in her throat.

"Does he look familiar to you at all?" Eric asked, calm and steady, the voice of reason in the middle of her storm.

"How could I possibly answer that? He's never facing the camera."

"Going by build, mannerisms?"

"Not that stands out to me. No." She had a good memory, but it was too much to expect she'd pick him out of the slew of people she put away. At least not without context.

"Why don't you go back to when he enters the store? We can reference the height indicator tape to determine how tall he is."

She did that, and the tape marked him as six foot one with his head hunched forward. "Say six two or three. Lakisha could probably establish his exact height from this video. She might even be able to gather something we're not seeing."

Eric nodded and left to retrieve the manager. They came back together.

Sandra got up, pulled her card from her pocket and scribbled Lakisha's name and email on the back. "Please email the video to that address there."

"I'll do it right away."

"Thank you." She quickly tapped out a text to let Lakisha

know she should be receiving a video and that she was interested in knowing the height of the man in the flannel-lined jean jacket and anything else that stood out to her. She had a response within a few seconds from Lakisha that she would look out for it.

Sandra and Eric had just made it to the sidewalk when her phone rang. Elwood Rowe's name flashed on the screen. "It's Elwood," she told Eric before picking up.

"Sandra, does the name Duane Novak sound familiar to you?"

Fifteen years ago, Novak and his brother robbed a downtown convenience store, but things fell apart quickly. The clerk had managed to raise a silent alarm, and police showed up, sirens screeching, before the Novak brothers could make off. There was a standoff, and Sandra had been the lead negotiator. She'd given Duane, the shot caller of the two, every opportunity to surrender peacefully, but he'd wanted nothing to do with it. In the end, SWAT breached the store. The clerk and customers remained unharmed, but Duane's brother was shot during the extraction. The bullet punctured his spinal cord, making him a paraplegic for the rest of his life. "Yes, I remember him."

"Well, apparently, Duane Novak was just released this past Friday."

She became cold. The Duane Novak of fifteen years ago would have fit the build of the man they'd just seen on the DiversaBlend video. Had he found out about Olivia and gone after her as payback? She reached for her pendant, pushing through the collar of her coat to get there.

"Sandra, did you hear me?"

"I did. Ah, Novak had a brother. Do you know if he's still alive?"

"He's alive, residing in an assisted living home. What's this telling you?"

"I was just curious." In truth, she wanted to know what

bearing this might have on Olivia's well-being. Was Novak inflicting the same damage on Olivia that had been done to his brother? But another thought occurred to her. Assisted living didn't come cheap, let alone keeping up the payments for the last fifteen years. Could he have taken Olivia for ransom? Considering the alternatives, that prospect didn't sound as bad. He'd treat her well to better ensure a payday.

"Do you think Novak could have taken Olivia?"

"He hates me enough, that's for sure, and I think I just might have seen him on video." She brought him up to speed.

"So he left right behind her. And you're sure this man could be Novak?"

Hit with the direct question, doubts moved in. Was it the context that helped her to see the similarity or a desire to rush things along? "If he looks like he used to, yeah. There were no clear shots of the man's face though."

Elwood mumbled something that resembled, "That would make it too easy."

"Do you have an address on him?"

"His parents were contacted. They want nothing to do with him, but apparently he reached out and told them he was staying at the Sands Motel if they changed their minds."

The flea-infested dive fit Duane Novak. It was also a good match for someone up to no good, such as a kidnapping for ransom. "We need to get units over there right away."

"Agents are heading there as we speak, same too for a house owned by his parents. They moved to a condo a few weeks ago, but the place hasn't gone on the market yet. The parents said Novak would likely still have a key. Agents Radcliffe and Shaffer will have a cursory look around, see if there is any probable cause to take things further."

This might not be about money then. Not if the parents could afford to leave their house before it was sold. Though it might long be paid for. She really had too little information to form any solid theory. "He might be holding her there," she said, not wanting to think about another possibility. Such as, he disposed of Olivia's body on the property. "Where is this place? I want to go."

"Hmm. I'm not sure if that's a good idea, Sandra. You're rather close to the situation."

"Well, I'm not just going to stand back and wait, or I'll go crazy. I need to feel useful. This is my daughter we're talking about. If that man took her and has her somewhere..." She didn't dare finish verbalizing her intent. It was best that her boss had deniability if it came down to it.

"I get it, but you must understand that I can't let you run lead on this."

She'd propose a compromise. "Fine. Let Brice take it, and I'll take the backseat. I just need to be there for the questioning."

Silence stretched across the line.

"Assistant Director?" she prompted, pulling out his formal title. "I know you want Olivia found."

"Of course I do."

"You can trust me to keep my cool, boss. Just let me be there to talk to this guy. He knows me."

"He also hates you."

"Let me use that."

Seconds passed, but eventually Elwood said, "Okay, but Brice takes lead. Even though it goes against my better judgment."

That was a decision she could live with. "Thank you."

"I do want to make this very clear. This is a federal case, not one for the MPD, so don't let this Detective Birch get in on the interview. Am I understood?"

"Understood."

"I'll call if anything flags at the property." Elwood hung up.

Sandra turned toward Eric. "That was Rowe, and we have a suspect. Some guy I had a role in putting away fifteen years ago."

"That's great. Let's go."

"Here's the thing..." She hated to squeeze him out, but she also foresaw Elwood benching her immediately if he found out Eric was involved after he'd just given her an order. She wasn't willing to take that chance. "This is a full-blown FBI investigation now." She paused there, just a fraction too long.

"So I'm getting the boot?"

"Please, don't put it like that, Eric. I don't have a choice. If you came along with me to chat with Novak, you'd be seen as interfering with an FBI case. If Rowe wanted to be a prick, he could have you arrested, and I'd be benched from looking for my own daughter. I can't have that happen."

He squeezed her shoulder. "I'll step back. Is there anything else I can do? I can't just stand around and twiddle my thumbs." His cheeks were flushed, and his eyes hardened.

He was pissed about being pushed out yet showing her empathy. It was endearing. And loyal. Two things she admired about him, along with his ambition and drive. "Could you sit at the penthouse in case Olivia comes back?"

He didn't say a word for a few beats but what wasn't being said was plenty. He didn't expect Olivia to magically turn up any more than she did. "If you think that would help."

"It would help me to know that if she does by chance turn up, you'd be there for her."

"All right then. *For you.*"

"Thank you, Eric. This means a lot to me." She kissed his cheek, but he pulled her to him and took her mouth.

When they parted, she licked her lips. "You might not be standing next to me when I question our suspect, but I'll feel you there."

He dipped his head. He might never realize how much she appreciated his support and unwavering strength. She'd take that with her as she confronted Novak. What she didn't let Elwood know was she had no intention of taking the backseat.

TWENTY-TWO

The motel's parking lot was full of G-rides, or cars belonging to the FBI. Brice was standing next to one and waved at Sandra when Eric pulled in. She thanked him for dropping her off, got out, and joined Brice. "Any updates on the K-9 search?" she asked him.

Brice shook his head. "I would have called you if there had been."

She figured as much but had to ask anyhow. Her daughter's backpack and violin still hadn't been recovered, but they could be with her. "And her shirt?"

"I folded it and put it on your desk."

"Thank you." She proceeded to tell him about the video from DiversaBlend and how the man tailing Olivia could have been Novak. "What room is he in?"

"Seven."

"You ready?" She didn't wait for a response but strode toward the door with the silver 7 on it. She knocked, and the curtain on the window was lifted back, then left to fall. She pounded on the door. "FBI! Duane Novak, surrender!" With that last word, she was jettisoned to the past.

"Go away. I haven't done anything wrong."

"Open the door, or we will breach," she threatened.

A few moments passed, and the door was slowly opened. Brice swiftly wedged himself through the crack and slapped cuffs on Novak and pushed him back on the bed so he was sitting on the edge of the mattress.

"What are you doing?" Novak was pleading, not so tough in the face of FBI agents storming into his room.

Sandra searched for any sign of Olivia or a flannel-lined jean jacket. He could have gotten rid of the latter. *Olivia too...* Sandra swallowed roughly, walked around the bed and stopped in front of Novak. Brice stepped aside. No doubt Elwood had made it clear Brice was to take the lead, but he was deferring to her. Brice just went up several pegs in her opinion. As for Novak, his looks had hardly changed from fifteen years ago. Her heart pounded, realizing now more than ever he could be that man from the video. "Where is she?"

Novak glared at her. "Why am I not surprised you're here? Are you back to screw me over a second time? You do know my brother will never walk again because of you."

"I never pulled the trigger, but thank you for confirming motive."

"Huh? What do you people want? Should I get a lawyer?"

"Shut your face, Novak," Brice told him.

"Where is Olivia?" she said, in a voice so cold, it chilled her.

"I don't know any Olivia."

His claim did nothing to tamp down her suspicion. Criminals lie. Fact of life. She brought up Olivia's photo on her phone and shoved it in Novak's face. "Take a good, hard look."

"Why should I?" Novak shrugged.

"You want to go back to prison? Fine, let's go." Brice grabbed Novak's arm, and he bucked free.

"I'm not going anywhere. *Lawyer*," he said slowly.

"Olivia. Tell us where she is. Now!" she barked, but Brice

glanced at her, a warning look in his eyes. The request for a lawyer should have shut her down. But there was no way. *Use his hate for me...* "You clearly blame me for what happened to your brother, don't you?"

"Damn right, I do," he seethed.

That smacked close to *that's right.* He'd feel she understood him, but she was more interested in how this worked against him. "And it sounds like you want to keep your freedom and stay out of prison."

"Yeah," he said slowly, scanning her eyes as if trying to understand her sudden shift in approach.

Throwing a suspect off was interrogation gold when it could be done. "Great, then all you have to do is tell us where this girl is." She held up the screen of her phone again.

"I don't know her."

"Her name is Olivia."

"As you keep saying."

"Something I'm pretty sure you already knew." She studied his eyes, disheartened they were blank. Again, that didn't necessarily mean anything. He could have that deadpan look for many reasons, including to sell his lie. After all, he didn't want to return to prison.

"I've never seen her before either," he offered up.

"But this is you, isn't it?" Sandra kept her tone nonconfrontational and replaced the photo of Olivia with a still of the man from the DiversaBlend video.

Brice caught her attention from across the room where he was holding up a garbage bin with gloved hands.

"Ah, no, it's *not.*"

She was distracted by what Brice was getting at, but it all became clear when he lifted a DiversaBlend cup out of the trash. "This only works if we're honest with each other, Duane." She pointed a finger behind Novak, toward Brice.

Novak looked over his shoulder. "Okay, I was at Diversa-Blend today. Is that a crime?"

"It depends. Why did you follow this girl?"

"I didn't."

"But that's you coming out of DiversaBlend right behind her," she countered.

Novak studied the picture. "That's not the one I went to."

Brice was rooting in the garbage, and if she read his mind, looking for a receipt. He shook his head, set the cup back in the trash and set the can on the floor again.

"So if we showed your picture to them at this DiversaBlend, they wouldn't recognize you?" she asked.

"Where did you say it was?"

"I didn't, but..." She gave him the location.

"They wouldn't know me, so go ahead."

"Duane, I thought we were starting to connect." Skilled as she was, she couldn't pull that line off convincingly. "All right, fine, we weren't. You see, I think you took this girl. I want to know where she is and what you want."

"I didn't do anything. I've been here all day."

"You're forgetting about the cup," she pointed out.

"That was around noon at the one just down the street from here. I never took that girl. You've got nothing on me. Lawyer," he spat. "If you need me to, I'll spell it out for you. L. A. W—"

Sandra shook her head and signaled for Brice to get the man out of her face. She'd already steamrolled past his first request, and if she wanted to keep her job without a reprimand on her permanent record, she'd better not risk doing so a second time.

She left the room behind Brice and Novak, staring through the back of his head. That man had her daughter somewhere. He had to because she couldn't entertain the thought that he didn't. That would take the search back to ground zero.

TWENTY-THREE

Before Sandra and Brice left the area, they went to the DiversaBlend that Novak had indicated. He was being transported by another agent back to the WFO where he'd spin in an interview room waiting for his lawyer to show up.

The door chimed when they entered the coffee shop, and a friendly woman behind the counter smiled at them. "What can I get for y'all?"

They both ordered Americanos, and then got right down to their real reason for being there.

Sandra held up her FBI credentials as did Brice, and the woman shrunk back.

"Nothing to worry about, ma'am," Sandra assured her. "We just need to know if you saw a man come in here today around noon. Were you working then?" It might be a stretch given the hour now.

"I was. What man?"

This was where Brice stepped in with a photograph of Novak on his phone. Sandra was just going to describe him.

"This one." Brice held his screen toward her, and the woman shook her head.

"Nope, I never saw him. He come in, though? We have a drive-thru too."

Brice glanced at Sandra, then said to the woman, "He doesn't have a vehicle, so he would have come in."

"Then, no, I never saw him. Sorry."

"Thanks for your help," Brice told her.

"Don't mention it. Enjoy your coffees."

Sandra plucked her cup from the counter and took a long sip as Brice pushed the door open and they left.

"Novak has us chasing our tails, but he made a huge mistake sending us here. This gives us enough to get a search warrant rolling for the Novak property. You drive, and I'll call Elwood." She pulled her phone as they walked to their car.

Brice got into the driver's seat, and just as Sandra did up her belt, Elwood picked up. She recapped their visit with Novak ending with, "I think there's enough for a search warrant."

"By a stretch, Sandra. I imagine you want this over with, but just because he recognized you, which we thought he would, that doesn't solidify motive and support cause for a search warrant for his parents' place," Elwood argued.

It wasn't the response she'd expected. "For which Novak has a key. And he wasn't recognized at the DiversaBlend where he sent us. Doesn't any of this mean anything?" Her voice built in pitch as she continued to talk.

"I can't argue about the key, but the person you spoke to at the coffee shop could have stepped away when he came in."

She didn't respond to that.

"I hope you understand why I'm being this way," Elwood said.

If this way *means difficult...* But, no, she didn't understand.

"It's just if he has Olivia," Elwood said, "you want everything to stand up in court."

"It won't much matter if she's dead, when I had a chance to

save her but didn't." Her voice cracked, and Brice looked over at her.

There was silence on Elwood's end of the line.

She pinched the St. Michael pendant, drew some solid breaths. "I shouldn't have..." Her head was spinning, and her mouth was dry.

"No, I understand. I'm just on both sides of this."

She couldn't let herself travel down the empathy path. Not right now. Not when she was flaking apart inside. "I have a good friend who's a judge," she started. "He might be able to get the warrant through."

"Go ahead, but I don't think you have enough. And let me express my reservation about all this, Sandra."

She braced herself for what he might be about to say.

"Why would Novak hold Olivia at his parents' place and stay at a motel? Why not just stay out there too?"

"I don't know. I guess I'd counter with why not? You didn't make it sound like the parents were around the place anymore. You said they moved out weeks ago and haven't even put it on the market. It would be a good place to keep someone," she reasoned. "Let me share what else I was thinking. Novak's brother needs special care. Who's paying for that? I suspect it would cost a lot of money."

"So Novak's motive is money?"

"It's possible. At the same time he gets some sense of payback for what I did to his brother all those years ago."

A beat or two passed, then, "You didn't do anything to his brother, Sandra."

She remained silent. There were times she had a hard time separating the consequences of an incident from herself. She just held herself to such high standards, scoring herself on some imagined philosophical report card. What would her brother think of her performance? Would her actions have made him proud?

"You might be on to something here though," Elwood said when he must have realized she wasn't going to speak. "This gives me a bit more to work with. Let me run this past a judge, see if we can get that search warrant."

"Thank you." Her lungs expanded just a bit farther.

When he was gone, she looked over at Brice. "He's going to push this up the ladder, see if a judge will sign a search warrant. And the good news is he never even told me to stay away from it."

"Just because he didn't say it... I'm not sure I like that sparkle in your eye," Brice told her.

"It's all good. You're going back to the WFO and waiting with Novak for his lawyer, and I'm going to the Novak property. I want to be there and ready when that warrant hits."

"Assuming it does."

"It will."

"And until it comes in what will you be doing there?"

"Nothing. I'll be a well-behaved agent minding her Ps and Qs."

"Uh-huh."

TWENTY-FOUR

Duane Novak would be getting comfortable in an interview room at the WFO while she was pulling into the driveway of Novak's parents' place. Elwood had made the mistake of telling her the agents' names who were headed out there. She'd called Agent Gabe Radcliffe and got the address. This saved her the trouble of looking it up in the system and needing to defend the search to Elwood. As she and Brice had agreed, he was staying back at the WFO.

The property was in Alexandria, Virginia, twenty minutes from Washington. The house was a backsplit with an acre of land bordered by a six-foot-tall privacy fence. There was only one car in the driveway, and the exhaust was billowing plumes of white into the cold night air. Two silhouettes were in the front seat. Agents Radcliffe and Karl Shaffer must have carpooled, but why were they just sitting there?

She parked the fed car she was driving behind theirs and got out. There was a streetlight right out front, but she grabbed a flashlight anyhow. She rapped on the driver's window of the other vehicle, and Radcliffe put it down.

"Why are you just sitting here?" she asked him.

"We finished looking around, Sandra, and there's nothing that gives us probable cause to take things further," Gabe said. "We were just waiting for you to turn up."

"Well, thanks for that, but AD Rowe's working on a warrant. Just curious, but are there any outbuildings on the property?"

Karl leaned forward in the passenger seat and looked over. "Two, both fairly large."

"So a warrant's coming through then?" Gabe asked. "My first time hearing of it."

"Fingers crossed that we'll have it any minute. But in the meantime..." She turned on her flashlight and cast the beam toward the front of the home.

"We'll accompany you," Karl said, tugging on his door handle and getting out.

Gabe shut the car off and joined them.

She led the way to an opened gate. "It was like that?" she asked her colleagues.

"Yes, it was. That's why we could justify going in the yard. That, and seeing the outbuildings," Gabe added, and she was grateful he didn't elaborate on what he meant by that. Her imagination had already veered down that path. They would make a good place to hold someone.

There was an upper deck attached to the back of the house with steps down to the yard. To the side of it was a walkout from a full basement. She walked over there, but it was futile to think she could see inside. It was dark in there and out here. If she shone the flashlight toward the glass, it would just reflect like a starburst.

Her phone rang, and she flinched first, fumbled later, as she tried to fish it out of her pocket. She tucked her flashlight under her arm and finally got a hold of it. Elwood's name was on the screen. "Tell me you have the search warrant," she answered.

Gabe and Karl, who had turned their backs on her and started into the yard, stopped and turned around.

"I do," Elwood told her. "It covers the entire property, including all structures."

She pinched the pendant. If her girl was here, they'd find her, and it would all be above board.

"Where are you, by the way?"

"I'm..." Did she confess to being here? As Brice had pointed out, while he never told her to stay away, he didn't exactly tell her to come here either. Surely, he could appreciate she'd want to be here when the warrant came through.

"You're at the Novak property, aren't you?"

There's no fooling him... "I am."

"How did you know where it was? I never told you, and I know you didn't run a search, or I would have seen that."

She might be imagining it but could swear she detected some amusement and pride coming through. "You told me you sent Agents Radcliffe and Shaffer, so I called them."

Both their heads perked up, and she could feel them drilling her with their gazes through the darkness.

"But they're not complicit in any wrongdoing," she rushed to add.

"Neither are you, that I know of. Just tell me you didn't cross the line."

"You should know me better than to ask that."

"Good." With that, Elwood was gone.

"We're clear to breach and search this entire property, including the outbuildings."

"I'm going back to the sheds," Gabe told her, and she didn't care for the somber note of his voice.

"I'm coming too," she told him, and Karl also tagged along.

They got outside of the nearest one, and she called out, "Olivia?"

Gabe and Karl exchanged a look.

"You tried that?" she asked on a hunch.

"We did," Karl admitted.

He didn't need to say more as she took the following silence to mean there had been no answer. She tried the door handle, expecting and fearing that it would be locked. It turned without resistance. The Novaks must have forgotten to lock it behind them when they moved. *Or Duane had been here with Olivia and left...* The latter thought had her trembling. After all, where would he have taken her from here? And even if he had kept her here, there were neighbors close enough to hear screaming. And just like that her whirling mind intensified her fears.

Just think positive...

She stepped into the shed, flashing her light over the space. Patio furniture and lawn decorations filled most of it. As she rolled the beam into all the corners, desperation was rising within her. "There's nothing here." She turned to leave, almost bumping into her fellow agents, not sure if she was relieved or disappointed but sided with the latter. It still left her girl out there. Somewhere.

She checked the second shed next. This one was locked, but Karl picked the lock. Inside was lawn equipment, bags of potting soil, and garden tools. No sign Olivia had ever been.

The garage was searched next and gave up no obvious secrets, even as Sandra continued to inhale deeply to see if she could pick up even a subtle trace of Olivia's perfume.

Her colleagues trailed behind her, more than capable of branching out on their own, but she respected that they stayed close to her. It communicated they had her back literally and figuratively. Neither of them had commented on Olivia or expressed their sympathies about the predicament, but she could feel it coming from them.

They entered the house, flicking on the lights there, and she found the stairs to the basement.

"Olivia!" she called out as she took the steps down.

The lower level was finished in this area, but the absence of furniture made it quick to work through. She entered the utility room and tugged down on the chain attached to a simple overhead fixture. This room housed a furnace and water heater, but there was also a washer and dryer, a fridge, and an upright freezer jammed into the space. She moved to the back of the room, catching sight of a door there.

Her heart was pounding as she reached out to pull the handle.

A loud banging came from upstairs.

"Son of—" Sandra laid a hand on her chest.

"Sounds like someone's at the front door," Karl said.

"Go check it out then," Gabe told him.

Karl's steps thumped up the stairs, sounding like he was taking two at a time. Not a challenge for his long legs.

She stood there, her heartbeat sounding in her ears, and faint voices joined the rhythm.

"You can go ahead," Gabe gently prompted her, and when she looked at him, he gestured toward the door.

She'd almost forgotten what she was about to do. Almost. She pulled on the door. It was cold storage, and it was empty.

Gabe put a hand on her shoulder but didn't say a word. She nodded, getting his expression of camaraderie and support.

They left the basement and found an older man standing in the entry with Karl.

The man pointed at them, and Karl turned around.

"This is Tim Hewitt. He lives next door," Karl told them. "He was curious who was here because he knows the Novaks have moved."

"Just being a good neighbor." He winked at Sandra.

She smiled at him but was struck by the oddity of having this flirtatious old loon hitting on her right now. Especially considering her reason for being there. She left the area and swept through the main level, but it took just about as long as the basement had.

When she returned, Karl and Gabe were deep into conversation with the older man.

"I did see the younger fella park in the driveway earlier this evening," Tim said.

That was enough to lure her over to join in the discussion. Duane Novak would have no reason to come here and, from what she knew, he didn't have a vehicle. "Duane, their son?" she asked to clarify.

"Uh-huh, that's right, ma'am."

"What time was this?"

"Around six thirty. I'd finished dinner and was settling in."

"Did he say why he was here or was he with anyone?" She knew the second the double question slipped out that she was steamrolling the poor man. She added a smile to soften the assault, which seem to work.

"I never spoke to him, and he was alone."

Duane could have had Olivia lying in the backseat or in the trunk. "Did he go into the house or onto the property?"

"Not that I saw."

That wasn't reassuring. Duane could have moved Olivia without the older man seeing. "Did you catch a look at the vehicle?"

"Yes, ma'am. A Ford sedan, powder blue, older."

Could be a Taurus or other model for that matter. She wasn't up on cars. But where did Duane get the wheels? Brice had told that woman at DiversaBlend he didn't have a vehicle, which Sandra took to mean as he'd looked at Novak's record. So did this blue sedan belong to a friend? Where was it now? And would finding it get her any closer to Olivia?

TWENTY-FIVE

Sandra returned to the WFO, gutted that she wasn't any further along in finding Olivia. Brice had texted before she left the Novak property to say that Duane's lawyer had arrived. She'd fired back a message to ask him to hold off until she got back. She received two letters in response to that. *O* and *K*. Somehow it felt loaded in what wasn't being said. Then another text, *Rowe's here.* And that explained it. Brice was fine stepping back and letting her run with things at the motel but not with the assistant director in the audience.

She parked in the lot, and sat there for a minute, letting the car idle. She'd put off making a certain phone call for long enough. She pressed his name before she could conjure more reasons to procrastinate. By now, she'd hoped that Olivia would be back, and everything would be somehow okay. This entire nightmare would be something they could relay to Olivia's father after the fact. But the truth was far from that.

She landed in Nolan's voicemail. "It's urgent that you call me back. It's about Olivia." It was enough detail to prompt a quick response but not so much as to give him a heart attack.

Next, she called Eric to let him know where things were

with Novak. She could have easily texted him instead, but she longed to hear his voice and soak up his strength and confidence. With every passing minute of Olivia being out there *somewhere* it was slowly shredding her sanity. She kept coming back to one question. *What does Duane want out of all this?*

Every time it came up, all she could land on was revenge. Did that mean he'd permanently injure Olivia like had happened to his brother, as she thought before? But if this was about payback, wouldn't Novak have boasted about hurting Olivia? Instead, he claimed no recognition of her. Or was this about money? Even still, none of this explained the other anomaly of why he'd shown up at his parents' empty house in a mystery blue Ford sedan.

She entered the office and went to her desk. The sight of Olivia's folded shirt sent a sharp pain through her chest.

"There you are," Brice said.

She stuffed the shirt into a drawer and said, "No sign of her."

"I had a feeling when I didn't hear from you," he told her.

Then she filled him in on what the *good neighbor* had told them.

"All right. Well, as I told you, Rowe's here and he'll be watching my conversation with Novak."

"*Your* conversation?"

"Rowe made it clear to me that I'm the only one he wants questioning him."

She made a move to find their boss, but stopped when Brice held up a hand. "No sense pleading your case. He told me to tell you nothing you could say was going to work on him."

Except he wasn't confident enough to face me... "Okay. There are some things you need to ask." She ran through them fast and then said, "Let's go." She brushed her arm through the air in a sweeping motion, hoping it would encourage him to get moving.

He quickly caught up and kept his strides even with hers. She entered the observation room and found Elwood standing near the one-way mirror looking in on Duane Novak and a portly fellow with a bad combover.

"That's Otto Richardson, Novak's attorney," Brice told her.

"Thanks, but I figured as much. By that, I mean, his lawyer. I didn't know his name," she added.

Brice smiled at her. "I understood. Okay, so do I know everything?"

"You do."

Brice left them and showed up on the other side of the glass a few seconds later. Both Richardson and Novak sat straighter when Brice knocked and then turned the door handle. Richardson touched his client's shoulder briefly. Brice entered the room and no sooner sat down than the lawyer spoke.

"You might as well dismiss my client right now. You have had no right to hold him and have violated the law."

Sandra could feel Elwood staring at her profile, but she refused to acknowledge him.

"What did you do?" he said quietly.

"Please, shh."

"*Shh?* I'm your boss and you shush me?"

She looked over at him now. "I didn't mean any disrespect. I'm just... frustrated, disheartened. The hours are flying by, and I'm no closer to finding Olivia. But that man in there"—she jabbed a pointed finger toward Novak—"knows where she is." *He has to!*

"And if he doesn't?"

She pinched her pendant. "Let's not even discuss that possibility right now."

Back in the interview room, the conversation had carried on with Brice and the lawyer. Brice must have rebutted with something, and Richardson was red-cheeked and on the defense.

"My client says that he requested a lawyer *three times* before the questioning stopped."

"Is that true?" Elwood's entire body was facing her now, and she turned to him.

"It's not true." Technically the first time the word *lawyer* was framed by a question about whether he should get one. Not a request. "It was once."

"My God, Sandra." Elwood looked up at the ceiling.

"I just need to know where he has Olivia."

"By breaking the law. If this guy took her, he might never go away for it."

"I told you before my priority is Olivia." She'd deal with Novak in her own way if it came down to it, or at least she liked to think she could take the law into her own hands. Her dead father might come back and haunt her from the grave though. He was a good cop. She'd strived to be that all her career. So what the hell...? This situation with Olivia was knocking her off balance.

"We were just talking with your client," Brice said in response to the lawyer's accusation, drawing her and Elwood's attention back to the room.

"It doesn't look like 'just talking' when we're both sitting here across from a fed, my client suspected of kidnapping a teenage girl. And all the while you're harassing my client, he told me that he made it clear he has no idea who the girl even is."

Brice set out a photograph of Olivia and pushed it across the table in front of Novak.

He shook his head and looked at his lawyer, who shoved the picture back.

"He doesn't know her. What proof do you have against him?"

Brice took out a photo plucked from the coffee shop's video. "He followed her out of DiversaBlend on M Street NW."

"I told you I never went to that one," Novak said.

Brice leveled his gaze at him. "Well, you didn't go to the other one either. The lady at the front counter didn't remember you. Yet one of their cups is magically in your garbage."

"This is bullshit," Novak swore, and Richardson held up a calming hand at his client.

"Where were you this afternoon between four thirty and six thirty?" Brice countered.

Richardson gestured for his client to answer.

"At Sands Motel, in my room."

"Can anyone corroborate that fact?" Brice asked.

"Umm." Novak started squirming and faced his lawyer, who nodded. "I was with a hooker."

"A sex worker," she murmured, unable to let the other term go. It wasn't politically correct, and she had the insatiable need to keep things accurate.

"Where would we find her?"

"Just down the street from the Sands. She's really skinny with red hair and smells like an ashtray. Goes by Lucy."

"Okay, we'll have a talk with her. It must have been at the earlier end of the time I gave you. We were told that you were at your parents' old place around six thirty. Did we hear wrong?"

Novak wriggled in his chair and shook his head at his lawyer.

"What's the relevance?" Richardson asked, stepping in.

Brice settled his gaze on Novak. "Why were you there?"

Novak rubbed his jaw. "I... I was just there because of senti-mental reasons. That's all. It was after... well, the hooker."

"Sentimental reasons. Can you elaborate?"

"Maybe once you elaborate on the relevance," Richardson slapped back.

"All right then. The thing is, your client has no need to be hanging around the place. One of our agents spoke with your client's parents, and they had no interest in a reunion. They turned him away. That's why he's been staying at the Sands Motel."

"Still waiting on the relevance." Richardson tapped a hand on the edge of the table.

"We think he took this girl"—Brice pointed at Olivia's face—"to that property and held her there for a time."

A complete fabrication as there was nothing to support that. Elwood looked at her, and she shook her head, to which he gave a puzzled expression. She pointed into the interview room. He should know that interrogation was a game and if the criminals could lie, so could the good guys.

"I went for sentimental reasons!" Novak burst into tears.

Brice gave him a few moments to compose himself before continuing. "Which are?" he gently prodded.

"I grew up there." Novak sniffled. "Everything wasn't perfect, but it was all right. Jimmy could walk. I talked him into... into..."

The bank robbery where he wound up a paraplegic, Sandra finished in her head.

"My client needs a break," Richardson said. "Or let him go. I still haven't heard any compelling evidence against him."

"Just one more question, and we can cut out for a break. Where did you get the Ford sedan from, Duane?"

"I borrowed it from a friend."

"What friend? What's their name?"

"No, Agent, you said one more question. He answered it," Richardson shoved out.

Brice gathered the photographs back into a folder and left the room. A moment later, he joined her and Elwood.

"You did well in there. We'll get him." Her phone rang, and she pulled it out to see it was Lakisha and answered. As she listened to her message, she was smiling. Then she said, "We'll be at your desk as fast as possible." She hung up and signaled for

Brice to join her. "You're on a break from the interview, so you might as well join me."

"Hold up," Elwood called out. His authoritative tone had her stopping in the doorway and turning around.

"We need more proof against Duane," she said, "and we just might have it. That was Lakisha Hester from the Science and Tech Branch. She has CCTV footage ready to watch from the area around DiversaBlend."

"Go. In the meantime, I'll dispatch agents to find this Lucy, see if we can poke a hole in Novak's alibi. I'll also send some to canvass the neighborhood surrounding the Novaks' property to see if anyone else saw Duane at his parents' place with someone or caught the plate number on that Ford."

"Thanks." She hustled out, not about to wait around in case he changed his mind.

TWENTY-SIX

Sandra and Brice got out of the car and passed through the security measures at FBI headquarters and then on to where the Science and Tech agents were holed up.

Lakisha waved them over when they were close to her desk and got up to hug her.

Sandra wished she hadn't done that because she could feel herself flaking apart. "Thank you, but we should probably just watch that video."

"Yeah, of course." She dropped back into her chair, clicked on a file, and M Street NW came onto the screen. "Oh, just one quick thing. I was able to determine the man from the Diversa-Blend video was six foot two inches. I couldn't make out anything else that was useful. All right, so are you ready?" Lakisha made eye contact with Sandra.

As I'll ever be... Sandra nodded, and Lakisha hit play on the video.

The footage was a sideview and captured Olivia leaving DiversaBlend, wearing her backpack and carrying her violin case. She started to move down the sidewalk. The man in the fleece-lined jean jacket was only about ten feet behind. Others were on the sidewalk too, and Olivia was weaving between them. It could certainly be Duane Novak, but none of the angles captured the man's face directly, and he'd put on a ballcap. His head was facing slightly downward, not affording a strong profile shot either. Likely intentional.

Olivia continued to walk down the sidewalk and picked up speed. There was a black van parked at the curb, and Sandra wished she could climb into the video and travel back in time, because she had this sixth sense of what was about to happen.

She continued to watch as Novak swept behind her daughter and pushed her toward the side of the van. Likely inside. The video didn't have sound, but Olivia would have likely been so startled she hadn't a second to scream. And if the people behind this were anywhere close to being professional criminals, they'd have silenced her by some means the moment she was tucked into the vehicle.

The van merged into traffic seconds later, and no one on the sidewalk seemed to pay any attention.

"Liv." Her daughter's name left her lips in a whisper.

Lakisha hit pause. If she or Brice had heard her, they respectfully gave no indication. Both kept their gaze on the screen and were silent. But what was there to say? It was a scenario she had pictured, even expected, but watching it take place was surreal. In fact, until now a tiny part of her clung to the hope she was somehow misreading things. That Olivia would miraculously turn up unharmed with an explanation for her disappearance. That was the mother in her begging for a reprieve. What she'd seen just confirmed what the fed in her knew all along. Her daughter was kidnapped.

"Sandra." Lakisha was the first to break the silence.

Now Lakisha and Brice looked at her. Sandra was numb as her heart raced. "We knew someone took her. We just have the irrefutable proof now." The more affirmative she spoke, it might sink in.

"It might not have been the Ford sedan, but that guy's build and gait sure looks like Duane Novak's," Brice put in.

She nodded but wavered in confidence. The man on the video was without a face. Was it Novak? Regardless of whether it was or wasn't, what did this man want? So far, this person was a coward without a voice who'd snatched a child from the street.

Thankfully her mind continued to work, but thoughts were forming so rapidly, it was challenging to grasp one. "The van could belong to another friend. Any shots of the license plate?"

"Let's find out." Lakisha reversed until the black van pulled up and the angle made it possible to see that the front plate was blacked out. The tech forwarded and the same applied to the rear plate.

"They thought this through," Brice said.

Sandra shot him a look. If he wasn't going to offer something helpful, she'd rather he kept quiet. "We need to know where they went."

"Already on it." Lakisha clicked here and there, but it didn't take long to see the van headed out of the city, across Key Bridge.

Lakisha slumped in her chair. "I'm sorry, Sandra. I wish that..."

Sandra put a hand on her shoulder and took a shuddering breath. "We'll figure this out even if Novak refuses to talk. We'll find his friend." After all, tracking people down was what she was good at, and it always started with a base of facts. "They were waiting for her," she said. "They must have known about her routine of going to DiversaBlend after school. They waited until she was alone and snatched her."

"It seems we all agree there were at least two," Brice said. "Novak and the driver."

"It's possible there's a third in the back, but it isn't neces-sary," Sandra said.

"It kills me that no one called nine-one-one," Lakisha put in.

"People are too absorbed in their own lives to see what's going on right around them." It was a sad observation that Sandra had made over the years. "Can you go back to where the van pulled up?"

"Absolutely." Lakisha did that, and they rewatched that part.

"Pause." Sandra pointed at the screen. "If you zoom in, we have the driver's profile. It might be enough to identify him through facial rec databases."

"Worth a try." Lakisha panned in and captured a closeup and got the system started on doing just as Sandra had asked. It would search through several linked databases for a photo showing similar characteristics. Sometimes the hits came back fast. Sometimes they took time. The only thing was a person needed a criminal record to be in the database.

"Can you replay the part where Novak pushes Olivia?" Sandra was just wishing for one split second that captured the man's face. If they could prove this was Novak, they'd be well on their way to getting Olivia back.

Brice turned to her. "You sure you want to do that?"

Lakisha was watching her expectantly.

"I don't have a choice if I want to save Olivia. Please play it in slow motion," she added.

Neither of them said a word as Lakisha did just that, and they were rewarded. In the seconds after the man pushed Olivia into the van, he lifted his head, his face looking right into the camera.

"That's not Novak," Brice said.

Sandra's stomach clenched. "Nope, but I know who he is."

TWENTY-SEVEN

The moments following Sandra's realization swelled and stretched. She couldn't stop staring at the man's face. She'd seen him for the first time a few days ago, but what possible reason could he have for taking Olivia? "We need to cut Novak loose," she said. "And call off the agents Elwood would have dispatched."

"I'll call Rowe in a minute," Brice said. "But you said you know him?"

She nodded while her mind tried to unravel the riddle. Why had he taken Olivia? What did he want from her?

"Sandra?" Brice prompted. "Who is he?"

Brice and Lakisha were watching her with eyes full of worry and expectation.

She saw her insecurities reflected in them and stiffened. She filled them in on her past, including mention of the recent parole hearing and its verdict. "This man's a friend of Darrell Patton's. He was at the hearing and spoke to his character."

"His name?" Brice prompted.

Her mind was blank under the pressure. Despite the adrenaline coursing through her, the sound of her heartbeat in her ears, she was finding it hard to focus.

"We can call the parole board and find out." Brice pulled his phone.

She held up a hand. "No, I know it. Just give me a minute to think..."

Brice and Lakisha shared a glance. She didn't much like that it communicated their concerns over her welfare, her capabilities. It didn't help that she felt their apprehension was valid in that moment. Her memory never let her down.

Focus, Vos... She snapped her fingers. "Lonnie Jennings."

"Okay, good. We'll look him up in the system, track him down," Brice summarized, and Sandra could only hope it was that easy. "But why would he take Olivia?"

"To extract revenge for his friend not getting released?" Lakisha put in, leaning back in her chair and looking at Sandra.

Sandra shook her head. "But what does he expect me to do about that? And it can't just be about revenge. Kidnapping is usually done for leverage. He wants something from me, but what?"

"Would he know you're FBI?" Lakisha asked.

"Yeah." Now she regretted making that clear during her statement. She'd thought it would make her sound more authoritative.

"He could think you have the power to have the decision reversed." Lakisha curled her lips, clearly wanting to offer something, but not confident with what she said.

"Surely, he would realize Sandra doesn't have that authority," Brice countered. "There has to be another endgame here."

The energy of the room intensified. If she was reading it right, they might be thinking that "endgame" wasn't good for Olivia. That she might be the victim of spite, but Sandra knew better. From all her years with the Bureau, and talking people down, one thing was clear. People acted the way they did for a reason. There was always motivation and a goal in mind. She looked at the screen, concentrating on Jennings's face. "He's smug, arrogant, challenging. He's taunting me. He deliberately looked at the camera knowing I'd be watching."

"Rather brazen," Brice put in.

"He's also intelligent. He calculated the risks and took some precautions on being tracked down. He blacked out the plates on the vehicle."

"Except that tinted covers could get him pulled over."

"Which again confirms he's smug and brazen. As we've established, he'd know I'm FBI from the hearing, but he took Olivia anyway. Then he stares right at me. He's obviously after something he thinks I can get for him and is using Olivia to force my cooperation." Surprisingly that admission eased her stress. It put her in familiar territory. If she could keep her emotions out of it, she'd be able to navigate the terrain with skilled practice. The big part being *if*.

"To go to this trouble, whatever he's after must be high stakes," Lakisha put in, and turned to her computer and started pecking on the keyboard.

"All right, well, he knows you're FBI, but does he know what you do for the Bureau?" Brice asked.

She thought back to her statement at the hearing and nodded. "I said I was a negotiator for the FBI, but what could that matter?"

"You don't seem to think this is about revenge, so that brings us back to leverage. Why you? Why Olivia? I don't think this is just because you spoke against Patton's release. It has more to do with who you are, what you're capable of, or what he thinks you can do. In sticking with your skillset, is there something he needs to get out of Patton that he's not giving up until he's a free man? He could have taken Olivia to coerce you into getting Patton to talk." Brice pressed his lips as if that was an easy conclusion and the resolution was just as simple.

Her colleague made a good point, but until she heard from Lonnie Jennings, it was risky to make assumptions. She could demand an audience with Patton but that would sacrifice time she didn't have. Getting to Olivia was more important than trying to predict what Jennings was after. "Not going there yet. If we're right, and Jennings wants me to do something, I'll be hearing from him. When he's ready." Forcing her to wait was a form of torture but also a means of trying to establish control. Jennings wanted her to believe he was in charge, so she'd be more willing to comply.

"I've got the guy's info," Lakisha said, and the screen split to show the background on Lonnie. "No criminal record. Single, fifty-eight, living in Brentwood. He does have an older GMC van, black. Too old for GPS tracking."

"Cell phone?" Most people had a satellite on them.

Lakisha shook her head. "Good thinking, but nothing on file for him."

"Guy like him probably has a prepaid phone," Brice said.

Sandra would like to disregard the "guy like him" comment but Brice was right. At least from a statistical viewpoint. Brentwood was an older neighborhood and one of the roughest in DC. It boasted high records of violent crime, but the city was working to revitalize it with new housing developments. Most residents were poor and lived in rowhouses, some of which had been around since the late 1700s. This reflected George Washington's intention for Washington to be a rowhouse city. But more noteworthy than that was it was where Darrell Patton had grown up. It was possibly the same for Lonnie Jennings. He had said at the hearing they'd been friends since childhood. But what about the driver?

An alert popped in the middle of the screen at the same time as Lakisha's computer beeped.

"It's a hit from facial rec," Lakisha said.

As much as Sandra wanted to know who she was dealing

with, the fact he was in the system sank in her gut. "What's his sheet say?"

"One second..." Lakisha brought the results up on the screen. "The driver was ID'd as Dennis Eaton, fifty-seven. He has a record for assault in his twenties and served five years."

Violent crime... She hugged herself.

"Address?" Brice asked when Sandra didn't speak. But she was frozen. She'd never heard of Eaton so why was he doing this to her? To Olivia?

"Brentwood. Looks like him and Jennings are roommates. No phone for him either."

"Let's go." Sandra was the first out of the room, her heart pounding. They had the names of the men who took Olivia but still had no idea where she was or why they were doing this. And their first stop to gather more intel was a neighborhood that hated cops.

TWENTY-EIGHT

Lonnie put the plan together so fast that he was beyond pleased with himself. From the moment he spotted Vos on the news and found out that she had a teenage daughter, all the pieces clicked together. After all, he'd need strong leverage to get a fed to help the likes of him. The next morning he'd roped Dennis in on what he was thinking and got on the road to confirm the place he had in mind was still abandoned. When it turned out it was, Lonnie took that as a sign he was good to go ahead. He was certainly finished playing victim. He'd leave that to the FBI agent. All her whining because her twin brother had died, but he was going to give her something fresh to sob about. Besides, he'd lost people. It was a fact of life that we all ended up in the dirt at some point. And the fed's brat would end up there soon if Mommy Dearest didn't come through. He'd been more than patient. So much so that it was ridiculous.

They wouldn't even be here if it wasn't for his quick thinking and following his intuition. But now he had a great chance of getting what he and Dennis had lost when Darrell held those people hostage in that pizza place. The stupid moron!

It felt incredible to finally take his fate back into his own hands. There would be no more uncertainty about the future. He was due the pay-off on the sacrifice he'd made years ago, and he could smell that it was getting close now.

He looked in the back at their bargaining chip. The girl was resting, still knocked out from the rag soaked in chloroform he'd put over her face. All it took was one swift thrust and he had her in the van. She'd barely let out a yelp before the side door closed and his friend was pulling them away from the curb. No one on the street seemed to pay them any attention. Even if some do-gooder had, they'd be long gone before anything could have been done to stop them anyway. And the plates were blacked out. He punched Dennis playfully in the shoulder. "I've got such a good feeling about this."

"Not me." Dennis glanced at him from the driver's seat as he drove them to their holding spot. It was a location far away from the posh Washington suburb of Georgetown where they had snatched the girl.

"Nah, no need, man. It's all going according to plan." Lonnie leaned back against the headrest and shut his eyes but was jolted awake not long later by some ruts in the road. Only it wasn't the road but the mouth of the parking lot. They'd arrived at their destination. He must have drifted off to sleep, but he was certainly wide awake now.

Dennis stopped at the locked gate, and Lonnie hopped from the van with a pair of bolt cutters. He used them to snap the chain securing the gate and opened it. His friend drove through, and Lonnie swung the gate shut again behind them. He put a new padlock on to secure the gate. At quick glance, should anyone even care, they'd think the place was still locked up tight.

He hopped back into the passenger seat. "See? What did I tell you? Nothing to worry about at all."

Dennis bobbed his head. He was such a mindless idiot. He

was never diagnosed with a mental illness, but Lonnie wagered he'd been struck by his mother hard and often enough to cause permanent damage. That, and the drugs took care of the rest.

They drove around the back of the building, and Dennis cut the engine. No one would see the van from the road if they happened to drive by, but this area had little to no traffic. That was just one reason he had selected it for lying low. Another was any connection to him was barely a thread.

Dennis got the door unlocked and signaled they were in. He popped back a thumbs-up and opened the rear door of the van.

The girl flew out, all hair and limbs, and jumped him.

Lonnie was pushed backward and slammed to the ground. "You little bitch." All he saw was red, and he grabbed her upper arms and flipped her over.

She screamed. He laughed.

"No one's going to hear you, sweetheart. It's just me and my friend to keep you company."

She was squirming beneath him and spit in his eyes.

He cried out and released his grip, just long enough that the girl squirmed free and was now running through the lot yelling.

"What the—" Dennis came out of the building and was looking after her retreating form.

"Don't just stand there!" Lonnie scrambled to his feet and took pursuit. But it seemed his friend finally shook his coma and kicked into action. He was dumb but physically fast. It was an advantage to his long, lean frame. He caught up to the girl and got a hold of her.

"Let go of me!" The girl jerked her upper torso trying to shake free but to no avail.

Lonnie caught up to them and put his nose to within an inch of hers. "Try anything like that again, princess, and I'll kill you with my bare hands." He laid the chloroform rag over her face, and she dropped like a lifeless puppet in his friend's arms.

TWENTY-NINE

Sandra ended up filling Elwood in on their recent discovery, and he was going to handle everything associated with Novak. Elwood had tried to talk her into letting other agents take it from here, but she resisted and he eventually complied. Not that she was holding her breath that anyone in the Brentwood neighborhood would talk to them. From a statistical standpoint most of the residents here would have a criminal record or be friends or family with someone who was put away. Suffice it to say there would be few, if any, fans of law enforcement.

Be-on-the-lookouts were issued for the men and Lonnie Jennings's van, and Lakisha was doing a deeper dive into both Jennings's and Eaton's backgrounds. She'd be looking for relatives, known associates, workplaces, other registered vehicles or properties. But given the neighborhood they both called home, it was unlikely they owned anything. It was that thought that scared Sandra the most. There was little likelihood either of them had a property on record, leaving Olivia out there, only God knows where. It was likely someplace isolated and out of state given that they went over the bridge. Her only relief was knowing her daughter was both smart and a fighter. She just hoped the former superseded the latter and didn't have her taking any chances with her life.

It was one thirty-eight AM when Brice stopped the car in front of the house shared by Jennings and Eaton. There wasn't a single light on inside or out. In fact, most of the neighborhood was swathed in darkness aside from some dull streetlights and random porch lights. Even the moon was too weak to penetrate the cloud cover, but the shadows had eyes. Amber lights from cigarettes burned and waved through the air from the street corners.

Sandra had called Nigel Morse on the way over, and he was rushing through a search warrant for the home. Chances were something inside might lend a clue as to where they took Olivia. But they couldn't have been planning this for long. A day, day and a half.

Sandra checked her email and found two new messages. One was from Lakisha, and another from Judge Morse.

"We have what we need?" Brice asked her.

"And more..." She opened Lakisha's first. "So we have more info on Jennings and Eaton. Jennings is currently unemployed, but Eaton works at Boats N More, a boat factory, where he's been for the last ten years. Neither of them have any living relatives or other properties linked to them. The address in Brentwood is a rental."

"Can't say any of that's a surprise," Brice said quickly then held up a hand. "Not what you want to hear, I know."

"Facts are better than assumptions. The search warrant came through, and Lakisha also included the number for the property owner. She said she tried to reach him unsuccessfully. Guy's name is Jerald Booth."

"I say we try knocking first."

Brice banged the tarnished brass knocker against the door. Chills ran down Sandra's spine as she had this sensation of being watched and encroached upon. She looked left and right, over her shoulders, her head on a swivel, while Brice repeated the knocking.

"FBI! Lonnie Jennings or Dennis Eaton, open up!" Brice called out. His voice pierced the cold early morning air like a raid siren.

The inside of the house continued to be silent, but the neighbor's light popped on and the door cracked open.

"What the hell? Some of us are trying to sleep here." A squat and rotund man in a ratty bathrobe stepped onto his front landing.

"FBI Special Agent Vos," she said, holding up her creds. "And you are?"

"The property manager." He put his meaty hands on his hips.

How convenient... "Jerald Booth?"

"What's it to ya? And what do you want with Lonnie and Dennis?" He came closer to them, and his breath was coming out in puffs of white.

He appeared to be wearing thick pajamas beneath the robe, but his feet were in thin slippers. He must be freezing. They were straightforward observations, but they kept her grounded in the present.

"It's an FBI matter, but when did you last see either of them?" Brice asked.

The man smirked. "So I answer your questions, and you don't have to answer mine? Is that it?"

"It's how it works, Mr. Booth," Brice said firmly. "That's if you don't want to be seen as interfering with an FBI investigation. Personally, I'd suggest you be more cooperative."

Jerald simpered, crossed his arms, and angled his head. Unless they changed their approach with him, the man wasn't going to say anything. After all, he had no reason to do so.

Threats were often ineffective at motivating people. "Mr. Booth, you look like a standup guy," she began.

"I try."

"We're just trying to protect the neighborhood and people like you."

"*Pfft*. Police, feds, you all forgot about this area a long time ago. That is unless it's to storm in here and arrest people for no good reason."

She refused to get sucked into a debate. The truth was bad cops were out there. She'd try another tack. "There was an incident..." She almost said *earlier today* but caught herself. In some ways it felt like time had stopped, but framing this statement reminded her it marched on. "Yesterday afternoon, early evening, involving Lonnie Jennings and Dennis Eaton."

"Are they"—the man gripped the front of his robe, clenching it tighter together, seemingly having caught a chill—"okay?"

"We're not sure and need to find them to know for certain."

"Oh please." The man flailed his arms in the air. "You're playing with me."

"I assure you I'm not." Her calm tone alone made the point he could trust her. His shoulders relaxed. "They are potentially in danger," she added, not stretching the truth by much. Once she found them, they would be. Even more so if they hurt Olivia.

"Let's say I believe you. What am I to do about it?"

"To start, could you answer Special Agent Sutton's question about when you last saw either of them?"

"Let me think. I saw them yesterday morning. Lonnie anyhow. Dennis goes to work early and is done around three in the afternoon."

They'd track down Eaton's employer tomorrow once the sun came up and find out when they last saw him, talk to his coworkers and boss, see if they had anything to offer. They might even be able to provide another friend's name who they could question. "Do you have phone numbers for either of them?"

"I should have on their lease. Want me to go find out?" He jacked a thumb toward his house.

"That would be great." Even if the number linked back to a prepaid SIM card, Tech had ways of tracking it down.

"One minute then." Jerald ducked back into his house.

"Great job turning that around," Brice praised her.

"Job hazard, but you should know. We're wired to see things from the other person's perspective." It was certainly embedded in her after all these years. And focusing on this as her job, removing the personal, helped tamp down thoughts of Olivia.

"I have the lease." Jerald returned holding up a stapled packet of legal-size papers. "Here." He walked to them, and she and Brice helped close the distance too.

She took the papers with thanks and flipped through as Brice held his phone's flashlight over the pages. She scanned until she found a number and then juggled the lease with her phone as she punched in the digits. Her breath paused as she waited for the line to ring.

A mechanical voice answered, "You've reached a number that is no longer in service."

Click.

She shouldn't have gotten her hopes up. Blame that on the mother in her that just wanted this resolved and her daughter safely home. The fed in her realized it was likely the number was tied to a prepaid phone. In that case, it was easy to change them out and switch numbers with new SIM cards. "Is that the only number you have for them?"

"Yeah. I take it no luck?"

She shook her head and handed the papers back to Jerald.

"Well, I hope you find them, and they're okay."

"We are going to do our best," she said, still pulling on her training to remain diplomatic and neutral. It was taking more out of her as the minutes passed standing there. While she was slogging through this minutiae, her daughter was... No, it was best that she didn't entertain any thoughts pertaining to her welfare. No good would come from that. "You wouldn't happen to know where they like to hang out, or names of any of their friends, would you?"

"Nah. We're not chummy."

Sandra had a feeling that was going to be his response, but she had to give it a go. If they could track down friends of the men, they might be able to get their current numbers and a lead. She brought up a photo of Olivia on her phone and held her screen for Jerald. "Does she look familiar to you?" It was a reach, a long shot, but she had to ask.

The man narrowed his eyes and shook his head. "She's not from around here."

"So you've never seen her?" she volleyed back.

"No. But what does she have to do with Lonnie and Dennis?"

"You've been very kind and generous with your time, Mr. Booth, but I can't disclose that as it's an FBI matter," she said.

"Huh. Okay."

She closed Olivia's photo but not before catching a glimpse of her daughter's beautiful face. But there was no time to wallow in fear or sorrow. Focus was going to be her savior. "We have a warrant to search the residence of Lonnie Jennings and Dennis Eaton." She brought up the document.

Jerald waved her away. "First you ask about Lonnie and Dennis, and now this young girl... I'm just sickened by my own imagination. I can put things together, Agent. Do what you have to do." He put his hand into his robe's pocket and came out with a key. "This should help." Then he turned to walk back into his house, but she stopped him.

"Just take this." She gave him her business card. "Call if either of them comes back but don't approach them."

Jerald nodded and retreated into his house. The sound of his deadbolt clunking into place could be heard from down his front walkway.

His response did little to settle her stomach. "What did he mean by...?" She couldn't bring herself to finish the question. Did the property manager have reason to question the morality of his renters?

"Don't pay that attention, Sandra," Brice encouraged her. "People get a bit touchy when it comes to kids."

"Me too." *Especially when it's my kid!*

"That's why I'm here. You can lean on me to help you through this."

She looked over at him, and he raised an eyebrow. She'd never opened herself up to the guy before but that may have been her loss. "Thanks."

"Don't mention it."

They returned to the rental and let themselves inside. The place was stale with the faint smell of bacon. Brice flipped on the light switch and revealed a plainly decorated home with scuffed beige walls, white trim, and little furniture. They went through the house, and for each step Sandra took, her gut curdled to think she was in the home of the men who had her daughter.

It didn't take long to sweep through the two stories, and nothing gave them any clue as to where they had taken Olivia. What they did have was dried bacon grease in a fry pan on the stove and skinned-over coffee in the pot. She pointed out both to Brice. "They haven't been here in at least twenty-four hours. Longer than that I'd suspect we could see mold."

"That fits with what the landlord told us."

She nodded, though this tidbit didn't get her closer to

Olivia. It was time to talk things out some more. "There's nothing to indicate they planned to take Olivia for a while."

"And they couldn't know about you before the hearing or that the parole would be denied," Brice weighed in.

"Right, so their decision to take Olivia was impulsive." It was something she'd considered in passing and feared. Impulsive people were unpredictable and steered by emotion. With that, logic and reason took a back seat. *Not good.*

"That might not be a bad thing. They could slip up."

She appreciated Brice's positive bent on the situation. "We could be looking at this wrong too. They could have prepared some, established a backup plan in case parole was denied. The judgment just came through Thursday morning and Olivia was snatched before five on Friday afternoon. They'd have to know about her, where and how to get to her... Even have a place in mind where they could take her." Premeditation was somewhat more soothing than impulse driving the crime, but it still didn't answer the primary question about what they wanted. Were they simply after revenge, or did they want her to do something? Her mind flipflopped the two options. Or was it a blend of both? Either way, the realist in her knew she had to consider that Olivia might even already be... No, she couldn't accept that she was gone. And, surely, she'd feel it, as she had with her brother.

"Whatever the case, they've got some balls going after the daughter of a fed," Brice said.

"That right there is the part that scares me the most." If they were that daring, did they have limitations on what they were capable of?

"We'll figure this out, but for them to take such a risk there must be the possibility of a high payoff."

"As I said before. But what bearing could Patton's release have on Jennings and Eaton?"

"Still a mystery."

She was running this all through her mind and was chilled by a new thought. "We talked about them finding Olivia online, but that doesn't explain how he knew where to find her in person."

Brice's face shadowed. "Well, if Jennings was preparing in advance and latched on to you at the hearing, he could have followed you home from the prison."

She suddenly felt chilled right through. "But I didn't go straight home. I had the hostage incident, but before that I— Shit. I visited my mother." She pulled her phone and realized the time. It was nearing four in the morning.

Brice put a hand over hers. "You can call if it makes you feel better, but I think she's safe."

She met his eyes and considered his implication. They had taken Olivia. Her weakest point. And she was much easier to manage than an older woman. But could she be satisfied with assuming all was well? "I need to call."

She did just that and woke the nurse, who confirmed her mother was safe and sound asleep in her room. She'd even had Dana duck down the hall and peek inside.

"I see her and hear her soft snores, Ms. Vos," Dana told her.

"Thank you."

"Don't mention it. Good night now."

She never got into it with the nurse as to why she was concerned about her mother, or brought up Olivia's situation, so there was no reason to ask that she keep this call quiet.

"So?" Brice said when she tucked her phone away.

"She's safe. Thing is though, if Lonnie was following me, he'd have hung around at the standoff too. That lasted for hours." A determined person could never be underestimated, but it still seemed extreme when all that effort might not even be needed.

"Right, and that was a long one, wasn't it?"

"Until the wee hours of Thursday morning." She was

grateful for sleeping in that day, as she didn't count on getting much until Olivia was home. Then she'd sleep for a month, and maybe the two of them could take a vacation together. "There's no way he hung around. An officer would have noticed that. Besides, as we touched on before, people can find things online these days."

"We didn't find a laptop," Brice pointed out.

"Unless it's with them, but even a phone accesses the internet these days." She had made efforts to keep her private life just that, but there was only so much she could do being the daughter of a Davenport and the twin sister of a brother who was murdered in a tragic hostage situation. That was all public record. Again, she thought once this was all over, she'd hire someone to make them invisible online.

"True enough."

The back of her mind waded through the vehicles in the area when she'd first arrived at the hostage incident. There was one thing coming through. "News vans were there when I got on scene at the grocery store. I even had one reporter knock on my window."

"All right, so Jennings may or may not have planned to take Olivia, or even consider a backup in case Patton's parole was denied. He might have hatched his plan when he saw you on TV. Maybe during a recap or replay the next day even."

"Either way, he had from the hearing on Wednesday until Friday afternoon to find out about Olivia and devise a way to take her. But we're back to why he's even doing this." She grimaced, hating unanswered questions.

"Well, we've speculated on this already. He must want you to get something out of Patton. Most likely *talk* something out of him. And now it would seem whatever it is involves Dennis Eaton. But how is he rolled up in all of this? What's at stake for him? Is he just a friend who wants a cut of whatever it is? And I say *cut*, but it's not like we know if it has anything to do with money."

"The problem is we can't be absolutely sure what this is about," she countered as her mind gnawed on Brice's words. *Anything to do with money...* Was that what all this boiled down to? But how did that link to her negotiation skills? Or Patton for that matter? Her phone rang, and she fumbled to get a hold of it. Her heart raced at the sight of the text in place of the caller's identity. *Blocked Number.* She answered.

THIRTY

The moon hung outside the broken windowpane like a giant beachball. Lonnie was looking at it, imagining he could reach out and touch it but knowing it was a fool's errand to try. But this, what he was doing with this girl, had to work out. It just had to. He was done waiting for his time to come. He was seizing the day.

The girl was asleep next to Dennis, who had also nodded off. As they say, good help is hard to find. His friend had good intentions, as stupid as he was. Probably the only reason he kept him around. That and possibly some modicum of loyalty.

Lonnie pulled out his phone and woke the screen. It was approaching five in the morning, and a fine time to call the girl's mother. She'd probably been up all night trying to chase down leads to find her daughter. Her nerves would be shattered, and she'd be tired and vulnerable. Hopefully malleable and in a cooperative mood.

He called Sandra's number, something he'd obtained from the girl. He smiled imagining her reaction to hearing her phone ring and seeing *Blocked Number*. It rang twice before it was answered. Silence.

So she was playing a game too... "Do you know who this is?"

"Lonnie Jennings."

Her voice was calm and cold. It was also level, like the welfare of her child wasn't at stake. She knew his name, something he wasn't sure she'd figure out this fast. He may have underestimated her, but he wasn't about to give up. He was already in too deep. If you take a fed's kid, you commit to seeing it through. "You know who I am already. Kudos." He hated himself for acknowledging this much and wished he'd just kept quiet or got to the point.

"You've taken my daughter. You don't have a criminal record. If you return her safely now, we can work something out. I'm sure that Dennis doesn't want to go back to prison either."

So she knows about him too... Lonnie looked over at Dennis, who had a trail of drool in the corner of his mouth. She certainly didn't waste time making her request. She'd even disguised it as concern for his welfare. He was pleased he'd recognized this. "Always the negotiator, I see."

"So you know I'm a negotiator with the FBI?"

She was still cool and collected, and he was finding it unsettling. He had her daughter. She should be terrified and unhinged, willing to do whatever he asked of her. "Listen closely. You fucked everything up at that parole hearing, and this is your penance. But you have a chance to make things right."

"Tell me how, and I'll do what I can. But before I do anything, I need to know that she's still alive."

He looked over at Olivia, whose head was tipped forward, her chin to her chest. "Very well." He walked over and grabbed a mittful of her hair.

Olivia screamed so loudly, the gag barely muffled her outcry of pain.

"You hear that? It's your precious little girl. Is that enough proof for you?" Lonnie asked this as he stared into the teen's eyes. He'd kill her if he had to. No compunction. He'd lost his conscience with his baby teeth. After taking her, he regretted not breaking the law more often. It was exhilarating.

"I want to talk to her." The woman's voice remained level.

Lonnie removed the gag from Olivia's mouth.

"Mom!" the teen shouted, and he replaced the gag.

"You'll have to take that as proof."

A minuscule stretch of silence, then, "Tell me what you want."

"Happy that we've come to an understanding. You do as I want, then I'll return your girl to you. You don't, then she will die. Painfully." He was smiling, unable to help himself. As often as he could twist the blade, he would. Figuratively and literally. He had a gun, but he could switch things up.

"Tell me what you want," she repeated.

He didn't miss the fact she made no promises, but her phrasing and tone were misleading as if that was implied. For now, he didn't care. Saving her daughter should be motivation enough. "You need to get Darrell out of prison."

"I need to get Darrell out of prison?"

Why is she parroting me? "That's right. You suddenly develop a hearing problem?"

"There's no way I can—"

"You will if you want to see your daughter alive again."

"I'm sorry, but I don't see how I can do that."

Lonnie gripped his phone. What was he? The world's problem solver? "Figure it out."

"I'm sorry, but without more I don't see how I can—"

"He has something I want," he roared. "You do as I ask, or your daughter is dead." He ended the call, consumed by rage, and turned his phone off.

"What's going on, LJ?" Dennis had come to from his sleep

coma. He hadn't stirred when the girl had cried out twice but Lonnie's raised voice had roused him.

Lonnie lowered himself down and put his face in the girl's. "Your mother is a stubborn bitch."

The teen glared at him with contempt and balled up her face. There was no doubt she'd have spat in his face again if it wasn't for the gag. He reached out and slapped her. Her head lolled to the side and blood poured from her nose.

"Hey, hey, hold on." Dennis stepped up next to them and wedged himself between him and the girl. "Do we really need to hurt her?"

"Are you kidding me? She needs to learn some respect."

"We got into this without thinking it through, and now we're in over our heads. Her mom is the freakin' FBI, for God's sake."

"You're losing sight of the goal here. She's a mother first. She'll do what we want her to if she ever wants to see her kid again."

"Did she say she would?"

Lonnie replayed the conversation. Lots of talk, no outright promises. "I'll make her see the light."

"Uh-huh, and if she does what we want, are you going to give her the girl?"

Lonnie looked at the teen. The blood from her nose was now dripping from her chin, and her eyelids were fluttering. Was the plan ever to return her alive? He wasn't so sure he saw that future anymore.

"LJ, you're kind of scaring me, man."

"I guess we'll see, but for now this girl is our best bargaining chip. We use her to get what we want."

"And then what? You still haven't said. We give her back, right?"

"We get rid of her." He looked his friend in the eye, serious in his commitment.

"But none of this is her fault. She didn't ask to get caught up in this."

"Then her mother should have thought through the consequences of her actions. Patton's still in prison because of her. She's why we're still waiting on our due from decades ago. My patience has run out."

"No." Dennis shook his head and stepped back. "I didn't sign up for this. Not murdering a teenage girl."

"What are you saying, Dennis?" Anger was rising in Lonnie's chest and making it hard to take a full breath, but he put his hand into his coat pocket, wrapping his fingers around the grip of his gun.

"I'm just saying it's not necessary."

"Huh, but as you just said, her mom's a fed. We get caught, we're going away for the rest of our lives. Not that I have any intention of getting caught, but I say we give the woman something that will stay with her forever."

"Nah. I want out, LJ." Dennis was shaking his head like the brain-dead idiot he was.

But maybe Dennis was handing him a gift. After all, he'd already played his part by getting the van in place and driving them here. And if he was going to whine at every turn, he'd be more hindrance than help. Suddenly any bit of loyalty he felt toward Dennis was gone. "Fine, you want out, you're out." He pulled the gun and shot Dennis between the eyes.

One yelp, and he dropped to the ground.

The girl screamed behind the gag, her eyes wide and full of tears, as Dennis's blood sprayed her face.

"Don't worry, princess, your time is coming."

THIRTY-ONE

Sandra's legs buckled, and Brice caught her.

"I've got you," he said.

She heard his words, but they barely penetrated. Her mind just kept replaying her poor, sweet Olivia's screams. As a baby, she had lungs that could rival any headline singer, and each time her girl opened her mouth, Sandra went running to her, to make things better. Being a reliable mother was something she prided herself on. But now, when her daughter needed her the most, she was out of reach. The other side of the line might as well be on the other side of the planet.

"You did great, Vos. You held it together."

"Better than now."

"Understandable, and behind the scenes doesn't matter. What did you learn?"

"This is about Patton's denied parole." She shared this as if from a catatonic state. It might be easier to operate from here without being inundated and blinded by emotion. It was isolated here. Safe. A hiding place.

"What did he say?"

You fucked everything up at that parole hearing, and this is your penance...

"Sandra?" Brice prompted.

"This is my fault."

"Enough of the self-pity," Brice snapped. "Lonnie Jennings and Dennis Eaton are to blame here. No one else. Now talk to me."

She met his gaze, thankful for his bluntness. "He wants me to get Patton released."

"One of the things we theorized about, but why? And how does he expect you to do that?"

"I don't know. We didn't get that far." Her calm approach had clearly toppled him. She feared what he might feel pressured to do to assume control again. She let out a deep breath. "Olivia sounded so... terrified."

"Put that out of your head."

"Easier said than done."

"Sure, but if anyone can, it's you. Just focus, or he wins."

It already felt like he had, but she still refused to surrender. She couldn't afford to. "Thanks, wise guy," she volleyed back with sarcasm.

He held up his hands. "Just trying to help here."

"I know. He hung up when I tossed the scenario back to him to solve. He wants Patton out, says Patton has something he wants, but Jennings doesn't want to tell me what he expects me to do about it."

"That tells me the plan is half-baked right there."

"Not reassuring." And they were back to the kidnapping being an impulsive act with volatile emotions running the show. "Jennings is definitely the leader of the two, and he has a temper."

"Understandable. He took a fed's daughter. That's a lot of pressure right there."

"Thinking about things from his standpoint is the only thing keeping me sane, yet threatening my mental stability at the same time. If that makes any sense. He's put himself in a losing position. Once he realizes that, well, I don't want to think what that could mean for Olivia."

"And there's no need to. It accomplishes nothing. Since he hasn't fully laid out what he wants, he'll be calling back."

She wished she had Brice's confidence, but as she thought about it more, he was right. After all, Lonnie Jennings still hadn't had his need fulfilled. For him to go to these measures, he must have seen her as the only means of getting there. That meant Olivia wasn't disposable yet, and Sandra had more time. "If he hadn't blocked his number, I'd try calling him. Wait... we have people who could help with that." She got back on her phone, and the line was ringing. Lakisha answered, and Sandra didn't waste time with pleasantries. "Jennings made contact."

"I'll trace the number. When did he call? This to your cell phone?"

"Yes, just a few minutes ago. You'll have to unblock it first."

"I'm sure it's nothing I can't handle. Consider me on the case."

"Thank you." Sandra hung up and shared the update with Brice.

"Lakisha's good. She'll get the number and track it down. Chin up."

"Chin up?" She smiled at him, impressed that even though she was sick with worry, he managed to lighten the mood, even if for a moment. But as it passed, the shadows rolled in. There was no forgetting that her daughter was with a madman.

THIRTY-TWO

After Sandra updated Elwood Rowe with the latest, he sent her home. It wasn't a suggestion but a direct order, which he made abundantly clear. She only relented when he said he'd arrange for other agents to go to Dennis Eaton's place of employment the moment they opened for the day. She let herself into her penthouse, and Eric came to the door.

"Have you heard anything?" he asked her.

She nodded and fell into his arms. He didn't prod her to elaborate but let her be. Her dam of emotions burst, and she cried against his chest while he stroked her hair. She eventually pulled back, licking her lips. "I should get some sleep."

"That sounds like a good idea."

He still wasn't pushing her, even though he must have been eager to learn more. She told him, "We know who took Olivia now, and they called me."

"*They* did? There's more than one?"

Sandra nodded and told him the men's names.

"Okay, well, that's a good start, right? Are they looking for a ransom?"

She appreciated why his mind went there. "This doesn't

seem to be about money. Though I don't even know exactly what it is about." The admission made her feel so helpless, but that might be Jennings's intention. Had he simply called to tease her, manipulate her emotions, and make her believe there was a way to get her daughter back when her future was already written? She filled Eric in on the little she had.

Eric was quiet for a few beats. "Huh, so whatever they want from Patton is worth kidnapping a federal agent's daughter over. But no idea what that is?"

"Not yet, but I'm going to figure it out." *Ransom... worth kidnapping...* Her mind was working, and she needed time to explore the chains of thought. But before she could dig in too deep, exhaustion rolled over her.

"I'm sure you will. Want me to stay?"

"I'd like that."

Eric kissed her forehead, and they sauntered down the hall to her bedroom where they fell asleep in each other's arms.

For Sandra, it felt like she'd just shut her eyes when her cell phone rang on her night table. It jolted her upright, but she took a few collective breaths. If this was Lonnie Jennings, she'd best serve her purpose by being calm.

"Is it the kidnappers?" Eric had stirred awake beside her.

She looked at the screen. It wasn't a blocked number, but it was a name that put a knot in the pit of her stomach. She shook her head at Eric, and he settled back again, and she answered, "Nolan."

"What's this about Olivia? Sandra, talk to me. I'm her father."

Her ex, Nolan Copeland, laid into her the moment she picked up. His tactics clearly hadn't changed over the years. "I would talk if you gave me a second to speak," she bit back, and then proceeded to tell him everything.

"So you know who took her?" he asked.

She didn't miss the implication, the personalization, as if

Olivia being taken was all her fault. And maybe it was. Jennings had told her it was her penance. If she hadn't gone to the parole hearing and spoken against Patton's release, maybe they wouldn't be in this position. But how could she not defend her late brother? There was no way she could have seen it coming to this. "Lonnie Jennings and Dennis Eaton. Jennings is the leader. He's the one who called."

"He thinks you can get Patton released. Heck, then, let's get him out."

Her ex was always a pie-in-the-sky dreamer, who thought anything was possible. If it didn't come easily, he forced it. "You and I both know that's not going to happen. And are you forgetting this man killed my brother?"

"I'm sorry, Sandra, but now he could save Olivia. And maybe we don't really get him out, but make these assholes believe that's the case. You could set up a meeting between the two, have it surveilled and when it's the right time, FBI SWAT moves in."

He really hadn't changed in their time apart. He was still about brawn over brains. Just one way that made them such different people. "And get Olivia killed in the process?"

"Forget it, Sandra. I'm coming home. We'll talk when I get there."

"Where are you?" His job with the FBI's Hostage Rescue Team took him all over the world.

"Istanbul. I know there's a military transport heading back to the States later today. I'll be on it. I should be in sometime tomorrow morning."

"I don't know if you need to do that. There's nothing you can do, Nolan. I'm on it. The FBI here is on it."

There was silence from his end. Her ex wasn't the type to sit back and wait. He was suited for his job because he was a man of action, not words. But sinking into his perspective, she couldn't imagine being on the other side of the world with Olivia in danger. "I understand your need to come home."

"Thanks, because I am." He ended the call, and she was left holding her phone and staring at it.

His words hung like a threat more than they glittered with hope. Sometimes too many hands didn't lighten the workload but made it worse. But brooding over the conversation wasn't going to change anything. She had to get up and get going. Elwood might not be happy as she'd just been down for a few hours, but it was all she could give him. She got ready to go into the field office, but before Eric would let her leave, he told her she should grab something to eat from the kitchen first. She made toast and ate half a piece smeared with peanut butter.

It was two minutes to nine when she got to the WFO. Agents should already be at Dennis's place of employment, or she'd head right there.

She'd start with knocking back coffee though. Caffeine was the only hope she had if she was going to be awake when Lonnie Jennings called back. Because he would. He had to. He hadn't made his demands clear.

Her phone rang, and she jolted like she'd been shocked. Then she took a few steadying breaths and looked at the caller's ID. "Special Agent Vos," she answered.

"Special Agent Hester, if we're being formal."

"You're still in?"

"I wanted to see what I could find out on that number before heading home, and my work paid off. I was able to unblock it." She rattled off the digits as Sandra hurried to scribble them on a notepad in front of her.

"That's good news. Could you track it?"

"Unfortunately, no. It is a prepaid number serviced by Digitech. I opened a trace on it, but it's currently inactive."

"I don't understand then. You tracked it but you didn't...?"

"Jennings must be using a mobile VPN to throw off the tracking. The phone traced back to Antarctica."

Panic rose in her chest. Had he taken Olivia there? Though for two guys without money, that was unlikely.

"Which is clearly a con," Lakisha picked up, "because the coordinates lead to an old research station that's only in use for five months of the year. Technically until next month, but I think we can agree he's not there."

"Son of a bitch."

"I'm sorry I couldn't have helped more."

"You did all you could."

"If anything changes, I'll keep you posted."

Sandra pinched her eyes shut for a moment. "Thanks." But the relief only lasted until she opened her eyes, and Lakisha was off the line.

Brice came in holding a takeout tray with two coffees and laid his coat over the back of his chair.

"What are you doing here?" she asked him.

"I had a feeling you would be. Here, this is for you." He walked over with a coffee extended to her.

"Ah, thanks."

"Don't get used to it." He winked at her. "So how are you holding up? Stupid question I'm sure, but I'd look like an insensitive prick if I didn't at least ask."

"I'm holding up. That's about it." She filled him in on the tracking results.

"For one, Lakisha is gold. Two, does this Jennings fella think he's a comedian?"

"If he does, I'm missing the punchline."

"Makes two of us."

She got up with her coffee and walked over to a clear markerboard and wrote *Darrell Patton denied parole*. Then she tapped the capped end of the marker to her chin. "Let's work backwards. What was the original inciting incident?"

"If we knew that..."

"I know. Then what does Patton have that Jennings and Eaton want? Is this an item or information?"

"Either way, it would seem that Patton isn't handing it over as long as he's in prison."

"That we can agree on. It seems equally plausible then that whatever this is might be something Patton came into possession of not long before going away."

She added *Original inciting incident: before Darrell Patton went to prison/has something others want* to the board. "And for Eaton to also be involved, it stands to reason that the three of them have a stake in whatever this is."

"There does seem to be some sense of entitlement there."

She stepped back and stared at the board, as if it would magically offer up some solution. But her mind was a whirling dervish. The last twenty-four hours were a blur for their intensity and fullness. Chaos. Though even thoughts of the standoff at the grocery store earlier in the week worked their way in there. That hostage taker's claim about being a failure in life and that his family would be better off without him. There was a familiar ring to those words. She was quite sure the transcripts from Patton's standoff included something similar. The exact words skirted around her brain. Instead of caving to frustration, she'd again focus on what she had. "Patton, Jennings, and Eaton grew up in the same neighborhood."

"Okay, so they go way back. And Brentwood has always been a predominantly Black neighborhood. Now you've got three white guys. They would have stuck together. Times were different forty years or so ago."

"You really think it was that different? Sadly, I don't think enough has changed. There's still racism, bigotry, and hate crimes."

"I was just schooled and given a reality check by Vos."

Sandra laughed, clearly desperate to relieve some tension. Though the topic itself wasn't a laughing matter.

Brice stood next to her, holding his coffee, and taking a sip. "I'm just saying they would have bonded over that alone, but it would have made them strong. They might have even thought they could accomplish anything together." He was clearly talking out his thoughts, and she understood the reasoning and had no plans to interrupt the process. "If Patton took something that by all rights belonged to all of them, I'd guess it has to do with something illegal they did together. We could be talking coming into product, information, or cash."

Cash... That one word pinballed in her head. "The thing is Darrell Patton had nothing of value. He had a rough upbringing, poor. Dead-end jobs all his life, some alcohol and drug use. He had moved out of home when he got his girlfriend pregnant at eighteen. They were together for a few years, then separated for a year or two, but the girl's mother finally pushed to get full custody when he arrived late to pick her up for her birthday, 'hungover and stinking of cigarettes and a cheap whore's perfume,' as per her statement. And, before you ask, I'm quite familiar with the investigation files. And all this was only a few weeks before he took his daughter." *And killed Sam...*

"Huh, because I would have pinned this down to money. It makes people crazy more than anything. Well, love does too, but..."

Love... People had different views on what that looked like. She could feel an epiphany creeping on the edge of her brain, but for now, it teased her, just out of reach, hazy without definition. It had something to do with another piece of the transcript for the incident involving Patton... Her phone rang, and it evaporated. She answered on speaker after seeing a colleague's name on the screen. Brice moved closer to her. "Agents Vos and Sutton."

"Agent Radcliffe. So Agent Shaffer and I just finished up at

Boats N More, and had an interesting chat with Eaton's boss and coworkers," Gabe said. "To start, Eaton never showed up to work yesterday, but I guess Eaton has always done a lot of smack-talking about how he wasn't going to be sticking around forever, that his ship was coming in soon."

"Did any of them know what he meant by that?" she asked.

"I pressed them on it, but nope."

"Were you able to get a phone number for Eaton?"

"Sure, but there's no answer. I'll get Digital Forensics on it to see if they can get anywhere with it."

"But it's in service?" She latched on to the rainbow in his comment.

"Far as I know. It just rang to voicemail like it was turned off. For what it's worth, Sandra, I should have told you this before, but I hope we find your girl safe and sound."

His genuine sentiment unnerved her. "Thank you."

"Don't mention it. If you see Rowe, tell him we're on the way back."

"Will do."

Gabe ended the call, and she looked at Brice.

"His ship was coming in?" he said, beating her to it.

"Uh-huh. Eaton spent time for assault, but what were the surrounding circumstances?"

"Let's find out." Brice logged on to his computer. A few keystrokes later, he said, "Looks like the assault took place during the attempted robbery of a convenience store. He hit the clerk when he tried to block the way to the register."

That reveal made her feel a bit better about Dennis Eaton in one sense. Assault was a broad label, subject to intent and level of violence. This sounded more reactive than downright violent. "Was he armed?"

"No, but..." Brice pried his gaze from the screen. "An eyewitness said there were three men involved. Only Eaton was caught. Were the other two Patton and Jennings? After all, you've got three amigos, all from poor households. Did they talk each other into it, a way to change their futures?"

Change their futures... But nothing was fully clicking. It felt like her brain had stepped out, like the years she'd spent obsessing over the transcripts from the incident that killed her brother had never happened. Additional recollections from the recent grocery store came to her more easily though. Gavin McConnell had wanted to prove himself to his girlfriend by being a better father and taking care of his daughter when she was ill. Essentially providing for her... Then her thoughts clicked into focus. Darrell Patton had said something along the lines of providing for his daughter. She'd read the transcript at least a thousand times and should be able to recall this readily. Then finally it came to her. The statement was also one repeated in court. "During the standoff with Patton, he claimed he could be a better provider for his daughter than the girl's mother. He also claimed he did what he had out of love."

"How could he be a better provider? You just said he had no money. Even the cash from the robbery Eaton was implicated in was recovered from his person. A measly five hundred dollars."

"That's the thing. At the time, Patton had a dead-end job at a body shop. No one could understand how he could claim to provide for his daughter better than her mother. She held a steady corporate job with good pay and benefits, and it allowed her flexible hours to work from home. And Patton refused to answer the question when asked directly during his trial."

"All right, so did this guy come into money somehow? Possibly by shady means?"

"And does it have anything to do with Dennis Eaton's ship coming in?"

Brice cracked his knuckles and started typing.

"What are you doing?"

"Searching for any unsolved robberies in the area. Let's say the three were involved with the convenience store. They could have worked other heists together."

"Great idea. I'd focus on the time after Eaton's release and before Patton killed my brother."

Brice looked over his shoulder. "What would I ever do without your brilliant mind?"

She nudged his arm, and he laughed as he continued to enter parameters.

A few seconds later, Brice sat back and pointed at the screen. "The week before Patton kidnapped his daughter, Liberty Bank was hit by three armed suspects. The crew made off with nine gold bars, a value then of one-point-four million. No arrests have ever been made, and the gold bars never resurfaced. It would be worth much more today." He pulled up an internet screen and looked at the present-day values and let out a whistle. "The bars are worth nine point eight mil now."

"I'd say the gold was taken out of the States or melted down, except so far this seems the strongest possibility of what Jennings is after. If he, Eaton, and Patton robbed the bank maybe Patton stashed the bars someplace only he knows about. All I know for certain is he didn't have gold bars in his car when he was arrested. He could have planned to pick them up after grabbing a bite to eat with his daughter."

"Only he didn't get that far. But this could explain why Jennings and Eaton want Patton out. They need Patton to take them to the gold."

"If we're right about this, Patton could be refusing to disclose the location until he's out of prison. Something I can't blame him for. How much do nine bars of gold even weigh?"

Brice googled that and read off the answer. "Two hundred and forty-seven pounds."

Two hundred and forty-six point six, to be precise... He'd rounded up from what she saw on his screen. "They must have divvied it up to be able to carry the weight. Three guys, three bars or eighty-two-point-two pounds each."

"Are you going to talk to Patton about this? Or I can?"

She shook her head. "He has no reason to talk to us yet. So far, we've only got a theory. To sway him to talk, we'd need proof and some leverage. Both of which we don't have."

"Any ideas how we get either?"

"I do. When Patton went to prison, he left two close relatives behind. One of them would have become responsible for his possessions. We chat with them and gain access to his things. We could find something to support our theory. Possibly the gold itself. If not, we might find that Patton confided in her."

"You talking about the daughter now?"

"Yep."

THIRTY-THREE

As Brice drove, Sandra felt quite confident in her suggestion they speak to Patton's daughter. Natalie's last name was Roth since she married seventeen years ago. If they were right about Patton being involved in the bank robbery, he was likely motivated to do so for his and his daughter's futures. In that case, it would stand to reason if he was going to confide in anyone it would be her. He'd said in the parole hearing he hadn't spoken to his daughter, but that could have been a blatant lie to protect the gold's whereabouts.

Sandra and Brice stood at Roth's front door, and she knocked. A small, yappy dog started barking and jumping at the window. In the background, a woman was yelling for the animal to shut up. As she headed toward the door, Sandra could feel the vibration on the floorboards of the porch.

It cracked open, and a boy about ten ran behind his mother with a toy gun, calling out, "Pew! Pew!"

"Ryan, stop that right now!" The woman spun and held up a sternly pointed finger at the child. "Go, get your things together."

The boy ran out of the room, still yelling, "Pew! Pew!"

"Yes?" The woman turned to them with raised eyebrows.

Sandra stepped back. She looked so much like her father, it was eerie. From the shape and spacing between the eyes, the slight hook of the nose, and the dimpled chin. To think she was looking at his flesh and blood while he'd taken hers, stabbed like a knife. And there was no way in hell she was losing two people she loved because of the same man!

"Natalie Roth?" Brice said, stepping in when Sandra remained silent.

"Yeah..." She dipped her gaze back and forth between them.

"We're FBI, here to discuss your father." Brice held up his credentials, and Sandra followed his lead though she felt out of body.

"You're mistaken. I don't have a father. Good day." She started to shut the door as a teenage girl walked up behind Natalie. She had long brown hair like Olivia.

"Mom, Ryan's hid my gloves," the girl said.

"You kids are going to be the death of me." Natalie pushed on the door, giving them one more look.

"Please, Mrs. Roth," Sandra said, stepping in. "It's important and..." She lowered her voice before adding, "A teenage girl's life is at stake."

That had Natalie stopping all movement. It might have been a low blow to play, but Sandra wasn't apologetic. The woman locked eyes with Sandra, and it was like they saw into each other's souls. Mother to mother. Time slowed down.

"I've got five minutes, but that's all. Jodi has a hockey game out of town today, and I've got to get us on the road."

Jodi must be the teenager. And no wonder why the household was so chaotic midmorning on a Saturday. "We just need a few minutes, so all good."

Natalie stepped back to let them inside, and Sandra and Brice wiped their boots on the mat in the entry. The woman stood there like she was prepared to have the conversation on the spot.

"It might be best if we could talk sitting down." Sandra was thinking of Natalie here just as much as she was her weary bones. Brice had to be running on fumes and coffee too.

"Sure, but like I said, I don't have long." Natalie took them to a kitchen table. The neighboring countertops looked like a hurricane had passed through. From initial count, there were only two kids in the home, but there might as well have been ten from a quick assessment of the damage. There were dirty plates and bowls, frying pans and dried egg on the stovetop. A piece of toast was up in the toaster, abandoned or forgotten.

"Mom!" The teenager popped into the room.

"Ryan, give your sister her gloves back," Natalie yelled out.

The boy's cackling traveled from another part of the house.

"Do you have kids?" she asked and didn't wait for an answer. "They're why I'm sprouting gray hairs early."

Sandra wondered where her husband was given all the excitement in the home and why he wasn't pitching in, but she wasn't here to dissect their domestic life. "How well do you know your father?"

"You said a teenage girl could be in trouble? But you want to discuss my dad?" She narrowed her eyes. "I'm not sure how they're related. Besides, he's in prison where he's been most of my life."

"Please, tell us whatever you know about him."

"I mostly only know what my mother told me. She's gone now though. Breast cancer took her a few years ago."

"I'm sorry for your loss." It was an automatic response but also genuine.

"Thanks. She meant the world to me. She was always reliable."

The children seemed to have calmed down, and the resulting silence made Sandra's ears ring.

"Mom made me promise on her deathbed that I'd never speak to Dad. She'd told me all my life that he was trouble. If he wasn't looking for it, it was finding him."

Maybe Patton was telling the truth at the hearing and hadn't been in touch with his daughter. "Is that why you weren't at his parole hearing?"

"I'd have nothing to offer. He endangered my life that day, best intentions on his behalf or not."

For her to tag on the latter bit, a part of her must have thought Darrell had her interest at heart, even if his way of showing that was misguided. Whatever the case, Natalie's conflicted feelings toward her father kept her from testifying for him at the hearing, and that might have been a good thing. If she had, Lonnie Jennings and Dennis Eaton may have taken her. Though maybe they didn't think she had anything to offer. Maybe coming here was a waste of time. "You think he took you from your mother because he had good intentions?"

"My mother said that, but I think it was to make me feel better for the risk he placed me in."

Sandra nodded. "Your mother also said your father was trouble. Did she ever say what kind?"

Natalie licked her lips and didn't meet Sandra's eye when she responded. "I gathered it was the illegal kind."

"A bank robbery possibly?" Brice put out there and earned Natalie's gaze. She blinked slowly a few times and crossed her arms.

"Honestly? I think Mom suspected something like that. She never came out and said it, but there were subtle hints she dropped throughout the years. They usually came when money was tighter."

"Did he send money to your mother for you?" They could be wrong to think the gold was just hiding somewhere untouched.

"Don't think so."

"What sort of comments then? I'm not sure I understand," Brice said.

"Just that she wished she could rob a bank and get away with it like Dad."

Sandra glanced at Brice, then back to Natalie. "Nothing really subtle in that."

"Is it true? Is that also why you're here? You mentioned a girl being in trouble though."

"We're just gathering information right now, but we have our suspicions. But he never mentioned any of this to you? Tried reaching out over the years?" From Natalie's standpoint if she knew about the gold's location, she'd do her best to keep it to herself. Sandra studied the woman's reaction to the question. A slow shake of the head, steady eye contact.

"I swear to you I don't know anything about it. As I said, I've never talked to him, and I don't have any interest in doing so now. I've gotten by just fine without him in my life. But, yes, he has reached out over the years. I've always rejected his collect calls and put any letters he sent in the trash."

Patton may have been trying to tell Natalie about the gold. The letters may have even contained some clue as to its loca-tion. But Sandra could appreciate that Natalie had sided with her mother and moved forward in her life, even if that didn't help find Olivia. "Were these letters sent more recently?"

Natalie shook her head. "It was before I got married, so over seventeen years ago. He wouldn't know where to find me now unless his mother somehow knows."

"I see," Sandra said. They were left with one other play here. Patton's possessions. "Where are his things, do you know?"

"As far as I know his mother has his stuff locked up in a storage unit. Where, you'd have to talk to her about. I'm not exactly in contact with her either. But I'm still a bit lost on how your questions about the robbery and my father pertain to that teenage girl you mentioned." She narrowed her eyes and studied Sandra.

"We're just gathering information," Sandra reiterated in a soft tone. "Do you know a Lonnie Jennings and Dennis Eaton?"

"Ah, kind of... well, I very vaguely remember having an Uncle Lonnie."

"Have you been in touch with him?" Brice asked.

Natalie shook her head, and her forehead bunched in confusion. "No. As I said I *vaguely* remember a Lonnie. I was just a kid when he was around."

It would seem when Patton went away, Natalie's mother made sure to shield her from the man's friends too. Sandra's earlier thought gained more credit. Jennings and Eaton wouldn't have reason to think Natalie would be helpful in recovering the gold. "I appreciate these questions must be coming out of left field for you," Sandra said, showing empathy, "but the men I just mentioned are suspects in an FBI investigation pertaining to the abduction of a teenage girl. We believe they were friends of your father's and that the three of them were involved in a bank robbery thirty-three years ago."

Natalie paled and wet her lips. "I... I don't know what to say. I wish I could help more, but as I said, my dad and I aren't in contact. At all."

"We appreciate you taking the time to talk to us," Sandra said, getting up. "I realize you have a lot on the go today."

"Oh, shoot. Kids!" Natalie bopped up. "We've got to leave!"

Sandra and Brice saw themselves out.

"I'd say she's telling the truth," Brice said as he slipped behind the wheel.

"I agree, but why do you think that?"

"It's in her name. *Nat*-a-lie." He smiled at her.

"Very funny." She smiled back, despite herself.

"But in seriousness, she seemed genuine to me. If she had

something to share that could help us find Olivia, she would have told us."

"I think so too. I'd still like to check Patton's visitor records from the prison just to make sure."

"We could also check her phone records."

Sandra shook her head. "I don't think that would fly at this point, but at least it wasn't a waste of time coming here. Our theory about the threesome doing the bank robbery gained more traction."

"We also know who to talk to next. The grandmother. I assume now that Patton's mother was the other living relative you were referring to?"

"Yep."

"Well, she might even be able to give us more than access to that storage locker. She might be familiar with the haunts Patton had as a kid. There's nothing saying he didn't return there as an adult to hide the gold bars."

"It's worth a try, but from what I recall as part of Patton's sob story, the woman loved the bottle back then. It's hard to know what she might remember, if she was even paying attention to her son at all." Her phone rang, and she rushed to pull it out. The screen showed *Blocked Number*. "Jennings." She took a deep breath, answered on speaker, and said nothing. By doing so, she was making a move for control, but it was taking all her willpower to pull it off.

"How much does your daughter mean to you?" Lonnie's voice came across the line, but Olivia's muffled cries could be heard in the background. There was a garbled word that sounded like *Mom*. He must have her gagged.

The mother in her wanted to react and dole out threats, but the fed part knew she wouldn't get anywhere with that tactic. Responding strongly would have the opposite of the desired result and weaken her position. She sidestepped his question with, "I told you that I'm willing to do what you want. Tell me what that is."

"You're a negotiator. Use those skills to get the verdict overturned."

He had a lot of unfounded faith in her abilities. Even if she wanted to, this request was beyond her scope. But she didn't need to come right out and tell him that. "I can work with that if you tell me what it is you want from him. We all want this to end peacefully, and there's no reason why that can't be the case. What are you after?" It was best that she played dumb because it would give Jennings the illusion of control.

"Just get him out of prison."

"I'm sorry, but I don't know how I'm supposed to do that. Just tell me what you're after."

Silence for a few beats, then, "Let's just say that Patton owes me. But you do talk for a living, don't you? Some hotshot negotiator with the FBI. If you can't get him out, just get him to talk."

"I can do that." She impressed herself with the confidence she conveyed. Even putting her skills to work might not have any effect on Patton. She tamped down the anxiety that rose about facing him again. "What do you want to know?"

"There's money he's been holding on to. Half of it belongs to me."

Hard to split nine bars evenly... She shared a look with Brice. There had been no mention of Dennis or his share. "Half of it belongs to you?" she parroted.

"That's right. Darrell will know what I'm talking about. Gold bars, and he owes me half. Actually, never mind that, I want all of them. Tell him it's interest for waiting so long."

If it came down to talking with Patton, she'd be sure to hold that back. "And he knows where the gold bars are?"

The more he spoke, the more he implicated himself in the robbery. "Yes," he hissed. "But I don't think any of this is a surprise to you. So just get me the location of the gold, and you'll get your daughter back."

"I'll get my daughter back if I just hand over the location of the gold?"

"As easy as that." His smugness traveled the line, and she had to swallow down the rage it ignited. "That's if you're as good as your reputation makes out. But don't be fooled. I'm not actually a patient person, but I'm also not completely unreasonable. I'll give you until tomorrow at noon. When I call then, you better have the location of the money."

Tomorrow at noon... Though it wasn't the deadline playing on her mind. It was the fact that Olivia would remain with that madman for another twenty-four-plus hours. "I'll do this, but in the meantime, promise me you will not touch one hair on her head."

"Too late for that."

Click. The line went dead.

She'd throw her phone if there was somewhere to toss it, but it was also her only link to Olivia. Her hands were quaking, and Brice put his hand on her forearm.

"Don't let him into your head," he said gently.

"Too late for that." She inadvertently recycled Jennings's words. He'd said them with such menace. He'd better not have hurt Olivia, and if he'd touched her sexually, she'd... Well, her thoughts skittered into the darkness, dredging up all that she'd known man to do to another. Being a career FBI agent, she had a catalog of heinous crimes to pull from.

"Kick him out then," Brice said with force, popping her into the light again. "You let him set up in there, it won't do you or Olivia any good."

"I know that, but this is my daughter."

"Sure, but you've been down this road before. For other people's daughters, sure, but the stakes have been high. Lives at risk. You show up and get the job done. That's the Vos I know anyhow."

She looked at him, not realizing before how much respect he held for her. "And now I've got a clock over my head." The time on her phone said it was eleven thirty. She had until tomorrow at noon. That's what Jennings had said. She'd justified putting off a conversation with Patton, but now she wished she'd seen the future and had the visit already set in motion.

"Hate to point this out, though I don't think you missed it. Jennings is escalating. The way you looked at me I think you picked it up too. Is Dennis Eaton even in the picture anymore?"

"Jennings sure didn't make it sound like it. He talked about Darrell owing him *half*. There were three suspects in the robbery. At minimum that makes for a three-way split. And presumably that third person was Dennis Eaton."

"I also hate to say this, but if he did kill Eaton, a friend since childhood..."

"You don't need to finish that sentence." *Killing Olivia would be easier...* She could feel herself spiraling despite all the training and years of experience. All the *keep it calm* and cool demeanor that she put on like a suit didn't fit right now.

"Deep breaths, all right. We don't need to go there yet."

"Don't need to, but it's hard not to. This is my Olivia, not a stranger."

"I get that, and it's also why I have complete faith that you'll get her back. The stakes are higher than ever before."

"I'm going to do everything I can, that's for damn sure. I need to get on the approved visitor list ASAP and in to talk with Darrell Patton. There's no more putting it off."

"Here's the flaw in that though. You really think he's going to want to talk to a fed about a bank robbery he did? He comes clean to you and that's him admitting to it. You've already proven that you're against him with the parole hearing. Why wouldn't you find a way to make the armed robbery charges stick?"

Her colleague had a point. Darrell would fear being tried and sentenced for the bank heist next. *Which he deserves to be...* "He hid that gold and is probably counting on it as a payday when he gets out of prison. He may even have plans to share some with his daughter, Natalie, to win her back. I'll have him see me as a threat to that happening."

"But is he going to buy that a fed will let him ride off into the sunset with the money?" Brice smirked at his turn of phrase.

"I'm going to have to talk to him on his level. He took his daughter thirty-three years ago because he thought he was showing love for her. I'll appeal to that emotion, while I also share the stakes involved for me." The recent standoff in Woodbridge also taught her this. Gavin had held people in the grocery store because he was desperate to prove himself a good father and provider. She had the recent reminder that a parent's love knew no bounds. She was also living it.

"You plan to tell him Jennings has Olivia?"

"I see that as my strongest play here. Parent to parent."

"You're going to have to put on one hell of a performance."

"For someone just singing my praises a minute ago, have you changed your mind?"

"This just hits so close to home. Are you really okay with revealing Olivia's situation?"

On reflection, it wasn't ideal as Patton could see her desperation as a weakness to exploit, but she didn't see a way of working around that. "It's better than offering up some deal to the man who killed my brother." She hated feeling wedged between justice for her brother and her daughter's future. "I just can't do that. Not if you're suggesting I work something out for early parole."

"Not at all. I was just thinking immunity against robbery charges."

Her conscience might allow that. Surely there had to be another way… Then she had it. "There may be a different angle I can work."

"I'm listening…"

"I could make Patton think *his* daughter was taken. It works on the same premise, that Natalie is of utmost importance to him. Lying is part of the negotiation toolkit."

"That could work."

"I hope so. Because I'm going to hate every millisecond that I need to sit across a table from that man. On the upside, if I make this work, there might not even be a need to set up an immunity deal."

Brice smiled. "You just make him believe his daughter's in danger, he gives up the gold, he gets charged with the bank robbery, gets more years tacked onto his sentence…"

"He'll chalk it up to parental sacrifice. As far as I'm concerned, by the time all is said and done, he'll be happy if he ever sniffs freedom again."

"I love it, except it's likely that Patton will need to approve your request to see him."

"That's why I'm taking this to Elwood." She called her boss.

"What the latest?" Elwood answered.

"We're getting some momentum, but I need your help." She ran through where things were, and that she needed clearance to speak with Darrell Patton, and her thoughts on offering up immunity.

"Leave it with me. I'll get it cleared past the prison warden. It's Saturday, though, so it might take a bit to track him down."

"Time isn't on our side."

"I realize that and will get on it the second I get off the phone with you. I'll call once it's a done deal."

"Thanks."

"Don't mention it." With that, the assistant director was gone.

Sandra turned to Brice. "That's in the works, but it could take hours. I'm not just going to sit on my hands and wait."

"It might be a good time to catch some more sleep."

She looked at him, his statement striking her as serious, but found he was smiling. "Just get us to Darrell's mother's house."

"For that I need to know where to find her..." Brice punched into the onboard computer system. A moment later he confirmed, "Regina Patton's living in Woodbridge these days. Buckle up."

Sandra did, but the phrase took on so much more meaning. So much uncertainty lay ahead with nothing to be taken for granted. There was no guarantee of safety or a happy outcome. They were venturing into the unknown. All she had on her side was hope and a prayer. And solid instinct. Yes, she had that.

THIRTY-FOUR

The forty-five-minute drive from Washington to Woodbridge gave Sandra time to think. The approach that she and Brice had laid out should work on Patton. It was the *should* part that curdled in her gut. But she'd never been one to harbor a defeatist attitude, and she wasn't about to start now. Patton had been willing to risk his freedom by snatching his daughter, and Natalie said that he made efforts to connect with her. That was before she got married, but Sandra expected he'd still have a soft spot for Natalie that she could exploit.

Regina Patton had never remarried after her husband died of a heart attack several years ago. The address on file for her led them to a well-maintained trailer park. Empty flowerpots were stacked in the corner of the front garden near the walkway, but otherwise the place looked taken care of from the outside.

Sandra knocked, and a woman swung the door open rather abruptly, as if she'd been sitting right on the other side. The smell of stale beer and body odor wafted from the trailer.

"Whatcha want?" She hadn't aged well, but that's what rough living did to a person. She was also in her late seventies.

Crow's feet clawed out from her eyes like sunbursts, and her forehead was rows of wrinkles.

"Ms. Patton," Sandra began, holding up her badge.

"Wait a minute, I know you. You're that... *that* girl whose brother died."

Sandra's hackles rose at how she put that. It was stated as if something accidental had claimed Sam's life and not the actions of this woman's son. "My brother was murdered during the standoff between your son, Darrell, and police."

"Yes. I knew you looked familiar." The woman's gaze lingered on Sandra for several more seconds before it transferred to Brice. "And who are you?"

"Special Agent Sutton."

She leveled her gaze at Sandra. "You're FBI now too?"

She tucked her badge away. To answer that would be redundant. "We need to talk to you about Darrell."

"What about him? He's behind bars and will be there longer. Thanks to you." The woman smacked her gums, ill-fitted dentures snapping as they released from the roof of her mouth in the process.

I never saw you at the parole hearing speaking up for him...

"Then you're still in touch?" Brice wedged in. If he hadn't, Sandra might have lost her temper. Her insides were quaking with rage at how this woman made her out to be the villain instead of looking at her own son.

"Not really, but the parole board keeps me up to date on his status. Honestly, I can't stomach what he did all those years ago. Ain't no son of mine. Cuz of him, I've never had a part in my granddaughter's life either. Or great-grandchildren."

A moment ago, the woman pinned blame on Sandra as if her son did no wrong. The about-face was surprising. Coming here might not have been a wasted trip after all. "A situation has come up involving some childhood friends of Darrell's. We thought maybe you could help us."

"Let me guess. Lonnie and Dennis. Lonnie, especially, was always trouble."

Sandra was surprised by how sharp this woman was factoring in her age and that she'd been an alcoholic for years. If not for the smell of the trailer, she'd think maybe she'd given up drinking. "Well, we're trying to find them." For this conversation, she'd run on the assumption Dennis Eaton was still living.

"What have they done?" Regina leaned against the door-frame, suddenly appearing exhausted and chilled.

"Would it be easier for you to speak with us if you sat down? We could go inside," Sandra said.

Regina batted a hand in the air. "I'm fine right here."

"All right. Well, do you know where Darrell liked to go? Either by himself or with his friends?" It was possible if he had some special spot where he hung out as a kid, he might have taken the gold from the heist there.

"I wasn't the best mother when he was young." The woman's eyes became weepy, and it highlighted her advancing age. "My husband wasn't a good man and was hard to live with. He was old-school, expecting food on the table when he came home, a clean house, a submissive wife. That wasn't me, but I felt stuck. I drank to numb myself to my horrible life. Reggie died ten years ago, and I've been sober ever since."

The smell of stale beer contradicted her claim.

"Ah, I see it on your face. If you pick up on beer, it's from some gal pals of mine. They're a bit younger, and we play poker on Friday nights."

Sandra gave Regina a tight smile. This woman didn't miss a thing, not even a subtle energetic tell.

Regina continued. "But I do remember a phase when Darrell loved fishing. Don't ask me where he'd go, though it was clearly around home as he'd walk or ride his bike."

This was potentially helpful, but not a glowing lead to finding the gold bars. If they were going to set out to recover it, they needed a more pinpointed place to start than the vague summary they'd just received. "Okay, thank you for that."

"It help?" Regina narrowed her eyes but didn't come out and say she detected the opposite.

"It might have," Sandra said. "We were told that Darrell's possessions are in a storage locker. Would you mind if we had a look at his things?" She could request a search warrant if it came down to it, but one thing at a time. At this point they didn't even know where the unit was or whose name it was under.

"No skin off my back. I'll get the key." Regina retreated into her trailer and returned with a shotgun.

Sandra and Brice stepped back.

"Whoa, there," Brice said, holding his hands up.

"I've been nice, but get goin'. I'm not doing anything to mess up my boy more than I already have. Go. Scoot."

"Ma'am, you don't want to do this," Brice petitioned. "Think about what you're doing. You're holding a gun on federal agents."

"I know exactly what I'm doing, and I ain't got nothing to lose." She cocked the gun. "Now, scram!"

Sandra and Brice made the briefest of eye contact and carried on a silent conversation. They needed to act swiftly and in sync before this woman could get a shot off. They'd move in at the same time. *Now!*

Next thing, Brice gripped the handle of the gun to her right, and Sandra grabbed the barrel to her left. They pried the shotgun from the older woman's hands, and Regina cussed and stomped her feet.

"Get off my property!"

"That's it. I'm done playing nice guy, lady. You're coming with us." Brice handed off the gun to Sandra, who unloaded it while Brice cuffed Regina.

The visit didn't exactly go as planned. Worse than that, it meant a delay when time was already running out.

Once Sandra and Brice got Regina Patton into the back of their car, she disclosed the location of the storage unit housing Darrell's things. It was in Dumfries, a town about ten minutes from Woodbridge. Regina was handed off to another agent. She'd be booked and charged for threatening federal agents. Her incarceration would also keep her from talking to Patton. Before parting company, they asked for the key to the unit, and she told them to go to hell. At least there was a way to work around that.

It was one fifty-seven when they were showing a clerk at the storage facility a search warrant for unit 802, as registered to Regina Patton. The thirtysomething was eager to help, as he'd confessed to taking criminology and forensics courses after hours with the intention of working in a lab for law enforcement someday. He held a pair of bolt cutters in hand.

"You said eight-oh-two?" The guy looked over his shoulder, and when she and Brice confirmed, he didn't waste a second clamping down on the padlock. It popped open.

"Thanks," Sandra told him.

"Anything I can do to help." He smiled at her and backed up.

Brice tugged out what remained of the padlock from the loop and turned to the man. "If you could leave us to it now, that would be great."

"Oh, yeah, of course." He bobbed his head, as if self-satisfied, and walked back toward the golf cart they took to here with a breeze to his steps.

Sandra lifted the door on the unit and stepped back to look at the contents. The thing was packed tight with boxes and furniture. It wasn't likely any of Patton's things were tossed over the last thirty-three years, and she'd wager his entire apartment had been uprooted and moved here.

"This is going to take forever to wade through," Brice griped.

"No time like the present." She gloved up and dug in, disheartened there wasn't something else she could be doing. But this was it until she received approval to talk to Patton. On the upside, they could find something in this mess to lead them to the gold or give them an idea where Olivia was being held.

"We should also call for backup to come and help process everything. There's just so much here. If we do uncover evidence in the bank robbery, we'll want that to remain intact."

"I get that."

Brice put his hands on his hips. "Where do you even suggest we start?"

"I'd say the boxes. They might contain papers or photographs that can give us a clue."

Brice hauled out an end table and set it to the side. In the back of the unit there was a bookcase loaded with boxes, but it would take some work to reach it. "Help me clear a path," he said.

For the next fifteen minutes they took out a kitchen table, a set of four matching chairs, a couch, a recliner, a mattress, and a boxspring. When they'd finished, the front of the unit looked like a garage sale.

"Moment of truth." Brice snatched one of the boxes from the shelving unit and set it on the kitchen table and popped the flaps.

Sandra grabbed one for herself and set up next to him. Hers was full of DVDs. "Bust for me."

"Nothing much for me either. Some bric-a-brac." He lifted a sculpted wooden duck, then tossed it back into the box.

"We keep going until we're done." Even as she said this and grabbed another box, she was thinking of Olivia. If only there was some fast way of getting to her and bringing this nightmare to an end. But there weren't any shortcuts. At least none she could see. And where the hell was Elwood with her clearance to speak with Patton?

"I think I might have something here," Brice said, pulling her from her desperate thoughts.

She shuffled closer to him and saw that the box he had opened contained a lot of photographs. The prints were loose as if they'd been tossed inside without care. Brice shuffled through them, sharing several with her. There were shots of Natalie and a woman who looked strikingly like her and familiar. She was probably Natalie's mother and Darrell's ex. Sandra likely recognized her from early memories of the trial. There were also candid photos of Regina with a cigarette dangling from her mouth as she shucked corn, a beer bottle on a table next to her. A picture or two of a cranky-looking man who was possibly Darrell's father.

Brice fished out a framed photo and smiled when he dusted it off. "Ah, here we go..."

The photo captured a teenage Darrell with a similar-aged Lonnie Jennings and Dennis Eaton. The trio were holding fishing poles.

"Sadly, though, this picture doesn't tell us anything we didn't already know," Brice said. "Patton liked to fish and so did his friends. But even if we figured out where this picture was taken, why would Patton hide the gold there? It's probably public land, and there would be nothing stopping Jennings and Eaton from searching the area."

"They might have, if they thought of it. But this fishing hole might have been important to Patton and mean nothing to the other guys. If Patton did hide the gold somewhere in nature though, things change, landmarks, all that."

"Suppose so." Brice grabbed a small stack of prints and sorted through those.

They all showed a twentysomething Darrell with hiking poles and hiking boots in different poses. He was always smiling for the photographer. Whoever was behind the camera was someone he liked. Given his age, it could have been Natalie's mother before their separation. "He clearly liked nature."

"Seems so. Hiking particularly. But even if we narrowed things to DC, there are a lot of trails."

Hiking... "Huh. I remember now. It was so inconsequential to me that I must have kicked this out, but Darrell was wearing hiking boots when he was arrested in Washington. But he was living in Dumfries at the time. So why go to Washington with his daughter unless..." She met Brice's gaze, and they spoke at the same time. "He did plan to pick up the gold from his hiding spot. Probably before he left the state."

"Uh-huh. But you realize this would suggest the gold is likely hidden somewhere in DC," Brice said.

"Yes, and I'm going to guess somewhere in parkland or the woods."

"Jeez, good luck to us. There are a lot of green spaces. That money could be anywhere. Even if we were able to narrow it down to a trail or woods, where would we go from there?"

"No idea. Let's just hope that I can get Patton to talk." Her phone rang, and she held her breath as she pulled it out and looked at the caller ID. "It's Eric." She answered.

"Hey, I thought you'd want to know. It just got back to me, but Dennis Eaton's body was found at the labyrinth in Georgetown Waterfront Park this morning."

THIRTY-SIX

The news about Dennis Eaton didn't come as a surprise. Sandra was just a little aggravated that the body was found that morning, and it had taken until the middle of the afternoon to reach her ears. What she found somewhat reassuring was that it was the same park where they found Olivia's phone. For Jennings to dump Eaton's body there it suggested he wasn't holding Olivia that far away. There was a message in the location though. It was impossible to ignore that the park wasn't far from her home. It was where she took her morning runs. Was it a power move on Jennings's part? But what concerned her more was where had Olivia been when Jennings dumped Eaton's body? Was she left alone, tied and gagged, or caged? Was she drugged? Her mind was a whirlwind, and the possibilities were endless.

Eric had told her the body was found before seven AM, and there had been no eyewitnesses. That meant Jennings would have left him before that to avoid early joggers who braved the cold morning. But his action wasn't without risk. It proved yet again that he was impulsive and capable of anything.

The sky was overcast and made four-oh-two PM feel later

than it was. Sandra could barely wait for Brice to park the car and for it to come to a complete stop before hopping out.

Even these hours later there was a police presence, and curious gawkers were gathered behind a line of crime scene tape. A loudmouthed uniformed officer was continually barking, "Get back!"

"What makes this Lonnie guy snap and kill his lifetime friend?" Brice looked over at her and shook his head. He was walking beside her, keeping up with her strides. "Forgive me. Dumb question. Money. With Patton in prison, it would all be Jennings's."

"Precisely."

They approached the mouthy officer, who quietened down and stepped closer to them. "Closed scene. You'll need to get back."

She and Brice held up their FBI badges, and the officer rolled his eyes and huffed.

"Just because you're feds, that doesn't mean you can stomp around wherever you'd like."

Sandra squared her shoulders as she pocketed her badge. "Detective Birch on scene?"

"I'm not going to answer—"

"Hodges, let 'em in." It was Eric, and he was quickly making up ground to get to them.

The officer turned around and said, "I was told to keep this place locked down."

"Except they're with me." Eric waved for her and Brice to walk past the uniform.

"I'm just trying to do my job here," Hodges mumbled, then raised his voice to the blustering crowd again. "Back up!"

They walked into the park with Eric. Thankfully, Hodges's booming voice eventually faded into the background.

"We call the guy the Mouth behind his back, but if you want someone to get a point across, he's your guy," Eric said.

"He'd get it across all right," Brice snickered.

Eric laughed, but the expression was short-lived. "Any progress on finding Olivia?" His softened eyes and body language told her he was concerned about her. If they weren't surrounded by work colleagues, she imagined he'd be taking her into his arms. And she'd happily let him.

"Some. At least we know what Jennings wants now." She filled him in on the bank robbery and the gold bars.

"And you think you can get Patton to reveal the location?"

"I need to try." Before she was inundated by thoughts of Olivia, she did her best to push them away. Admitting uncertainty made her feel like a horrible parent, but she was focused on the endgame. Right now, Eaton might be a key to finding out where Jennings was holding her. "Where was he found exactly? By whom?" *Focus on business, push through.*

"By a jogger, around seven, as I told you on the phone, but he was laid out right in the middle..." Eric pointed to the circle marking the center of the labyrinth. It wasn't done with hedges but was set out on concrete with green pavement laying out the puzzle. CSIs were around snapping pictures and combing the area outside of the maze, to see if they'd turned up anything for evidence. "Obviously the medical examiner has long been and gone with the body. Identification was easy as he was dumped with his ID."

"What about his phone?" If so, they could get it over to Tech ASAP. They might be able to use the GPS tracking history on the device. That's if Dennis hadn't turned it off before reaching the holding point. Otherwise, it would do them no good.

Eric shook his head. "Jennings was too smart for that, but I'll reach out to digital techs to see if they can somehow access the phone's GPS history without the device in hand."

"Thank you," she told him.

"Still, he took a risk coming here to dump the body," Brice put in. "Early risers could have spotted him."

Sandra turned to her colleague. "I was thinking the same. We could hit the press and make a public petition asking for anyone who might have seen something suspicious here this morning to come forward. Not that I have a doubt who is behind this, but it can help build the case against him. Someone might have seen Olivia."

"We can't go to the media. It's too risky. It could push Jennings into doing something rash," Brice countered.

Eric was nodding when she turned to him. Guess her suggestion was vetoed, but Brice had made a good point. She said to Eric, "Obviously, you weren't on this case from the start?" She trusted that he'd have called her long ago if he had been.

"No. I called the moment I found out who it was. I became aware of it when I heard some uniformed cops talking about a DB found in the park related to a BOLO issued by the feds. I had a feeling and followed it up."

"Yet, MPD still worked the crime scene without calling the FBI?" she asked.

"I can't account for other people, Sandra. I called once I verified things."

"And I appreciate that." And she did. She was grateful to have him in her corner. "Time and cause of death?"

"TOD was pegged between four and seven AM. COD seems straightforward. Gunshot between the eyes."

"Execution style. And the time tells me that Lonnie must have killed him around the point of first contact." The thought of him being so unstable and having her daughter in his hands was too much to contemplate. *Squeeze it out... Focus on cold detachment. Paint the picture of a random kidnapping...* "Jennings has proven again that he can be unpredictable, while taking deliberate action. That of the murder itself, but also the dump location, were given thought. He chose here, close to my home as a power move. But to get Eaton's body here, he likely would have left Olivia alone wherever he's holding her. He must be confident that she can't escape." As she rattled this off, she realized just how frightened she should be that Jennings's emotions were driving him. Greed, anger, impatience... The latter might be the worst of them all. "And by leaving Eaton, his childhood friend there"—she flicked a finger toward the center of the labyrinth—"he's making it clear he's finished waiting. He will kill anyone who stands between him and that gold." Her mind flashed back to that photo of the three teens sporting smiles and fishing gear. If Jennings was willing to kill Eaton, the outlook wasn't good for Olivia. "But if he thinks he's in control, he has another thing com—" Sandra's phone rang, cutting off her brave statement. Just the sound of the trill sent ice through her veins. "It's him," she said at seeing *Blocked Number* on the screen. She turned away, and Eric stepped up next to her, standing so close their arms were touching. She appreciated his strong presence.

"I assume you found my friend by now."

She looked around her as goosebumps traipsed over her shoulders and down her arms. *Is he here now, watching from the shadows?* "Why did you do it?"

Jennings laughed. "Why do you think? The guy was as dumb as a stump, and I'm done playing Mr. Nice Guy."

"What do you want, Lonnie? I'm working on what you asked me for." Though she imagined the reason for his call was to gloat about Eaton's murder and to ensure she got the message. If Jennings was trying to communicate that he was a killer, she received it loud and clear.

"Glad to hear it. Then no one else needs to die."

She gripped her phone tighter, as tears of hatred pooled in her eyes. She nudged out her chin, a blister of defiance buoying her. "I plan to talk with Darrell and get you what you want, but how can I trust that you'll keep your word? That you will return my daughter safely to me? After all, you killed someone who was a friend."

"We talked about that. It boils down to the fact I don't have patience for people who piss me off or are no longer useful. Just make good on your end, Special Agent Vos, and you and your daughter will have nothing to worry about. And remember, *tick tock.*" He hung up.

She lowered her phone. A few tears fell as she stared into the distance, not focused on anything. Eric took her hand, his fingertips dancing over hers, despite their audience.

"Sandra," Eric prompted. "Talk to me. Tell me what's going on."

"I'll tell you what," she said with heat, removing her hand from Eric's. "Everything is taking too freaking long. Where's my approval to see Patton?" She paced in a circle. "I can't wait anymore. Not while my Olivia is..." She gripped her forehead, and she noticed Brice shrink away to let her have privacy with Eric. She was hyperventilating inside, and clearly losing it on the outside, but she needed to cut herself some slack. How could she expect to hold herself together every second with Olivia out there? Her phone rang again, and Eric tried to ease it from her hand. She started to release it but caught the name of her caller. "No, it's okay. It's Elwood." She picked up. "Tell me I've got the green light to talk to Patton."

"It's arranged. Patton's all yours tonight. No lawyers, no recordings, nothing. What time do you think you could get there?"

"Give me three and a half hours." That was the time it would take to drive there if she left immediately. She could try to do this by video, but some things were better handled in person.

"So around eight o'clock then. Are you sure this is something you need to handle face to face? Wouldn't a video conference do the job? You haven't slept for hours. Should you really be driving?"

She probably shouldn't be, but she was also hopped up on adrenaline. "I'll be fine. As for the deal on the table…?"

"The one that lets him walk from armed robbery? Only as the last resort."

"Understood. And thank you."

"Don't mention it. Godspeed."

She pocketed her phone and looked at Eric and Brice. "I need to get to the prison to meet with Patton."

"I'll drive you," Brice said.

She shook her head. "I'll take myself."

"I'll get him home," Eric spoke up.

"To the field office?" Brice said.

"Wherever you wish."

Brice nodded.

"You guys work it out. I just need to leave now."

"Just be safe. Are you sure you're okay to drive?" Eric asked her.

"You sound like Rowe."

"It's a valid question."

"I'll be careful."

"You better be." He pulled her into a hug and kissed her forehead forgoing their unspoken rule about public displays of affection in a professional setting. He pulled back and said, "I'll let you know if anything pops up here that might help."

"I wouldn't expect less. Thank you." She stood there for a few seconds, absorbing the contours of Eric's face and dipped into his eyes. This man brought out her strength. She could only hope it would be enough to see this through and get the crucial information she needed out of Patton so she could save Olivia.

THIRTY-SEVEN

The administrative staff at the prison were miserable with Sandra as they followed the standard protocol for visitors. She was stripped of her gun and anything that could be deemed a weapon, even patted down by a female corrections officer.

"You realize I'm FBI?" Sandra said.

The woman looked at her as if to say that was the only reason she was being admitted at this hour. "Just doing my job, ma'am."

"I'll take it from here." A man in his fifties with a lean, lanky frame approached. "Warden Synder," he told her as an introduction of himself.

"Special Agent Sandra Vos."

"Oh, I know who you are. Your boss too. I made something clear to him, and I'm going to do the same with you. This meeting is unprecedented and could be seen as violating the inmate's rights. He never approved this visit."

Did this man not know why they had an interest in speaking with Patton? "I'm not sure what Assistant Director Rowe told you, Warden, but Darrell Patton is of primary interest to the FBI pertaining to a kidnapping."

She left it vague, thinking that Elwood would have done the same.

"Your boss told me that much, but it still doesn't make it cool in my book."

The fact the warden so strongly defended the rights of a convicted killer didn't earn any respect in *her* book.

The warden continued. "Patton has the right to signal the guard to leave the room at any time, and if he does, you are to let him go. Are we understood?"

Elwood hadn't mentioned that stipulation, and she was curious if the warden had said this to him. "Understood. Now, I'd like to get started." She met his gaze, not backing down when his drilled through hers.

The warden held the eye contact for a few beats before nodding and saying, "Follow me."

As she traversed the linoleum hallways that she'd been down just days ago, dread washed over her. It was sinking in that she was about to come face to face and one on one with the man who had killed her brother. Her heart started thumping wildly in her chest, and her throat constricted. She must have been a fool to even think she could pull off talking to him while remaining calm. But she wasn't beyond trying. *Remember, this is for Olivia.* She'd repeat it until it flooded her with the strength and courage to see this through.

The warden stopped outside a door with a window and a guard standing next to it. "This is it," he told her.

She nodded, unable to speak, afraid to even try. She imagined her words coming out as a croak. She gave the guard a fast look before grabbing the door handle and giving it a turn. Her pulse pounded in her ears as a fresh shot of adrenaline flooded her system. Behind this door was Sam's killer. Unplanned or not, the result of his actions cost her Sam. This thinking ramped up her rage, overriding her anxiety and easing her doubts about her abilities. To hell if he was taking Olivia from her too.

One deep breath, and she swung the door open. She walked inside with confident strides, holding her head high and squaring her shoulders.

Darrell Patton was seated at a table and facing toward the door. He was chained to the table by restraints that hooked to cuffs around his wrists. Manacles were around his ankles and linked to hoops on the floor. He watched every step she took.

"You," he seethed. "They dragged me from my cell for *you?* Guard!"

The man popped into the window of the door, and Sandra shook her head at him. No way was Patton getting off that easy.

Patton's shoulders lowered when the guard didn't come into the room. "Listen, if you're here to berate me some more, I don't want to hear it."

"Berate..." She snapped her mouth shut. *Remember Olivia.* "This has nothing to do with you and me. It involves Natalie."

"What about her?" Tossed out with nonchalance. Not the reaction she'd expected, but it could be a performance.

"Your daughter," she stressed. "And she's found herself in a dangerous situation."

"I'm not sure why I should care." But his words and tone were in conflict with his body language. He shuffled forward on his chair if only a bit, and his shoulders tensed just enough to tell her he did care. *Good.*

"Because you're her father. Years apart doesn't change that. There was a time you put everything on the line just to be with her." She hoped that she wouldn't need to go deeper than that.

"Huh, and look where that got me. The brat won't even talk to me. I haven't seen her since that day. She's an adult now. She could come here and visit. As you pointed out, she wasn't even at the hearing."

His bitterness had Sandra believing his claim more than she had initially. Though it would have been in his favor to lie before, bolster up the hope for reconciliation. She released the need to check visitor logs, but she'd need to deepen her lying. "Natalie wants to reconnect with you."

"And how would you know that?" His tone softened a minuscule amount.

"Her husband told me."

"She's married?" There was a slight hitch to his voice, and she knew she had him.

"Yes, and she has two children. A boy and girl. You could meet them someday, but right now Natalie needs your help."

"Is she hurt?"

He was clearly invested now. "It's hard to say." The longer she was here, the easier it was getting to speak with him. Most of the time, she could even set aside that it was really Olivia who was in danger. She'd dipped into this world of make-believe, and it gave her the strength to do what she had to do.

"What do you mean by that?"

"Just that. Lonnie has her."

"Lonnie? Why the hell would he...?" But he abandoned the question there. His eyes met hers, and there was a moment of truth and understanding. He knew why he'd take her. "She's no good to him. Why is he doing this?"

"Why is he doing this?" she parroted, as if she didn't know and wanted him to provide the answer. Letting the silence stretch was tough. Jennings's deadline wasn't far from mind.

Patton narrowed his eyes. "Tell me what you think you know."

He clearly wasn't *biting*. "All right, I'll play along. A week before you kidnapped your own daughter, you and two friends, Lonnie Jennings and Dennis Eaton, robbed Liberty Bank in Washington, DC. You made off with nine gold bars. Lonnie said you hid them until things cooled down. But that didn't happen because you got yourself sent to prison. Well, he's run out of patience. It's the gold bars or your daughter's life, Mr. Patton." She set all that out there coolly, but her body stiffened.

Also for one tiny flicker of a moment, she'd lost the narrative and her voice fluctuated.

Patton met her eyes, smiled, and shook his head. "Nah, it's not Nat in danger. It's someone who means something to you. You want to know what I think?"

She splayed her hands as if to say, *By all means, tell me.*

"I'm starting to think it's *your* daughter, the way you keep throwing *daughter* around."

Her turn to shake her head. "Even if I had a daughter, why would Lonnie take her? I can't offer him anything."

"You're assuming I can."

"You know where the gold bars are."

"Says who? You're trying to rope me into confessing that I robbed that bank. But I ask you, what proof could you possibly have?"

He had her in a corner, and she didn't particularly like it there. They didn't have any solid evidence against him, but they had logic. "Why else would Lonnie be demanding to know the location of the gold if you didn't know where it was?"

"Lonnie's lost his mind? I don't know."

"Is that how you want to play this? If you don't tell me where the gold is, your daughter will *die*." That impactful word had her slipping back to reality, and her voice cracked, betraying her again.

Patton sat back. "I'm a little lost here. Lonnie takes Natalie and gets a fed to find out the location of gold obtained in a bank robbery. Why would he implicate himself? And what do you care about Natalie?"

"It's my job to care about people, Mr. Patton, and Lonnie doesn't intend to get caught. He just wants the gold, and he's tired of waiting for you to get out of here." She was surprised by her ability to hold it together.

Patton sat silently for a few beats. "I don't know. You can't even provide proof to back up your claim. Besides, *if* I was involved in some robbery, why would I bare my soul to you? You're the freaking FBI. I'd be lucky to see the light of day again before I die."

"I can help you."

"*You* help *me*? That's a joke. Days ago you stood in front of the parole committee and made it clear you think I'm shit."

I still do... "Tell me to save your daughter, and if not for that, because you found God. Isn't that what you told the parole committee? Don't you want a clear conscience before Him?" *Or Her...*

"Nah, I'm out. Guard!"

She looked over her shoulder, and the man was alerted and turning toward the door. "Lonnie will kill Natalie if you don't give up the location of the gold."

The door handle turned.

Darrell shook his head. "Lonnie doesn't even have Natalie. This is all some ruse to get me to confess to a crime I didn't commit, so you can ensure I rot in here. Well, I'm not in the accommodating mood."

"I can make you a deal," she rushed out. She had wanted to reserve this as a last resort, but she was pinned against the wall.

"Really?"

The guard was in the room, looking between Sandra and Patton. "You finished in here, Patton?"

Patton held up his hand. "I'm listening," he told Sandra.

"Just tell me where the gold is, and I'll give you immunity regarding the bank robbery."

Patton studied her eyes. "Nah, I don't believe you."

"I can have it put in writing before you tell me. Think of your daughter."

"I'm quite sure we both know it's not my daughter that he has. You're trying to manipulate me, but I'd suggest you plan a funeral for whoever Lonnie does have. The guy has always had a short fuse."

"I know. He killed Dennis." She threw that out to shock him, jolt him to reality.

"He... *He* killed Dennis?" The question scraped from his throat, and the impact of this news played over his facial features.

"Shot him in the head."

"Nah, I can't accept that." Patton looked at the guard, who started to release him from his restraints that bound him to the table and floor.

As Patton shuffled from the room with the guard, she remained frozen in her chair, numb. He'd already taken her brother from her, and now the same man just may claim her daughter. All because she'd messed up. She'd let emotion interfere. She smacked her palms against the table and roared at the empty walls.

THIRTY-EIGHT

Sandra must have been a fool to think Darrell Patton would take her word for it. But that, she realized, was her error right there. She hadn't convinced herself. Her compromised emotions screwed everything up, but there was no time to sit around wallowing.

She stormed down the halls of the penitentiary and reclaimed her gun before heading out into the night. The air was cold and bit her nose, ears, and cheeks, but she did nothing to make herself more comfortable. She didn't deserve comfort. She walked slowly to her vehicle and calculated a way out of the mess she'd created. If only there was some way of making Patton believe that Jennings had Natalie... Then it hit.

She called Lakisha through the Bluetooth system in the G-wagon, but it rang through to voicemail. She might not be working tonight. She hung up and called back, going through the back door of the phone system for the Science and Technology Branch and reached Special Agent Simon Pratt.

"It's Special Agent Sandra Vos from the Washington Field Office. Is Lakisha in tonight?"

"No, but she'll be back in tomorrow morning at seven. I heard about Olivia, by the way. I'm so sorry."

"Thanks." She let his concern wash over her, though she wasn't about to get bogged down by more emotion right now. It had already screwed her over enough. "Can you do a deep-fake?" She'd heard about these in the media and other channels, distasting the technology on impulse for its power to destroy people's lives if used for ill purposes.

"Child's play. Well, once I have footage and images to work from. Why? What are you after exactly?"

"I need to convince Darrell Patton that Lonnie Jennings has kidnapped his daughter, Natalie." She filled in the details for him.

"All right. I see where you're going. If you can convince Patton that Natalie Roth is the one being held hostage for these gold bars, her father will tell you where he hid them?"

"That's the hope. Sadly, he wasn't taking my word for it." She'd leave out the part where she'd been completely to blame for that. She was as see-through as sheer curtains thanks to her emotions getting the best of her. She wouldn't have believed her either. "How long would it take you to get this together?"

"Guess it depends on how long it takes to get the base images. Also if you want anything to be said, I'd need voice samples to pull from or a direct recording. And obviously I'd need clearance to do something like this."

"And would you get those images from online or need them supplied to you?"

"Everyone lives on social media these days. I'm sure the same goes for Natalie Roth." Simon clicked on his keyboard and said a few seconds later, "Yep, she has several accounts and a lot of selfies."

"Which you can use, and I don't know, combine with a green screen to make it look like she's in captivity?"

"Something like that."

"And how long will that take?"

"An hour or two. But since we're doing this for official reasons, the Bureau will need the subject's approval."

"I'll call Assistant Director Rowe and have him connect with your boss."

"Sounds good. I'll wait to hear."

"Thank you."

"Don't mention it. Whatever I can do to help a fellow agent."

Sandra cut off from him and called Elwood's cell phone. He answered before the second ring.

"Is it done?"

"I appreciate your faith in my abilities but not even close. Patton refuses to talk. He doesn't believe that Jennings took his daughter." There was no point bringing up her role in that.

"He's willing to take that chance? Guy's got thick skin. Did you offer him immunity for the robbery?" Elwood's voice was full of concern.

"I did, but he's not biting. He's refusing to admit to the robbery, and I can't say that I blame him. We don't have solid proof. Just the word of Jennings."

"Though clearly he wouldn't have taken Olivia if Patton didn't have the location of the gold."

"I know. It's a circle. But I've thought of something that will help convince Patton that Natalie's life is in danger." She told him about her idea and her chat with Simon Pratt.

"I've heard about criminals using deepfakes, but it's unusual for the good guys to use it."

"Unusual maybe, but if it helps us convince Patton to tell us the location of the gold, it's a win."

"I never said no." There was a second's hesitation on Elwood's end of the line. "It's just if we go down this road, it will be hard to get the robbery charges to stick. Any good defense attorney would knock it out as entrapment for Patton to confess to the crime."

"The way I see it we were offering immunity anyway," she volleyed back.

Elwood was silent.

"We're talking about saving a life." *Olivia's...* But she resisted the urge to say her name. Withholding it would serve Sandra's purpose by proving she was retaining objectivity.

He still didn't respond. Her training would have her letting the silence extend, but she couldn't.

"Why are you hesitating? What's the problem?" she pushed out.

"It's not typically how things are done. But if you talk with Patton's daughter and she agrees to this deceit, then I'll approve it. Fair?"

She shouldn't have expected him to say anything different. Even Simon had given her a heads-up in this regard. "I'll call her right now."

"No. You will get a hotel room and some rest."

She bristled. She had a go-bag in her trunk with a change of clothes and toiletries, but she didn't have her own car. "I'm just supposed to let this hang until morning? Meanwhile Olivia's out there with that lunatic."

There were a few beats of silence. "I feel for your situation, Agent Vos, but I remind you that I'm your boss. I'll excuse the outburst because I appreciate that the situation, coupled with exhaustion, is playing on your nerves and emotions. I will get an agent over to speak with Natalie Roth."

"When?"

"As soon as possible."

"Time's running out. I'll call her, get approval over the phone, and Special Agent Pratt can get to work on the video."

"I realize I can't physically stop you from calling her, but again—"

"I know you're my boss, but Olivia's my daughter." She threw that out, and it landed with a thud.

"Fine, go ahead and try calling, but I'll still need her consent in writing."

"But a verbal one should be enough so we can get the ball rolling."

"Now I know you're exhausted. Writing upfront. That's how the Bureau works."

"Protects its ass at all times. Check."

Elwood didn't respond to that, but she took that as a small mercy.

"If that's all, Agent Vos, I wish you a good night. Try to get some sleep." With that he hung up, and her chest pinched. What the hell was that supposed to be? Tough love? And where had things been left? Was he still getting an agent over to talk to Natalie Roth?

THIRTY-NINE

Sandra checked into a motel near the prison, taking Elwood's direction. She really was too wiped out to drive back to Washington. The choices weren't great in this area, but her body and mind were begging for rest. The place was seedy, and her room smelled strongly of cleaning chemicals and a fragrant floral spray. All of it was likely an attempt to override other unpleasant odors.

She'd tried reaching Natalie Roth several times without success and had finally given in and told Elwood. He said he'd dispatched an agent to the Roth residence, and no one was home, but he'd send another agent back in the morning. It was only after that she started to munch on a cheeseburger she'd picked up and brought to the hotel, but the patty had gone cold. Most of it wound up in the trash. Probably for the best as what she had eaten churned in her stomach.

The bed was firm, like lying on a board. She didn't expect sleep to come easily, but if she could just rest her eyes for a bit it might help. Instead, she found herself staring at the cracked ceiling. There had been a leak at some point given the discoloration in the corner near the door. Maybe there still was.

There was no way she was even going to rest. Not without any give to the mattress. Yet, she remained stretched out as she returned Eric's call. He'd left a voicemail when she was in with Patton.

"There you are," he said when he answered. "How did it go with Patton?"

"Don't even ask." She massaged her left temple. Her eyes were achy from exhaustion.

"Not well, then."

"Not at all." She told him that she was working to make a deepfake happen to convince Patton that Jennings had Natalie.

"It could work."

"It had better work. Listen, I'm completely wiped out. I just wanted to return your call, give you an update."

"I had a message for you too. It's why I called, otherwise I wouldn't have bothered you tonight."

"Right. You said you wanted to talk." She must be more tired than she realized. She was losing the ability to think clearly, and her memory was shit.

"The medical examiner took a closer look at Eaton. The round was a nine mil and fired at a range of between five and ten feet. There's probably nothing much left of it that would provide us with lands and grooves."

Also known as rifling, this was caused when a bullet traveled through the gun. They were unique to each gun, but there were also markers that were generic and could narrow down gun make and model. "Well, the picture's still a scary one. Jennings has Olivia, and now we have proof he's armed. What about Eaton's phone? Did that get us anywhere?"

"No. I was just going to get to that. Considering the urgency of the situation, everything was rushed through, but the short of it is the last location for his phone showed in Brentwood on Friday at seven AM."

"So much for that leading us to where Jennings is holding Olivia."

"All isn't necessarily lost though. There was some tar on the bottom of Dennis's shoes. But not any regular tar. Wood tar. It's used as a water repellant for boats."

"Dennis works at a boat factory, though, so I'm not sure how that helps us."

"I thought you might say that so I had a talk with them. There's no way Dennis came into contact with it there."

This finding piqued her interest, but she was still too tired to sit up. "Is wood tar used for anything else?"

"It can also be used in roofing construction, soaps, and in some medications for skin diseases."

"Right. So that's a lot. How can we narrow that down?"

"I'm just passing on what I've found out, Sandra."

"I know. I'm sorry. I'm just so exhausted, my eyes hurt, my back and neck hurt. Heck, even my nose hurts."

"Get some rest. Love you."

"Love you." She hung up, or believed she did.

FORTY

The fact Lonnie slept in a sleeping bag with only it between him and the concrete floor hadn't affected his rest one bit. He had the peaceful slumber of a baby with no concerns weighing him down. Though maybe he should have some reservations. Things could take a bad turn today. But if they did, he'd cut and run. Just not before killing the girl.

He got up and saw that she was staring at him from where he'd left her bound to the chair. Her sleeping arrangements were far more uncomfortable than his, and her mind would have kept her awake.

"Well, well. Good morning." He made a show of stretching out his arms overhead.

She said something behind the gag that he took as "Go to hell." That only made him smile.

"Someone's feisty. I must say that's far more entertaining than a lump resolved to their fate. Because you do know what your fate is, right?"

The girl's eyes shadowed, but she stared defiantly back at him.

Can't say she doesn't have spunk... "If your mother doesn't come through today, you're dead. Heck, I might kill you anyway, just for the fun of it. Maybe your mother too." Speaking of, he needed to get to work in case the day took an unwelcome turn. If somehow Special Agent Vos or other feds got to this warehouse, he was only wise to stand his ground. And if they were occupied scrambling to save their own or shaken by the tragedy, he'd at least be able to get away without company trailing him. He had the perfect thing in mind to cause the utmost damage with a high potential for casualties. Worst case he didn't get the gold, but he'd have some fun. Really, any way he viewed the day ahead, it held a sunny prospect for him.

Lonnie kept looking at the girl, and his gaze must have been making her uncomfortable because she wasn't holding eye contact. He heard Dennis's voice in his head about killing her, that she was just a kid. But those words didn't impact Lonnie at all. People moaned about premature death of the young as if it were some grand tragedy. He could flip that another way. Killing kids made for fewer whiny and controlling adults. And from their standpoint, should he care to consider it, the child wouldn't have to grow up to live a boring existence of slogging off to work and trying to make a living. He would be doing everyone a favor.

He took out his gun and traced the muzzle along the girl's jaw. She refused him all eye contact now, and Lonnie roared with laughter before putting his gun away again and getting to work. He didn't have any experience with what he planned to do, but the internet was a glorious fount of information.

FORTY-ONE

Sandra didn't even remember shutting her eyes when a ringing sound woke her. *What time is it? How long have I been asleep? Where am I?*

It felt like she was being ripped from another dimension. But as the ringing continued, it eventually penetrated her brain fog. It was her cell phone. *Olivia!* Had she overslept and it was noon? Was Jennings calling to tell her that Olivia was dead? She reached out to the nightstand, but her phone wasn't there.

"Shit!" She threw the covers back and flicked on the table-side light. It blinded her for a second, but she bounded from bed, searching for her phone through squinted eyes. She found it across the floor. It must have fallen there during the night.

Caller ID told her it was Elwood. Her eyes couldn't focus on the time on the top bar though. The font was too small. She sought out the alarm clock in the room. 5:03 *AM.* "Vos," she answered.

"Special Agent Little just called from the road. He got Natalie Roth out of bed, and she wasn't in a cooperative mood. Sum it up to say that she's not supportive of us deceiving her father."

"Did Little tell her that a teenage girl will die if Patton doesn't talk? And that the only way he's going to do that is if she agrees to this?"

"I'm sorry, Sandra. It didn't seem to make a difference."

"It didn't make a..." She swallowed roughly and rubbed her throat. "She's a mother herself."

"I'm sorry. We'll have to get Patton to talk another way."

Strangling it out of Patton wouldn't be effective. Dead men couldn't talk. But there might be *another way*. Her conversation with Eric last night felt like it had taken place years ago, but she remembered one finding he'd passed on that might help. "Wood tar was found on Dennis Eaton's shoes. Jennings needs to be holding Olivia somewhere isolated or remote, possibly an unused or abandoned warehouse."

"Already on it. Detective Birch contacted me at an ungodly hour, and I got an agent running a search in Washington and the outskirts. We figured that Jennings likely isn't holding Olivia too far away from the park considering where he dumped Eaton's body."

The van he took her in did go across Key Bridge, but it didn't mean he had gone far on the other side. "I'd do the same. By the way, thank you for being up so early and on this."

"No need to thank me, Sandra. I want Olivia back safely too and this scumbag behind bars. Or in a body bag."

She couldn't fault Elwood for that admission. It was impossible to feel empathy for the man who took her child. "I'm just going to freshen up and hit the road." As she said that she became aware she hadn't even changed before passing out. Then it filled in that she didn't have any toiletries or a change of clothes with her anyhow.

"See you soon. And drive safe." Elwood hung up.

While Elwood might be expecting her at the field office, she'd be making another stop first. Two, if she counted hitting a drive-thru for a coffee and a bagel to consume on the way.

. . .

Sandra raised her hand to knock a second time, not even concerned by her lack of makeup and rumpled clothing. It was nine thirty in the morning by the time she reached Natalie's door. She had two and a half hours left to get her approval, have Simon cut the deepfake, and convince Patton to talk.

The door eventually cracked open, and when Natalie saw Sandra standing there, she shook her head immediately.

"I told that agent I don't want to deceive my dad. I don't want anything to do with him. At all."

Her denial wasn't connected to any sense of loyalty toward her father. Sandra could work with that. "Can I talk to you mother to mother?"

"Ah, sure."

"And that agent told you that your father's friend is threatening to kill a teenage girl?" Not a question. Elwood told Sandra the agent had. She wanted to stress for Natalie what was at stake.

"Yeah. They want to know where he put the gold bars. But I don't know anything about it."

"It sounds like you don't want anything to do with this, but your help—"

"By which you mean deceiving my father and making him believe that I'm in danger? I do that and he talks, he's admitting to the robbery. He'll get more time. I don't have a relationship with him, but he is still my father."

"A father is someone who is by your side, Natalie."

She crossed her arms and shook her head. "No, I'm not doing it."

"If you don't do this, that girl might die." The words slipped out. A huge mistake, and Sandra rushed to backpedal. "None of this is on you. I'm sorry as I shouldn't have insinuated that."

"Please leave."

Sandra's heart was pounding. "That girl that he has... She's my daughter."

A dense energy swirled between them.

"Her name is Olivia, and she's sixteen," Sandra pressed on. "She's an A student, loves to play the violin, and volunteers at a nursing home two Saturdays every month."

Natalie's shoulders lowered slightly. Her facial expression softened. "I didn't know, and I'm sorry, but..."

"I get it. Darrell's your father. Family can be complicated, but you don't need to worry about implicating your father in the robbery. We do this video, even if he gives up the location of the gold, it would be fruit of the poisonous tree. Any DA would dismiss charges against him. It won't even get that far anyhow. The FBI is willing to cut your father a deal. He'll get full immunity."

Natalie worried her bottom lip. "You're telling me his sentence won't be increased?"

"That's exactly what I'm telling you," she repeated. "Will you authorize us to do this deepfake?"

Seconds ticked off, and Sandra felt like her heart was going to stop beating. Each inhale and exhale was painful as she waited for Natalie to respond.

"Fine, I'll help. Mother to mother." She met Sandra's eye, and Sandra could have cried, but she tamped down her emotions like she was programmed to do.

"Thank you." Sandra had her sign off her approval and left about an hour after she showed up. One point five hours remaining on the clock. Not enough time to return to the prison and show Patton the video in person. Besides, it still needed to be made. She might be cutting things too close in that regard alone.

She'd called Elwood with the news, and he was going to get the deepfake underway. She got on the road to the WFO, and her phone rang.

"Sandra, where are you? What's going on?"

It was Nolan, and she took a few breaths to steady her anger. Her ex could drain her at the best of times.

"You're back already?"

"At your desk as we speak, but you're not here."

"If you spoke to Assistant Director Elwood, you'd know I'm on my way." So what that she'd just hung up from him.

"Good. Because I have been speaking with Special Agent Sutton. I hope you have better news than Brice. You do, right? Where are you anyway? Our daughter is missing and you're not even—"

"Enough. Don't recap the situation like I'm some idiot, Nolan. I've been working on this since Friday and have hardly slept trying to get my girl back."

"*Our* girl."

She groaned and hung up. She had a low tolerance threshold for Nolan most of the time, but she did nothing to deserve being bullied this way. As if she didn't care about Olivia and was sitting on her hands. How dare he.

FORTY-TWO

Sandra was walking into the field office when a call came through from the lab. "Special Agent Vos," she answered.

"It's Renee from the lab. We finished processing that storage locker in Woodbridge, and you'll be interested to know that we found blueprints for Liberty Bank among Patton's things. They were marked up in his handwriting."

"Showing he planned the robbery."

"It sure looks that way."

"Thanks," Sandra told her. They had the proof they needed, and until they presented the deepfake to Patton, this discovery could still add years to his time in prison. Sandra hung up and placed another call as she entered the WFO. She passed Brice, and Nolan, who was sitting at her desk. She still hadn't taken time to change or put makeup on, and they did a double take at her disheveled appearance, but she kept moving with her phone to an ear. She was on hold while the prison administration put her through to the warden's cell phone.

"What are you doing? Where are you going?" Nolan asked, trailing after her. "Just stop and talk to me."

She kept moving, just as time kept chugging along.

"Sandra," he said, using a firm tone she was well familiar with and never cared for.

She looked over her shoulder but kept on her way to the conference room. "I'm not your dog. You have something to say, say it. I need to get on a video conference."

"You're right, I'm sorry."

His apology only slowed her steps.

"Who's the conference with?" Nolan asked.

"Darrell Patton. My deadline is noon. That's less than an hour from now, and if I don't have something to give Lonnie Jennings, he's going to kill our daughter. I'm not so sure he won't anyway, just for the fun of it. I'm quite sure the guy's a psychopath." She breezed into the conference room, when the other end started ringing.

"Warden Synder," he said drily. He didn't sound too pleased that she had his cell number and was cutting into his Sunday, but too bad.

"Special Agent Vos. I need to speak with Darrell Patton immediately, preferably over video."

"I'm at home, Agent Vos. Immediately is a tall request. Lots of moving parts."

Then get them moving! The thought passed through with such density, she was impressed she didn't verbalize it.

"I'd need the meeting link," he relented with a sigh.

"Should already be in your inbox." She'd taken care of that from the parking lot before heading inside the office.

"I'll make it happen. Give me ten minutes."

"Thank—" The line went dead. Only now did she face Nolan. He looked good, he always did, but there were more creases around his eyes and gray peppered the hair at his temples. "Wherever *and* whatever I'm doing is to get Olivia back." She stiffened.

"I know that and didn't mean to imply otherwise. I'm just..."

Emotionally compromised... "I know."

Nolan scooped her into his arms, and she let herself sink into the embrace. She might not always like the guy, but he was Olivia's father. If anyone could understand the hell she was going through right now, it was him. Only she'd never seen Nolan afraid of anything before. Uncomfortable, yes, and it usually emboldened him. She didn't feel that energy from him now though. It was possible he'd calmed down in recent months.

She pulled out of the hug. "Smooth flight?"

"As much as possible. Felt like a lifetime though, not just because it wasn't a straight shot."

"I bet it did."

"You're looking a little... rough. You doing all right?"

"Our daughter is with a madman, so you know the answer to that. As for my appearance, some things are more important." She set about logging on to the computer in the conference room and shutting the door. "You can stay but off camera, okay? I don't want to apply any more pressure on Patton than necessary."

"You saying I'm intimidating, Vos?"

"To some people you probably are." And she wasn't lying. Nolan was six four with a solid frame and all muscle. Part of the reason they never worked was his obsession with fitness. She was all for exercise and a healthy diet, but he had a grueling workout regimen. She sat in front of the computer, and Nolan sat across the table.

The video connected, and Patton was on screen. The warden had come through despite his protests.

"Mr. Patton," she said to signal Nolan she was connected and for him to remain quiet.

"I thought we said all there was to say last night."

"It seems I missed some things. Or namely one thing. You accused me of having no proof you were involved in the bank robbery. Well, you're wrong."

"This is just another attempt to incriminate me."

"We found the bank's blueprints among your things."

Nolan angled his head.

Through the video, Patton sat up straighter and leaned in toward the camera. "You went through my stuff?"

"We got a warrant. I assure you it was all legal and aboveboard."

"You said you'd give me immunity."

"I did, in the past tense." She was thinking with Patton not believing his daughter was in danger, concern over himself would win out.

"Well, if you put it back on the table, I'll talk."

She found it disheartening that his daughter's welfare didn't provide enough motivation. "I'm sure I can make my boss approve that."

"Is that a yes?"

"If you tell me where the gold is, and we confirm that it's where you say it is, then yes." Not that she had any idea how she was to pull all that off in time to benefit Jennings's encroaching deadline.

Nolan was punching one fist into the palm of his other hand. But violence and action were the go-to tactics in *his* negotiation toolkit. Another thing they'd never agree on. Her phone rang, and chills ran through her. "It's Lonnie," she said to Nolan and Patton. "I need to take this."

Patton made a gesture as if to say, *By all means.*

Sandra muted the video and answered Jennings's call.

"Time's up," Lonnie said. "Tell me why I shouldn't put a bullet in her head right now."

Olivia was crying in the background, and it tore at Sandra's soul. But Patton was watching. *Remember it's Natalie,* not Olivia, *Natalie...* "Because you want the gold." She could have pointed out that he was calling fifteen minutes early, but there was no advantage to stating the obvious. Jennings would have called early intentionally to shake her.

"Then you know where I can find it?"

"I'm in the process of finding out." She dared to look at Patton, who was saying something. With the sound off, she couldn't know what. She'd never been great at reading lips.

"Screw *process of*. Find out."

Olivia cried louder. "Mom!"

"Please, just one more hour. That's all I'm asking for." Silence grew on the line. She was hoping to extract understanding from a madman. He'd waited thirty-three years for the gold, so what was another hour? But was she insane to think she could trust Jennings to be reasonable?

Jennings eventually said, "I will call you back in one hour," and hung up.

"What did he say?" Nolan asked, rising from his chair, but he sat back down when she drilled him with a glare. She couldn't answer that without Patton asking who else was in the room.

"Darrell," she said after unmuting the connection, "Lonnie's going to kill Natalie if he doesn't know the location of the gold in one hour." *Natalie*, not Olivia... She had to immerse herself in the fabrication.

Darrell smiled. "I still don't buy that he has Natalie. He wouldn't do that or even know where to find her."

Where the hell was the deepfake video? But just as she thought it, her phone chimed with a message. She confirmed it was what she was after. "Here's the thing. You want proof, Darrell? Lonnie sent through a video. Here it is." She hit play, without even having a chance to vet it first, and held the screen to the camera so Patton would get a good view. She could only watch from a tight angle.

Natalie was strapped to a chair. She had a gag in her mouth, and her eyes were large and frightened. An arm moved in the frame and removed the gag. "Dad, please, do what he asks! He's going to kill me!"

Then the arm was back, and Natalie was sideswiped across the face. Natalie cried out again, and the video went black.

With the video finished, Sandra set her phone on the table. "You saw it with your own eyes. Lonnie has her, Darrell." She was doing all the mental coaching she could to remind herself that the dramatization was staged. It was so well done that she'd inserted Olivia's face there instead, and to see the restraints, the gag, the frightened eyes, the slap... It was almost too much.

"I can't believe he's doing this." Darrell's face morphed from shock to outrage. "I'm going to kill that son of a bitch!"

"As FBI, I can't condone that, but I understand why you'd feel that way. But I can bring all this to an end, save Natalie, and arrest Lonnie."

"And you swear I'll get immunity?"

"You have my word."

"Fine, I'll tell you where to find the gold."

Sandra listened as he laid out precisely where to go. It was an old fishing cabin in the middle of a wooded area in a Washington park, and she remembered seeing it before. "I sure hope you got that right because Lonnie's running out of patience."

"Trust me. It's there."

She disconnected the video chat with a promise to update Darrell. *As if.*

"We have the location. Let's go." Nolan popped up from his chair and pushed it into the table.

"All we need to do is hand this information over to Lonnie when he calls."

"You honestly trust that guy to give us our girl back on your word alone?" Nolan shook his head. "No, we need to get that gold in our hands, and then we have something to bargain with."

"You realize you are *bargaining* with our daughter's life," she flung back.

"I'm doing what I can to save her life, Sandra. Getting the gold is the smartest course of action. You must see the benefit."

She could imagine Jennings getting cold feet and wanting more than a dot on the map before releasing Olivia. Surely at some point he'd have to realize the location would be put under surveillance, and he'd be arrested if he showed his face. "I do."

"Then?"

"Well, I also see a million ways it can go sideways."

"Name one."

"He might not buy the FBI will just hand over the gold."

He shrugged. "You convince him."

As if there were nothing to it...

"Think of it this way, Jennings is a risk taker," Nolan said. "From what I've gathered, he's shown that from the start. It just shows how desperate he is."

Having Jennings's desperation pointed out wasn't soothing her nerves.

Nolan continued stating his case. He didn't realize she was already convinced. "This guy isn't going to give us Olivia back just because you tell him where the gold is. Surely even you must see that he'll want it in his hands first. I say we save him the trouble, get it, and show up with it, make the exchange. Simple and done."

That's how Nolan always saw life, an effortless flow where everything worked out. She'd like to argue that wasn't the real world, but for him, it seemed to come together that way. "Just like that?" She smiled and added, "It could work, but we only have an hour."

If Nolan was stunned by her agreement, he recovered quickly. "Then we better get to work."

"And nothing could possibly go wrong."

"I never said that, but let's not think that way." Nolan got the door for her, and they headed back to the warren of desks.

Nolan quickly started chatting to several agents, telling them they were headed out to search for gold bars.

"Agent Copeland, a word?" she said to him, drawing him into a quiet corner. "I'm not sure how it works in your unit, but here it's the boss who assigns the agents."

"I saw Assistant Director Rowe when I first got here and he said it was all hands on deck to get Olivia back, so I assumed..."

"I'll go have a talk with him." Before she left the area, she did ask Brice, "You in?"

"You couldn't stop me."

"Glad to hear you say that." She smiled at him and left to inform Elwood about the intended plan of action.

FORTY-THREE

"Maybe we rushed ahead with this. What's to say this guy didn't just send us on a wild goose chase?" Nolan vented to Sandra as they hiked down the trail toward the cabin. Brice was in tow, along with a few other agents, but they were farther behind.

"Nothing, but I don't think he did." If Nolan had seen Patton's face while he'd watched the deepfake, he'd be confident in that fact too. Patton went stark, clearly in fear for his daughter's welfare. *His* daughter's, though that wasn't exactly the truth... Poor Olivia must be so terrified. And what if they messed up by assuming they were making the smart move retrieving the gold first? "The only thing I'm second-guessing is us coming here."

"You've lost your mind then," Nolan said.

She shot him a glare. "Did you really just say that to me?"

Nolan didn't respond, and she caught Brice's eye. She read from his look that he was impressed by her restraint. "You realize that I have been here dealing with this the entire time?"

"Maybe that's why you've lost your nerve."

"*Lost my nerve?* What I do for a living involves brushing

against the wire all the time, toeing that line between working things out with words and guys like you pressuring me to move out of the way so you can rush in guns blazing. You can't put a deadline on things."

"Except for now, Sandy, there is one. You are working against the clock. And that's *not* something you're used to."

She opened her mouth, snapped it shut. He was right. Every time she turned up at an incident scene, she set her own internal clock. Time had run out for her brother, Sam. "I've asked you repeatedly not to call me Sandy."

"It won't happen again."

It would, and they both knew it. She checked the time on her phone. "Ten minutes out from that deadline you referred to. At least I'll have the location when Jennings calls."

"True, but we're here now, so let's find that gold," Nolan said.

He was beating a dead horse. They were still moving as they debated, getting closer to that cabin. She would be lying to say she didn't hate they weren't diversifying more, but where else could they concentrate their efforts? When she had her chat with Elwood, he'd informed her the warehouse search came back empty.

They crossed through a thick copse of trees and followed a worn path through some long grass. "We're almost there now," she said. "If I remember right, the cabin isn't much farther ahead."

They kept walking, but there was no sign of the cabin.

"Maybe you remembered wrong," Nolan said.

She shook her head. "It should be right around here. Not just from my memory of seeing it before but from Patton's description. Let's spread out and see if we can spot it."

"It's a cabin, Sandra," Nolan said. "If it was here, we should see it already."

"I'm telling you that Patton didn't lie to us," she said.

"He hid it thirty-three years ago. His memory could be a bit rusty," Brice put in.

Both Sandra and Nolan turned to him. Neither spoke. Sandra because she was afraid to admit there might be truth in that. There was also the changing landscape which she'd mentioned when she and Brice had discussed Patton hiding the gold somewhere in nature.

Her phone rang, and all the agents in the area stopped moving and looked at her.

She took out her phone and saw the blocked number. "It's him," she said. "Answering now." She wanted everyone to remain quiet while she spoke with Jennings.

"I have what you need." She pulled from her experience and exuded a confidence she wasn't feeling. There was no sign of the gold, but she'd have to sell the location anyhow.

"Well, I've been giving the matter more thought, and I've changed my mind. I don't just want the location. I want the gold."

Now that she couldn't find it, he wanted her to hand it over? "But—"

"Now, now, Special Agent Vos. Remember who holds the power."

"I got you the location. That's what you asked for." Her body was trembling, but thankfully she was doing well at keeping her nerves from hitting her voice.

"Good, then it shouldn't be too hard for you to get the gold and bring it to me."

"You tell me where and when, I'll be there." She squeezed out the cautionary advice in crisis negotiation. Talks in person statistically resulted in fatalities. Even more probable when she turned up empty-handed.

Nolan stepped beside her and touched her shoulder. She looked over at him, and he nodded. She shrugged him off. She didn't need his approval for the calls she was making.

"Georgetown Waterfront Park near the labyrinth. I assume you know the way."

A sick jab to remind her of Eaton's murder, that he was a killer. "What time?"

"One hour."

"One hour?" An arranged meet could be orchestrated with agents put in place but that took time. As did coming up with nine gold bars.

"What's the problem, Vos? You know where the gold is. It's just a matter of collecting it and meeting me."

It didn't take long to scramble for a reason he should be able to understand. "I need to get to the spot and then to the park. Traffic alone—"

"Fine. Enough whining. Two hours. That's it. Come unarmed. No police. No feds. I sniff one, and I'll put a bullet in the girl's head. I promise you that."

"Just bring Olivia. That's the deal. An exchange. Her for the gold."

Jennings didn't respond with words and hung up.

She cradled her phone in her hands.

"What does he want now?" Nolan prompted.

"He wants the gold." She wasn't about to bolster Nolan's ego and add it was just as he had suspected. "We have less than two hours. Let's find it!" She called out the latter part to the team of agents. Everyone spread out but Nolan and Brice.

"There's more you haven't told us," Brice said.

"I need to meet him at the Georgetown Waterfront Park labyrinth in two hours. With the gold."

"We haven't even found it yet. It might not even be here." Nolan drew in close to her, his words ringing with panic.

"And if it's not we deal with that then," she pushed back.

"I can go get things organized." Brice started to move, but Sandra caught his arm on a back swing.

"No. He said no cops or feds, or he'll kill Olivia." She

couldn't bring herself to verbalize the method. Too graphic, violent, *real...*

"Come on, Sandra, we can't agree to that," Nolan said.

"He's right," Brice chimed in, backing up Nolan for the first time.

She just imagined it going sideways and Olivia being shot. If that happened, how was Sandra supposed to carry on? There was no way she could withstand that burden for the rest of her life.

"You know we're right," Nolan softly petitioned. "I see the risk, but we know what we're doing. Agents will pose as civilians and the situation will be handled with the utmost discretion, so he doesn't get spooked."

He and Brice looked at her. "Fine," she eventually said.

"I'll get things rolling," Brice said.

"Go straight to Rowe, and let's start thinking about a backup plan if we don't find the gold." She stood where she remembered the cabin being. Her heart was hammering in her chest. It wasn't lost on her that she should be staring right at the building but wasn't. Had she somehow gotten turned around? She scouted the area and was grateful that Nolan branched out in the opposite direction. She could use some breathing room from him.

She heard Brice talking on the phone, and it sounded like things were moving along.

Where is that cabin? She stood still, hands on hips. She looked up at the sky through the bare branches of the trees. She wasn't religious, but she believed in a greater being and wasn't all that convinced He or She was interested in what happened down here. Otherwise why not step in? But now wasn't the time for spiritual thinking.

She took a few deep breaths and resumed the search. She rounded a clump of bushes that were still boasting green leaves.

Unusual, but she wasn't a green thumb to know how this plant should present this time of year. She looked closer and noticed milled stone and a piece of wood beam around the base. *No, it can't be!* But she hunched down, and there were more remnants beneath the bushes. She'd found what was left of the fishing cabin.

Her stomach sank, and she gripped her chest. *This can't be!*

Brice rushed over. He must have finished his call and noticed her. "Sandra? You okay?"

"There's the cabin." She pointed toward the remains. "What's left of it anyway."

"No way. You must be—"

She was shaking her head. "It's gone. The city must have ordered it to be demolished. I haven't been to this part of the park for years or I might have known."

Brice put a reassuring hand on her shoulder. "None of this is on you."

She turned to him. "What am I going to do?"

"What are *we* going to do, you mean? You've got the whole WFO behind you, and him." He jacked a thumb toward Nolan, who was with the small group of agents, all of them appearing oblivious to the truth of their predicament.

She smiled at her colleague.

"And off the record, for what it's worth, I like the new guy better."

"Me too." But there was a time she was wild about Nolan. In fact, head over heels if her pride would let her admit it.

"Hey, guys, call it off!" Brice yelled to the agents. "We found the cabin."

The agents swarmed toward them with Nolan in the lead.

"Either my eyesight is gone or..." Nolan said, looking around.

"It's been torn down, and the gold is gone along with it," she told everyone. "This is all there is." She kicked her toe against the piece of stone and wood.

"Son of a—" Nolan raked a hand through his hair. "You've got that meeting with that shithead in two hours. We need the gold."

She bit the urge to counter with something smart like *Thank you, Captain Obvious.* "We'll figure something out. We make some fake gold, make sure it looks and weighs just as much as the real thing. If anyone knows how to pull this off, please, I'm open to suggestions." She looked at the agents clustered around her. Nolan was quiet and appeared deep in thought. It was a surefire sign he was troubled. Otherwise he was always quick with something to say, whether it be sharp, cutting, or intelligent. He had his moments.

"We get tungsten steel and gold-plate it," Agent Gabe Radcliffe said. "It looks and weighs like the real thing."

"Let's make it happen," she said. "We need nine bars weighing twenty-seven-point-four pounds apiece."

Gabe nodded. "We'll also need to find out how those gold bars were hallmarked and their serial numbers. Every real gold bar needs both by law."

"I can find out," Brice said and got on the phone.

"I'll get started too," Gabe said.

"Thank you. Remember, I need it fast. Within the hour," she added.

"I'll make it happen." Gabe left with his phone to his ear.

The rest of the agents filtered out too, and she was left with a quiet Nolan. "It's a lot to take in, isn't it?"

"I just want our girl back safe. That's all." He met her gaze, and it was moments like this that had her trying to make their relationship work all those years ago. He could be kind and gentle. Too bad it was often smothered by his overbearing personality and ramrod mentality.

"I know. So do I." She stood there with Nolan for a few more minutes. Any composure she might have projected was a lie. Inside, she was freaking out. They didn't have the gold to give Jennings, and there were a million ways the exchange could go wrong.

FORTY-FOUR

Before setting out for the park, Sandra was back in the WFO. Nolan was researching the history of the fishing cabin, while she was getting prepared for the meet. She tucked a bug in with the underwire of one cup of her bra and a tracker in the other, in case things veered sideways. Then she got dressed in fresh clothes. She also powdered on some makeup and headed to her desk.

Nolan looked up at her. "Got some info on the cabin. Its demolition was ordered three years ago, and the contract to do so was awarded to GetRGone."

"Someone on that crew netted a good payday," she said.

"If the gold was there in the first place."

"Patton's my least favorite person, or at least one of." Jennings was vying for top of the list. "But let's give him the benefit of the doubt."

"That's a first. That never worked for me."

She wasn't touching that. "Let's find out who worked on that job and have a talk with them."

"I'll take care of it. You have someplace to be." He nudged his head toward the clock that was circling way too fast.

There were only forty-one minutes left before the meet. She still needed to get in place and confirm where everything stood.

"You're right. But don't let that go to your head," she quickly added with a smile. "I just need to confirm that Radcliffe has my 'gold.'" She was going to call him when he walked toward her desk.

"The nine bars are ready, totaling two hundred and forty-seven-point-six pounds. It's all fake, but we want the weight to feel real."

"And you checked with Agent Sutton on the hallmarks and serial numbers?" Nolan asked Gabe.

"Done and done."

"Where is the gold?" she asked.

"Ready to be loaded into a vehicle. Just point me to which one."

"That would be into mine," she told him. She turned to Nolan. "I'll leave the tracking down of the real gold to you?"

"As I said."

"Though, I could use some help loading it." Gabe looked at Nolan.

"Of course."

She put on a thick bulletproof vest, then her coat over that, and the three of them set out for her Mercedes in the lot. The two men picked up a wooden crate with rope handles on the way.

"Nice wheels," Gabe said at the sight of her Mercedes.

"Thanks. I like it." She kicked her foot under the rear bumper, and the trunk opened.

"Handy feature," Gabe said. "I've got that in my Hyundai too."

Gabe and Nolan lifted the crate into the back, and she closed the lid. The fact this box of fake gold was meant to pay for Olivia's life washed over her. What if she messed up and her girl paid the price for her incompetence? Her legs buckled, and Nolan rushed to help her remain upright.

"You've got this," he whispered in her ear.

That's all she needed. One expression of belief. She stood tall and nodded. "I'm off."

"Good luck," Gabe said, and the sentiment made her cringe. Probably for its accuracy. So much of what the future held was hinged on happenstance. When she worked a crisis incident, she had a roadmap to follow. Even when there were detours that were specific to that situation, she could find her way back. Where she was about to go was unexplored territory for her.

"Thank you." She got behind the wheel and drove out of the lot afraid of looking back. But her gaze traveled there anyhow, and she caught a glimpse of Nolan. It was candid and clear that he was just as scared as she was.

The afternoon was cool but sunny with not a cloud in the sky. It would have been a pleasant day if not for what lay ahead of her. Sandra would either get her daughter back alive or seal her fate.

She parked near Georgetown Waterfront Park and got out of the car. There was no sign of the black GMC van, but Jennings could have parked in an underground garage.

She had ten minutes until the meet, and every step she took toward the labyrinth was leaden. She spied the agents posed throughout the park as joggers and walkers. There were one or two pushing baby strollers. Civilians would have been cleared from the vicinity in a discreet manner when the meet was first arranged. While she knew the only people left were agents, hopefully Jennings would be fooled.

She was also aware that snipers were set up, but she didn't know where they were positioned. They'd be perched in their nests watching her through their optics right this minute. They were bound by FBI shooting protocol, which mandated a weapon was only to be fired when there was immediate risk to life or of or extreme bodily injury. Regardless, their presence still made her nervous, but Elwood insisted they be there. "Nonnegotiable," he had said.

She reached the center of the labyrinth, conscious of the fact a man's body had just been found there yesterday morning. Placed there by the man who had her daughter and who she was about to meet, no less.

A cool breeze whirled around her and had her tucking farther into the neck of her coat. There was something about being where death had been that brought with it a tangible sensation. It also clung energetically, as if the soul of the departed lingered, trying to make sense of their death.

Even with a vest, a wire, a tracker, and surrounded by agents, she felt vulnerable. While she waited for the minutes to pass, her head was on a swivel. She felt exposed enough without giving up her back to a gun or knife. No sign of Lonnie Jennings yet.

She kept looking around. After a bit of time passed, she received a phone call from Jennings.

"Look to the right of the labyrinth, to the cluster of bushes," he told her.

She turned and saw him. "I see you."

"Come over here." He hung up, and she walked over.

There was no sign of Olivia, and it curdled in her gut. She answered, "This was to be an exchange. Where is Olivia?"

"Where's the gold?"

She squared her posture. "It's in my car. I'll take you to it once I see Olivia." *Get proof of life...*

He reached into his jacket pocket, and she instinctively backed up.

Instead of pulling a gun, he took out a cell phone. "Say 'hi' to Mommy." He spoke to it and turned the screen toward her.

It was a live feed, and it showed Olivia tied to a chair. Her long hair was matted to her face from sweat and... *Blood?* Rage ran through her.

"Mom," Olivia cried out. "Help me. Please."

"Olivia, Mommy's coming for you, baby. I love you."

"I love—"

Jennings cut the feed and snatched his phone back to himself. "Reunion's over. Where's the gold?"

She was analyzing what she saw around Olivia. She'd guess an abandoned warehouse, wood trusses overhead. "You didn't bring her here. The deal was Olivia for the gold." She peacocked her stance despite how seeing Olivia had thrown her. Jennings's tactic to shake her had worked, but it also back-fired. Witnessing Olivia's dilemma fueled her with more deter-mination to see this through. This bastard in front of her was on borrowed time.

"Things change. You should know that by now. You hand over the gold, and I'll tell you where to collect her."

"I have no reason to believe a word you say," she spat, temporarily losing her cool.

Jennings pulled a gun, just enough that she saw his hand on the grip. She was unarmed, part of the deal. "Take me to the gold. Now." He prompted her to move with a nudge of the gun, with it still hidden in his pocket.

She started walking, not too thrilled about putting her back to him, but she didn't have much choice. She took him to her Mercedes and popped the hatch. "It's all there. We found it right where Darrell said it would be."

Jennings hesitated. Just briefly. But telling. Something was wrong.

"I told you to come alone," he hissed.

"I did. I swear I did."

"You just said *we* found the gold."

"I had help finding it, but I'm here alone." Served in a level and calm tone.

He scanned her eyes and shook his head. "You're lying to me, Special Agent Vos. Now it's not just your daughter's life at risk."

She imagined him taking the gun from his pocket and shooting her right there and making off with her Mercedes and the gold. Thinking about her life coming to an end didn't scare her. Failing Olivia did. "Please, don't be rash. Just take the gold. It's right there." She pointed at it and heard the pleading in her voice.

"Nah. Get in the car."

"What?"

"Get in the car," he hissed.

She headed for the driver's seat, catching the eye of an agent walking by with a stroller. Sandra subtly shook her head.

Jennings slammed the back shut and joined her in the vehicle. "Give me your phone."

She couldn't lie and say she didn't have one when he'd just called her on it not long ago. She handed over her phone, and he tossed it out the door.

"Now drive," he barked.

"Where do you want me to go?" She didn't know the destination he had in mind but was also stalling for time.

"Why are you being difficult? Just drive." He had his gun out now and was waving it around in the confines of the vehicle.

"Okay." She turned on the car and put it in reverse but didn't move.

"Drive!" Jennings shouted.

She pulled out of the spot and drove in the direction Jennings told her.

"Keep driving." He punched his back into the seat but kept the gun on her. "Go west on Route 29."

She did as he told her and put Washington in her rearview mirror. She looked for any agents who might be following, but if they were, they were doing a good job of keeping a low profile.

But Jennings had her taking a lot of turns, and he kept looking behind them too. Once she hit a more rural section, Jennings requested that she pull over.

"Why?" One more glance at the rearview. No one was there. The road was barren.

"I said, pull over."

"Right here? Where are we anyway, getting close to Gainesville, Virginia?" She was talking more for whoever was listening in on her wire. But if backup didn't show soon, this could be where she died. At the side of the road, her body tossed into the ditch. She pulled over, the gravel of the shoulder crunching beneath her wheels.

"Just get out of the car."

"Why? We have open road."

"Do it!" he screamed, and his voice battered her ears.

"I'm getting out." She undid her belt and opened her door.

He got out too and was around to her in a flash. He grabbed her arm and was nudging her onto the edge of the road.

Just before he got a hold on her, she spotted a metal nail file in the cubbyhole of the door. She snatched it before closing the door behind her. It wasn't a gun, but it could be used as a weapon, nonetheless.

"Strip," he told her.

"What? No." She was quaking. If she took off her shirt, there was the risk he'd find her wire and tracker. Then she'd be dead. "We can talk about this. You wanted the gold, Lonnie. I got you the gold."

"Just shut up! Coat, vest, and shirt off now!"

"It's nearly zero degrees out here. You don't need to be this person."

Jennings laughed. "I killed my friend, lady, I don't care if you get cold." He waved the gun in her face. "Take it off."

It was consent or fight for her life. Surely, if he found either device, he'd kill her. And all because she fucking messed up by saying *we* found the gold. She brandished the nail file and lurched forward. Her desire was to injure him and assume control of the gun.

But he jerked out of reach and pulled the trigger.

She dropped down. The report was deafening, and the round barely missed her. It was a miracle it had.

"What the hell do you think you're doing?" Jennings grabbed her arm with the file and squeezed her wrist until her hand released it and it dropped to the ground.

She cried out as her vision flashed white.

"Now, take off your damn shirt!" He thrust the gun toward her, adding emphasis to his verbal threat.

She held up her hand in surrender and started to stand. She considered attacking him again, but common sense filtered in. If she did and failed, he wasn't bound to miss a second time, and where would that leave Olivia? No, it was best she played along for a while longer.

"Fine. I'm taking it off now." She shucked out of her coat and let it fall to the ground. Then her bulletproof vest.

"Hurry up."

Next, she unbuttoned her long-sleeved shirt, revealing her bra.

"Off with it too."

She unhooked it from the back, slid out of the straps, and grabbed it down one of the sleeves.

"Hand it to me."

She did, not even caring that she was standing there half-naked at the side of the road. She didn't even feel the cold. She was more concerned that he'd find what she'd tucked into the underwire of both cups.

He licked his lips as he stared at her exposed breasts. Under his watch, she felt chilled, but she retained a strong stance. She wasn't going to let this creep play mind games on her. And if he had other ideas, he'd better pray to God because he'd need divine help if he decided to act on his base impulses. "Wait, what the hell is this?" He plucked out the small listening device. "You didn't think I'd find this? That means that your little fed buddies are listening in right now. Are they going to hear you die? I'm not a fan of a live audience."

"That's up to you." There was no point in denying that they'd be listening in. "You're in charge."

Jennings roared and threw the bug to the ground and smashed it under his boot, twisting his heel for good measure.

She remained quiet, clinging to silence as her ally.

"I should kill you, but get dressed. Let's move." He threw her bra at her, and she jammed it into a pants pocket, and scrambled to do up the buttons on her shirt. She bent for the vest, but he stood on it. "That stays."

She zipped up her coat and got behind the wheel of her car. No agents were within sight, but she shouldn't be alone for long. The tracker was still in the bra, which was on her person. But would help come before it was too late?

FORTY-FIVE

Even though Sandra had prepared for the possibility of being abducted, being in that predicament was surreal. Jennings had her drive to the rural outskirts of Gainesville, Virginia, and pull into the mouth of a rundown industrial building, which was blocked by a chain-link gate. Olivia was likely inside. *I'm coming, baby!*

"Don't think of trying to pull anything," Jennings told her as he got out. He freed the padlock and chain, opened the gate, and waved her through.

The thought ran through her mind to hit him with her car, but what if Olivia wasn't here? Instead she compliantly drove in and parked where he directed her to. He closed the gate behind them and walked over to the driver's side door and ushered her out.

She looked around, understanding why he'd chosen this place. It was isolated with the closest neighbor a couple of miles down the road. She wasn't sure how he knew about it or what connection he might have to it though. If this was where Dennis Eaton's shoes had picked up the wood tar, this place wouldn't have come up in any search that was done anyway. They'd looked closer to Washington. This was a fifty-minute drive away.

"Let's go." He had his gun out and was rushing her toward a door in the rear of the warehouse. There was a padlock on the outside of it that Jennings unlocked.

"Inside." Jennings pushed her, and she stumbled over the raised threshold but was quick to catch her balance.

It was a large open space with wooden trusses overhead. *Like where Olivia was bound to a chair.* She only had the chance to think that when she heard her daughter screaming.

Sandra ran in the direction of the noise. "Olivia?" she said.

"Mom!"

She rounded a corner and spotted her daughter. Olivia was tied to a chair with zip ties. Dried blood was on her face, and Sandra's stomach sank. It felt overwhelming witnessing Olivia's distress in person. "Oh, sweetheart."

"Not so fast." Jennings yanked Sandra backward and shoved her hard. The action caught her off guard, and she fell to the floor.

Sandra watched in horror as Jennings walked to her daughter, his gun out. He grabbed a fistful of her hair and put the muzzle to her head. "I did make it very clear, did I not? No cops or feds. But that park was crawling with them! And don't even think about lying to me."

She held up her hands in surrender. "Fine. You're right, and I'm sorry. But please believe me when I tell you that wasn't my doing."

"Ah, but you let it happen even though I told you what I'd do to her." He pushed his gun harder against Olivia's head, and she cried out.

All her training coalesced, trying to help her, but her poor, sweet, innocent Olivia was just feet away from her. Sandra scrambled to her feet.

"Stay right there. Or *boom!*"

Sandra stopped moving, dared not to even breathe. She couldn't pry her eyes from her daughter's. They were so full of fear. "You're right," Sandra rushed out. "I'm sorry. But, please, we can work this out. Take your gold, even my car, just let us live."

"Nah, I feel more like killing both of you. I've played fair. I've been more than patient."

"Lonnie Jennings, this is Brice with the FBI. Let's talk." His voice traveled over a bullhorn. "We all want this to end peacefully, and you want your gold, right? Special Agent Vos can give you my number. Call me, and let's figure this out together."

"What the hell?" Jennings crept next to a window and looked outside. He jumped back from the glass like he'd been burned. "Shit, they're everywhere. What did you do? How are they here so fast? It takes time to track a GPS in a car."

She was tempted to pluck the tracker out of her bra and stick it in his face, but that could be the last decision she made. No one took well to being made to feel like an idiot.

"Shit, shit, shit!" He started pacing and tugging at his hair.

Knowing there was an FBI response helped her envision a happy ending easier than a moment ago, but Jennings's mental state was far from ideal. She needed to work on setting him at ease. "You didn't want all this to happen. You just wanted the gold you worked so hard to get your hands on. Things have just gotten out of control." Sandra passed a quick glance at Olivia, so minuscule that Jennings could have missed it. A tear snaked down her daughter's cheek, and it nearly toppled Sandra.

Jennings leveled a nasty stare at her. "Which they'll have now," he spat. "They're all over your Mercedes back there. Fuck, I should have had us bring the crate inside. Son of a bitch!" He punched the wall and howled.

"It's not too late, Lonnie." She continued talking to him in a docile manner. If she could get him to calm down, she might be able to turn things around.

"It clearly is!"

"It's not over until it's over. The people out there want this to come to a peaceful resolution too. No one needs to get hurt. That call is up to you."

"No, it's over."

"It's not," she said firmly.

Jennings stomped back over to Olivia and put the gun to her head again.

The mother in her screamed.

Time stood still.

The negotiator in her came to life. "You kill her, there will be nothing stopping those people from coming in here and killing you. *Nothing*. That's not what *you* want." It was very clear that Jennings was more narcissistic than suicidal. "You want your gold. I can help you get it."

Seconds ticked off. One by painful one.

Jennings eventually said, "What do you propose?"

"The way this works is there must be a back and forth, give and take. You do something, you get something. It's how everyone walks away happy. I'm sure I can get you half of the gold—"

"Half?"

"Actually more than half, five bars, if you give up *half* of your hostages." She flicked a look to Olivia, and her stomach clenched. She couldn't think about what might happen when Jennings discovered the gold was fake.

"Her? No, I can't do that. I won't. And what good is some of the gold?"

"It's worth a lot, Lonnie. Now, I'm not outside, but I know from many incidents I've worked, some like this one, there's always guys with guns who want to rush in and put an end to things." She hoped he received the mental picture she was trying to project. A hail of bullets. A bloodbath.

Again, time slowed. Stood still.

"Fine," he said. "But any of this goes sideways, I will kill you both."

"I understand. Just give me your phone, and I'll let Brice know what you've agreed to."

"Okay." Jennings powered his phone, unlocked it, and handed it over to her.

She called Brice. At the sound of his voice, her heart lifted. There was hope for a happy ending. She just had to focus and do the job she was trained for. "Lonnie's ready to send out Olivia for five of the gold bars."

There was a delay to his response. No doubt he was considering how this would turn out once Jennings discovered the bars were fake. But that was her problem to worry about. "I hear you, Sandra. We'll get that together. Five minutes at the back door."

"Five minutes," she repeated. She'd normally set a timer, but she couldn't risk Jennings's phone chiming and jolting him. To Jennings, she said, "We have to get Olivia ready to leave."

"Cut the ties with this." Jennings took a pair of clippers from a pocket and handed them to her. He held his gun on them while Sandra removed the restraints binding Olivia's wrists and ankles to the chair. As soon as she was freed, Olivia popped up, arms open wide to hug her mother, but her legs crumpled before she got there. Sandra steadied her and squeezed her as hard as she could.

"That's enough." Jennings nudged Olivia's shoulder.

The girl stood taller, and Sandra caught the defiant glint in her eye. She subtly shook her head, advising her daughter to back down. She breathed easier when she saw Olivia's shoulders lower slightly.

"We need to go to the back door. That's where they'll make the exchange." She said all this to Jennings, not her daughter, and purposely spoke of her as if she wasn't there. Jennings needed to feel he had some power in this moment.

Jennings nodded and lightly pushed Olivia. "You heard your mother."

There was a knock on the door, and Jennings looked at Sandra.

"That will be them with your gold," she said.

"No way I'm getting that. You do it."

"Okay, I'm coming to the door." She spoke loudly, projecting her voice for the agent on the other side.

"I heard you," a familiar voice called back.

How does he do it? It was Nolan. She opened the door, and he was standing there with the crate. He set it at his feet.

"The girl," he said. "Then you get your gold."

Jennings's eyes trailed Nolan's huge size from his combat boots to the top of his head. "You unarmed?"

Nolan held up his hands, lifted his shirt to expose his waist. No holsters, no guns in sight.

"Go." Jennings ushered Olivia to the doorway, and she left with a quick look at her dad and Sandra.

She took a deep breath knowing that her girl was finally safe.

Jennings put his gun on Nolan. "Now bring the gold inside."

Nolan grabbed the crate and did just that. He gave one glance to Sandra, and she had a bad feeling he was up to something. It had probably occurred to everyone the risk involved of bringing in the fake gold. Nolan would be prepared to do something, and she had to be ready for whatever that was.

"Set it over there. Hurry up." Jennings was waving his gun around and slammed the door shut with a back kick.

"Did you want me to open it for you?" Nolan asked Jennings, as if he were offering to do a grand kindness for the man.

"That's not necess—"

Nolan had it opened and whacked Jennings on the head with one of the gold bars before he had a chance to react.

Jennings screamed and dropped his weapon.

Sandra swept in and grabbed the gun, and held it on Jennings. "Game over."

Jennings was writhing on the floor and bleeding from his head wound. "Is it?" He pulled something from his pocket, and by the time she got a good look at it, Jennings was telling them what it was. He flipped a switch on the device. "In case you don't know, this is a detonator. I've got this place rigged to blow, so if you don't want pieces of yourself everywhere, I suggest you listen and listen well. All I need to do is remove my finger from the button and the whole place goes, you along with it."

"You love yourself too much to kill yourself," Sandra told him.

"Quite an assumption you're making."

But surely, he was bluffing. Everything he'd done so far was with his own interests in mind, even killing his childhood friend. Also none of their background research or intel on Jennings revealed an understanding of bomb making. There was no laptop, tablet, or computer recovered from the house, but the worldwide web was accessible from any smartphone these days. It certainly made it easy to learn anything.

"I see your brain working, Agent Vos," Jennings said. "How could someone like me pull this off? The internet is a glorious thing. It helped me track down your daughter's school. She was posted in some picture wearing their branded shirt online. I just went there, waited it out, followed her. The rest, well, we're here, aren't we? The internet also taught me about mobile VPNs. Where did the trace take you, by the way?" He smirked.

She refused to satisfy him by answering. "Why are you doing this? You have your gold." She pointed at the crate. "The rest is outside. I came through for you."

"Well, now you're going to let all your buddies out there know to leave me alone or I will blow the place. It means nothing to me. I'm going to leave with all the gold in peace. Got that?"

"There's no way that's going to happen, pal. You're delusional," Nolan told him.

Sandra cringed at his approach. Always coming at people with a fight, not willing to compromise.

Jennings laughed. "The only one who is disillusioned is you."

"Agent Copeland misspoke, Lonnie. We can arrange whatever you need."

"That's more like it. You're starting to grow on me, but I'll be taking my gun back." Jennings held out his hand to her, and she put his gun in his palm. He pushed the weapon into his waistband and moved cautiously toward the crate with furtive glances over his shoulder. While he had that detonator switch in his hand, any moves would have to be strategically calculated. He picked up one of the bars. He was smiling at first, but the expression quickly faded. In a swift movement, he turned on her and wrapped his arm around her neck. Her airflow was instantly restricted, and she responded on instinct. She used combat training she'd taken and managed to duck and throw Jennings over her head. A move that was made on instinct and could have been a fatal one. Thankfully he retained a hold on the detonator switch.

Nolan came over and straddled Jennings. He pulled a gun from an ankle holster and held it on him. "You forgot a spot. Now carefully hand over that detonator to me."

Jennings's face scrunched up and next thing, he kneed Nolan in the groin. Nolan was stunned for a moment and groaned in pain. His gun was knocked out of his hand and skittered across the floor. All of this created just enough distraction for Jennings to butt Nolan off and do what he could to get to his feet.

What Jennings failed to notice was she had collected Nolan's gun. "Stop right there, or I'll shoot you and take my chances with the bomb."

Jennings turned around. He said nothing, but he pierced her gaze with his.

Had she called the situation wrong? Did he have a death wish? Before she had a chance to make an appeal, Jennings smiled and released his thumb from the button.

Nolan grabbed Sandra, and they ran for the door. She cringed expecting to hear the blast and feel the concussion, but neither came. The only sound she heard was Jennings wailing out in defeat. He should be running himself. The situation was certainly unstable. Just because the bomb hadn't gone off yet, didn't mean it wasn't going to.

She found everyone was on scene as Jennings had told her, including an ambulance where Olivia was being seen by a paramedic, but they were positioned far off from the building. Same too for everyone else. Fire rescue was also on scene. Sandra looked at Nolan.

He shrugged. "I have a wire tucked into the laces of my boot," he said to explain why everyone was bracing for an explosion.

"Good, but everyone needs to continue to stay back. We need to talk Jennings out."

"Everyone knows their jobs, Sandra."

She'd have to trust they did because she needed to get to Olivia. She ran to her with Nolan not far behind.

"I can't believe you're here, Dad. Aren't you supposed be in Turkey?"

"My girl needed me."

Sandra would let him have this one. He did come through in the end. Maybe he wasn't all bad, just better handled in small doses. They took turns hugging Olivia, and when Sandra had her back in her arms, she didn't want to let go. Ever.

"Lonnie Jennings, this is the FBI. Come out with your hands laced behind your head," Brice called out over a loud-speaker.

In response, a blast rocked the ground. The warehouse became an inferno, and debris hurled from the structure and rained down.

EPILOGUE
THE FOLLOWING SATURDAY

Sandra's doorbell rang, and she excused herself from the rest of her guests to answer. She found Eric already in the entry and hanging up his leather jacket. He was wearing a collared shirt, pleated pants, and dress shoes. He smelled as amazing as he looked. She smiled at him. "You have a key. Why do you insist on ringing the bell?"

"We've been through this. To respect your privacy, but I also like to keep you guessing. It's good for a relationship."

"I could handle fewer surprises, if it's all the same to you." She laughed, and she pulled him farther into the home and greeted him properly with a hug and a deep kiss.

"Well, then," he said, licking his lips. "Happy to see you too. You look beautiful as always."

"Thank you." She did a little dip, the amount her cranberry body-hugging cocktail dress would allow.

"And it sounds like everyone else beat me here."

There was a lot of chatter making its way to the door. "That they did."

Olivia came into the foyer and hugged Eric. Sandra swept a strand of her hair back as she did. She'd taken the week off work, wanting to spend every possible moment with her girl. She had her seeing a therapist already to help her process what she'd been through. Thankfully, aside from a few slaps, Jennings hadn't physically hurt her. He'd even fed her and gave her water. Her injuries were mental and emotional, which would take far longer to heal.

The timer on her oven buzzed.

"I better get that, or we'll be eating delivery pizza." Sandra went into the kitchen to take the roast beef out. Everything else was ready to go and set in serving dishes in the warmer oven.

"Pizza's fine by me, Mom," Olivia called out to her.

Leave it to her daughter to overhear *pizza*... "Two times this past week is enough." Sandra was laughing as she took out the meat and set about getting everything ready to cart to the dining table.

"Anything I could do?"

She looked up to see Nolan in the doorway. She resisted saying something sassy like her heart was tested enough this week and his offer to help might be the shock that sent her to the hospital. "Sure. Thank you." She directed him to what needed to be taken out and where to place it.

"Nothing changes." He smiled as he set off with a bowl of potatoes and carrots.

When he returned, he said to her, "You just had to call his bluff."

"I really didn't think he'd do it."

"Well, at least his detonator was faulty, allowing us time to evacuate."

"Yep. It worked out. And what can I say? Time had run out." *Maybe that sounded heartless...*

Nolan laughed. "Huh, and you're always the one asking for more."

"I see the irony. And what's up with you? Though I should have known you'd be packing a gun in an ankle holster, GI Joe."

"I'd prefer Rambo, but I'll accept the compliment. As for the backup gun, I wouldn't leave home without it." Nolan set off with two more dishes, and she finished slicing the beef. She took it out and found everyone was seated at the table.

There was only one person missing from tonight, though she wasn't invited. Sandra's mother, and she'd never know what happened to Olivia. With her failing memory, there was no reason to put her through that turmoil for the recollection to be gone the next moment.

Sandra sat at the head of the table and said grace. Even after she finished, she looked around the table at those closest to her digging in, and she was filled with gratitude. She smiled at Brice, and he mouthed, "Thank you," to her, but she was the one thankful to him. She'd kept him at a distance for so long, but after everything that took place last week, she'd adopt him as chosen family. He was by her side from the start, sacrificing sleep and his well-being for her and Olivia.

She lifted her champagne flute and softly tapped her fork to the glass. Everyone looked at her. "I'd like to say a few things, but I'll keep it brief. I don't want the food to get cold. But I just want to thank everyone at this table for helping get Olivia back home to us safe and sound."

Her table guests were Eric, Nolan, Brice, Elwood, Gabe, Lakisha, and Simon. As she took them all in, she felt her eyes warm with tears.

"We're just happy it worked out," Elwood said when no one else responded.

But there wasn't much else to say. It had been a grueling few days, but it had a happy ending. "Who knew that one little tracker from my bra could have helped get us home too." She smiled at her daughter and cupped her chin.

Olivia smiled.

"Tracker in your bra? I didn't know about that one. I thought it was the one I stuck to your Mercedes," Nolan said.

"You stuck one on my car?"

"I popped it in the back when I helped load the crate of gold."

"Why doesn't that surprise me?"

"And I assumed it was the tracker in the crate with the gold," Gabe put in.

Sandra laughed. "I guess it wasn't our day to die, huh, kiddo?" She winked at Olivia. "I'd like to make a toast. To Olivia!" Sandra touched her glass to her daughter's. She'd allowed her a full glass tonight.

"To Olivia!" everyone chorused, clinked glasses, and tossed back some bubbly.

After the cheers, people returned to eating and conversation began to roll again. Most of it was about the case still, the one thing that bound every person at this table, so it made sense. There was talk about the abandoned warehouse. It had been a roofing company where Jennings's father had worked when he was a teen, and they'd shut the doors about five years ago. Their trade explained the need for wood tar like that found on Dennis Eaton's shoes. They also retrieved Olivia's backpack and violin from Jennings's van.

"I've got something else to toast about. Recovery of the real gold," Nolan said.

There were some *oohs* and *ahhs*.

Nolan continued. "Or at least most of it. So it turned out the crewman in charge of demolishing the fishing cabin disappeared just after the job."

That much Nolan had filled Sandra in on before tonight.

"We finally tracked him down this week." Nolan nodded his head toward Brice, clearly identifying the partner in his *we*. "He was living it up in some mansion in Miami. Most of the bars remained in a huge home safe. He'd take out what he needed here and there. He'll be going away as an accessory after the fact."

"I'll toast to that," she said, raising her glass again.

"Wait," Brice cut in. "I probably shouldn't say this, but also to Jennings getting his comeuppance."

Knowing she wasn't the only one thinking that relieved her conscience some. "Salut," she said. At least where Jennings had gone, there wouldn't be any parole requests to protest. There was also justice in the fact he'd died by his own hand. He brought it on himself, but he never should have messed with her family. Same too, for Darrell Patton, who would remain behind bars for years to come, right where he belonged. "Actually, let's just toast to us." She smiled. She had everything she could possibly want right here. Eric on one side of her, Olivia on the other, and the rest of the table was filled with people who had her back. Who knew where life would take them next.

A LETTER FROM CAROLYN

Dear reader,

I want to say a huge thank you for choosing to read *Save Her Life*. If this book had you flipping the pages, you have every right to be excited because more Sandra Vos is on the way! If you would like to hear about new releases in the Sandra Vos series, just sign up at the following link. Your email address will never be shared, and you can unsubscribe at any time.

www.bookouture.com/carolyn-arnold

I hope you absolutely loved the first instalment in the Special Agent Sandra Vos series! The idea for this series hit during Christmas holidays one year, and it had me so inspired. It was something a little different to offer fans of crime fiction while not completely abandoning the adored genre. Not the typical detective mystery, but more a thriller with an infusion of police procedural.

As most writers do, I took some creative liberties, and not everything will necessarily be exactly as it is in the real Washington Field Office or Washington, DC, for that matter. I take the reality of a setting and sometimes give it a little creative twist. Same too for Corey's Grocer in Woodbridge. I created this store and plaza when writing Detective Amanda Steele.

If you haven't read any Amanda Steele books yet, I invite you to do so! For fans of Amanda Steele, you'll likely have noticed little Easter eggs. There's that grocery store, but there were other cameo appearances and name drops. I'll leave that mystery for you to figure out. Also who knows what crossovers will occur as time goes by? (You can always be there when Amanda Steele and Sandra Vos meet for the first time in *Hidden Angels*, book thirteen in the Detective Amanda Steele series.)

I'd like to thank everyone who helped me with this book. George, my husband and best friend, is always my first mention. He helps me keep balanced and sane. My editor, Laura Deacon, who is supportive and flexible. There are many others, too, and I appreciate everyone. And you, my beautiful reader, thank you for your support.

Speaking of, if you devour books, you'll be happy to know I offer several bestselling crime fiction series for you to savor, as well as series in other genres. In addition to Detective Steele, I write the Detective Madison Knight Series. She's another kick-ass female detective like Amanda, though Madison might speak her mind a lot more... But she'll stop at nothing and risk it all to find justice for murder victims.

Then there is my Brandon Fisher FBI Series if you like dark serial killer novels. It's also an extension of Amanda's world. Brandon lives in Woodbridge and is dating Amanda's friend. Now we have Sandra right in Washington... You'd almost think I gave some thought to linking them all...

And before I sign off, please, don't underestimate the power and influence of word of mouth. Talk to your family and friends about my books, your local bookstores and librarians, your neighbours, the people at the checkout counter, your dentist, your... well, you get the point. Thank you!

And last but certainly not least, I would love to hear from you if you're so inclined to drop me a note! You can reach me via email at Carolyn@CarolynArnold.net. You can also follow and interact with me on Facebook and Twitter (X) at the links below. To investigate my full list of books, visit my website by following the link below.

Until the next time, I wish you thrilling reads and twists you never saw coming!

Carolyn Arnold

www.carolynarnold.net

facebook.com/AuthorCarolynArnold
x.com/Carolyn_Arnold
goodreads.com/carolyn_arnold

PUBLISHING TEAM

Turning a manuscript into a book requires the efforts of many people. The publishing team at Bookouture would like to acknowledge everyone who contributed to this publication.

Audio
Alba Proko
Melissa Tran
Sinead O'Connor

Commercial
Lauren Morrissette
Hannah Richmond
Imogen Allport

Cover design
Head Design Ltd

Data and analysis
Mark Alder
Mohamed Bussuri

Editorial
Laura Deacon
Imogen Allport

Copyeditor
Jon Appleton

Proofreader
Becca Allen

Marketing
Alex Crow
Melanie Price
Occy Carr
Cíara Rosney
Martyna Młynarska

Operations and distribution
Marina Valles
Stephanie Straub
Joe Morris

Production
Hannah Snetsinger
Mandy Kullar
Ria Clare
Nadia Michael

Publicity
Kim Nash
Noelle Holten
Jess Readett
Sarah Hardy

Rights and contracts
Peta Nightingale
Richard King
Saidah Graham

www.ingramcontent.com/pod-product-compliance
Lightning Source LLC
Chambersburg PA
CBHW050549190726
48283CB00007B/2063